Wrapped in Seduction

Wrapped in Seduction

LISA RENEE JONES,

CATHRYN FOX,

AND

JODI LYNN COPELAND

HEAT

HEAT
Published by New American Library, a division of
Penguin Group (USA) Inc., 375 Hudson Street,
New York, New York 10014, USA
Penguin Group (Canada), 90 Eglinton Avenue East, Suite 700, Toronto,
Ontario M4P 2Y3, Canada (a division of Pearson Penguin Canada Inc.)
Penguin Books Ltd., 80 Strand, London WC2R 0RL, England
Penguin Ireland, 25 St. Stephen's Green, Dublin 2,
Ireland (a division of Penguin Books Ltd.)
Penguin Group (Australia), 250 Camberwell Road, Camberwell, Victoria 3124,
Australia (a division of Pearson Australia Group Pty. Ltd.)
Penguin Books India Pvt. Ltd., 11 Community Centre, Panchsheel Park,
New Delhi - 110 017, India
Penguin Group (NZ), 67 Apollo Drive, Rosedale, North Shore 0632,
New Zealand (a division of Pearson New Zealand Ltd.)
Penguin Books (South Africa) (Pty.) Ltd., 24 Sturdee Avenue,
Rosebank, Johannesburg 2196, South Africa

Penguin Books Ltd., Registered Offices:
80 Strand, London WC2R 0RL, England

First published by Heat, an imprint of New American Library,
a division of Penguin Group (USA) Inc.

First Printing, November 2009
10 9 8 7 6 5 4 3 2 1

Library of Congress Cataloging-in-Publication Data:

Jones, Lisa Renee.
    Wrapped in seductuction/ Lisa Renee Jones, Cathryn Fox, and Jodi Lynn Copeland.
        p.   cm.
    ISBN 978-0-451-22815-4
1. Erotic stories, American. 2. Christmas stories, American. I. Fox, Cathryn. II. Copeland, Jodi Lynn.
III. Title
    PS648.E7J66   2009
    813.60803538—dc22   2009023656

Set in Centaur MT
Designed by Ginger Legato

Printed in the United States of America

Contents

✦

Unwrapping Holly

by Lisa Renee Jones I

Hot for Santa

by Cathryn Fox 123

Mistletoe Bliss

by Jodi Lynn Copeland 229

Unwrapping Holly

BY

LISA RENEE JONES

Chapter One

Holly Reddy sat in front of the crackling fireplace of her parents' New Hampshire living room and sipped the decadent dark chocolate concoction in her Santa mug. How her mother made it taste so rich and perfect, she did not know and she didn't care. It was the closest she'd come to sin, or satisfaction, in about six months, so she planned to enjoy every last drop. With one more sip she finished it off, set the cup aside, and began unpacking Christmas ornaments from a box, the perfect ending to a quaint Thanksgiving dinner with just her and her parents.

Murphy, the family Labrador retriever, appeared by Holly's feet and nuzzled her hand. Well trained by her longtime pet, Holly absently stroked his head, thinking of the days to come. The rest of the Reddy clan would be showing up over the course of the next few weeks for the traditional holiday celebration; her two younger sisters, their younger brother, and a number of other friends and family members. It would be insanely wonderful and no doubt filled with a typical family rumble here or there.

Holly laughed as she thought of last year's Christmas. Prior to Christmas morning, Mason and Rachel had discovered that they'd gotten Mom the same perfect present, and the fight over who had to trade theirs in for something else had ensued. Holly and her youngest sister, Tori had been more than happy to volunteer to take credit for the gift and to let them pick another one, but as she'd suspected, they had suddenly managed to compromise and had then shared credit for the "perfect" gift.

Smiling to herself, Holly remembered how easily they had fallen for that little nudge and wondered if any other families the size of theirs were able to call a gathering anything but "eventful." Her family kept things interesting, to say the least. Still, the calm before the storm was enjoyable. Everything about the big sprawling farmhouse and its many memories said "cozy family holiday" to her. And as tempting as it was to tuck her feet beneath herself and snuggle into her parents' overstuffed brown couch, to simply soak in the warmth, there was a tree to be trimmed that could not wait. Tomorrow there would be no holiday playtime for her. The whole point in coming home a month before her siblings was to take advantage of the quiet, and break through a wicked case of writer's block.

After dreaming of the chance to leave her day job as a criminal attorney and focus on her next legal thriller full-time, she had learned that her fourth book had snagged a run on the *USA Today* list and had turned that dream into reality. That was sixty days ago, and she hadn't written a page worth reading since. It was as if she had simply lost every creative bone she once owned—a fact she secretly attributed to a burning desire to move home. That one was hard to admit, considering she had once said she wanted to escape small-town living, never to look back. But when her mother suggested she spend a month in her late grandma Reddy's cottage to write, she'd agreed. This was a chance to evaluate her urge to move home without any confessions required or any decision-making pressure. And since the cottage was only a short walk from the main house, she'd be close to family.

Holly dug through the decoration box, searching for the ornament hangers and finding none. She shoved her long, blond hair from her eyes and pushed to her feet. Where were Mom and Dad anyway? They'd been checking on that pie a long time.

She padded socked feet across the carpet and pushed open the kitchen door. Huh. The kitchen was empty. A muffled laugh drew her gaze to the pantry. Another muffled sound, this time a moan. *Oh my God! Mom and Dad are getting it on in the pantry.*

Blood rushed to Holly's cheeks, and she half ran from the kitchen. She rushed to the sofa and reached for her boots, shoving her feet inside. Good Lord, she was thirty years old, and her parents had a better sex life than she did. Of course, anyone who *had* a sex life had a better one than she did.

She darted for the door and pushed her arms into her white, down-filled parka. Reaching for her scarf, she wrapped it around her neck and snagged her purse and keys. Her suitcase was still by the door, since she'd arrived that evening just in time for dinner.

She hesitated and then yelled out, "Running to the store! Be back in . . ." How long did they need to, uh, finish? She wasn't taking any chances. "Be back in an hour!"

Ten minutes later, Holly pulled into The Tavern, a familiar

stomping ground for the Reddy siblings during their visits home. Big fluffy snowflakes floated around her blue Toyota Camry as Holly parked among numerous cars in front of what appeared to be a surprisingly busy establishment.

Holly shoved open the rental-car door, a smile touching her lips as she stepped into the winter wonderland of the snowstorm and stared in awe at the flakes glistening like crystal stars in the glow of the streetlights. This was how the holidays were supposed to be—wintry white. Back in Houston, the temperature was seventy degrees, and people were still in shorts. A glass of Irish coffee and a walk down memory lane sounded perfect right about now. She turned and stared at the white blanket of snow already covering her windows, walking backward as she did.

"You aren't in Texas anymore, sweetheart," she whispered with a laugh, shoving her gloved hands into the pockets of her coat as she turned to The Tavern and ran smack into a hard body.

"Whoa there, sweetheart," came the deep, rumbling male voice.

Holly rotated around and blinked at the man standing a mere two steps away, her jaw dropping at the pure heat he exuded despite the chilly winter night. At well over six feet tall, the hunky male transformed faded jeans and a dark jacket into the things fantasies were made of—*her* fantasies to be exact. The ones she'd been having when she should have been writing the next chapter of her book. She swallowed hard as she noted the snow dusting his dark, wavy hair. It was the kind of hair that a girl would want to run her fingers through while calling his name—or really just calling out, "Oh God." Actually, any affirmation that indicated immense pleasure would do quite nicely.

Inwardly, she shook herself and cleared her lust-laden throat. "Sorry about that," she offered. "I just got home and the snow, I . . ." She stopped herself. She was rambling. She was an attorney. She never rambled. Determined to gain some composure, she straightened her spine, standing taller. "I should have been watching where I was going."

For an instant, Holly thought she saw amusement dance in the deep brown eyes staring back at her but changed her mind at his reply. "Yes. You should have been." His square jaw was set firm, no humor in his ruggedly handsome face. "And I see only one way to solve this."

"Excuse me?" she asked, not sure what he meant. "Solve this? Solve what?"

"The need for a proper apology," he stated. "There is only one acceptable way for you to properly apologize."

She narrowed her gaze on him, certain now that despite his stern expression, she detected a sparkle in his eyes. "What would that be?"

"You can buy me a drink."

Unbidden, a fizzle of excitement zipped through her limbs. "I see," she said with one long nod, her best courtroom mask in place. "I can buy *you* a drink." She fully intended to press onward, when a sudden shiver chased a path down her spine. It seemed her blood had thinned a bit in those barely detectable Texas winters.

Responding instantly, the man pulled open the door and waved her inside. "Why don't we finish this conversation inside before you freeze to death?"

Holly found the idea of going inside and overheating with this man immensely appealing. But guilt stabbed at her. She wasn't here for play. She was here for family; she was here to work. Yet . . . she had promised herself a little slack time today. It was, after all, Thanksgiving. And it was just a quick drink. Plus, she had time to kill before returning back home.

Decision made, Holly stepped forward, but she didn't immediately go inside. She stopped directly in front of her newly discovered fantasy man and faced him, butterflies uncharacteristically fluttering in her stomach. Their gazes collided, his brow lifting in expectation and challenge. She'd known many a smooth-operating male in her courthouse days, faced them down both personally and professionally, and none of them had affected her the way locking gazes with this one did. She felt like melting butter warmed her insides.

Thankfully, she'd long ago learned how to adopt an easy facade of steady, cool composure. "I don't buy drinks for strangers," she informed him.

A slow, sensual smile tugged on his full, kissable lips. "Then I guess we should introduce ourselves."

"Better yet," she countered, casting him a not-so-innocent look, a look that she would never have dared before this night. She was really enjoying their little exchange. "*You* can buy *me* a drink." She didn't give him time to respond, darting inside the warm inviting Tavern, his deep laughter following her.

Smiling to herself, she tugged away her gloves and stuffed them in her coat pockets, surveying the dimly lit bar as she did. People were mingling here and there, none of whom she recognized, and she found that a relief.

Holly quite enjoyed the idea of this little game she'd entered into with a stranger, a secret flirtation. Sure, it had to end quickly— her mom and dad would miss her soon enough. But for now, she wanted to enjoy herself, to lose herself in the moment, and in the man responsible for that moment.

Holly calculated her best position in this game, passing the booths lining the wooden walls, and the tables in the open L-shaped seating area. Instead, she headed for the short side of the bar, where a four-foot Christmas tree adorned the edge of the long, wooden counter.

The jukebox kicked into play, the sound of Dean Martin's voice lifting in the air with "Baby, it's cold outside." The playfully sexy song fit her mood exactly. How long had it been since she'd simply had fun? She'd gone from workaholic to hermit. Not exactly inspiration for good writing. Living created inspiration and sparked creativity. The tingling awareness sparked by a stranger that she felt right here, right now, was the most alive she'd felt in far too long.

Excitement fluttered through her as Holly stepped to the bar and claimed a bar stool. She hung her purse on the back of the stool and then started to shrug off her jacket. Suddenly, he was there, pulling it off her shoulders, his hands gliding down her arms in its wake.

Holly shivered again, and it had nothing to do with being cold. Her nipples pebbled, ached. Heat swirled deep in her belly. She could smell a spicy male scent, mingled with a hint of vanilla. She could feel the heat of his body near hers. He slipped her coat onto the coatrack at the edge of the bar, and then leaned his arm on the back of her chair as the bartender appeared.

"What can I get for you folks?"

Her fantasy man removed his coat, and she forced herself to remain attentive to the bartender.

"Irish coffee," Holly ordered.

The sexy stranger eased to the side of her chair, his hands still strategically placed at the back.

"Make that two," he said.

She rotated in her chair to face him. He leaned on the bar, that one strategic hand still on the back of her bar stool. She was trapped and loving every second of it.

"You don't seem like an Irish coffee kind of guy," she commented.

"Is that right?" he asked. "What kind of guy do I seem like?"

He had on a black T-shirt that clung to nicely defined pecs. She smiled. "A Bud Light man."

Tilting his head, he studied her. "Guess I'm not as predictable as you thought."

"Oh, I don't think you're predictable at all." In fact, one of the things she enjoyed about this man thus far was how hard he was to read—well, beyond the primitive attraction simmering between them. She'd spent years learning to read the desire people hid beneath the surface. She'd made her living profiling people, learning to size up their inner desires. Rarely was anyone who they seemed on the surface. You had to ask questions, probe a little deeper to find the real person beneath.

The bartender set their drinks within reach, but Holly and her stranger simply stared at each other. God, she wanted this man. It was crazy. Insane. She was here to see her family. Her mom and dad were back at home probably wondering where she was now.

He lifted her hand into his, and she welcomed the touch. His hand was big, warm, strong.

"Cole," he said, introducing himself.

"Holly," she offered, feeling flushed all over. She'd thought she wanted to stay fully anonymous. And yet she liked knowing his name. There was a rich intimacy between them that couldn't be created. It had to exist naturally. The kind that came so rarely, when it did, it was like fine wine you wanted to savor and make last.

Without breaking eye contact, he reached for a cup and tasted the coffee. "Not bad," he said, a drop of that rich liquid clinging to his lips. She wanted to kiss him. She wanted him to kiss her.

She settled for another touch, covering his hand with hers, and sipped from the same mug. "Hmmm," she agreed, as warm liquid slid down her throat, heating her already sizzling limbs further. "It is good."

"You say that like you've never had Irish coffee before," he commented.

"I haven't," she explained, flirtation in her voice. This playful banter sparked boldness in her. She cast him a sexy look. "Seems a good night to . . . explore new things."

He stared down at her, the hunter in him silently vowing to brand this woman with pleasure. Her hands were warm on top of his, her mouth lush and temptingly close. Cole Wiley hadn't come here tonight looking for seduction, but he'd found it. And he'd be damned if he was walking away from it—from the she-devil of a seductress who could make a damned cup of coffee arousing.

He'd never expected to end this night hot and hard for a

stranger. He'd come to The Tavern to fulfill a holiday tradition of football and beer with his two younger brothers. In fact, with the bed-and-breakfast that he and his brothers were in the process of buying, and a contracting business still in full bloom, seduction had been the last thing on his priority list. But lingering a few minutes longer than his brothers had set him directly in Holly's path and changed that list.

Cole could honestly say that not only would exploring new things with this woman be a God-given pleasure he would heartily embrace, he fully intended to make sure it happened. He wanted her in a bad way. Wanted her naked, hot, and calling his name. She possessed a combination of innocence and naughtiness that had him burning to find out more about her. Oh yeah. Holly got to him in a way no other woman had in a very long time. She reached inside him and drew a response that he could no more control the necessity of his next breath.

"Exploring new things makes life interesting," he said finally, all too aware that she was awaiting his reply.

A smile hinted at the corners of that lush mouth. "I do believe I like 'interesting,'" she murmured, and then lifted the cup to her lips, sipped the beverage, his hand still beneath hers. Her sweet floral scent, unique and sultry, mingled with the scent of coffee.

He lifted the cup from her hands and set it on the bar so that he could step closer to her. "The night is young," he commented. Her jean-clad knees now touched his thighs, and he forced himself to resist the urge to press her legs apart and step between them. He wanted to enjoy every single second of this game they were playing, take it slow, savor the burn, until it became pure fire.

He set his palms on her legs, and her hands went to his. They stared at each other, arousal darkening Holly's eyes, telling him what she had yet to say—about her desire, need. His hands began to inch up her legs, his thumbs tracing the line of her inner thighs. Her lips parted, and he sensed her hesitation a moment before she pressed down on his hands. "No. We can't. I—"

"Wanted to explore new things," he interrupted. She greeted his words with a prim look of shock that did nothing to conceal the arousal lurking in her eyes. That she pretended to be appalled when she was not, well, that downright had his balls high and tight. Turned him on in a hot, hard way and told him she'd never dared anything sexual beyond the bedroom. He intended to change that. And so he challenged her. "Why not start exploring with pleasure?"

As the seconds ticked by, seconds laden with sexual tension, a magnetic force slowly lowered their heads together. Anticipation charged through Cole; the warmth of her breath teased his face. Would her lips be as soft as they looked? Would she taste sweet like her heart-shaped face and delicate features said she would, or spicy like her attitude? He was seconds from the answer when her cell phone rang once and then started to vibrate. They froze a hair from seeing that kiss become reality.

"Proof," she whispered. "The night is not so young." The phone rang again and she pulled back, though her hesitation was clear. "I have to go."

He didn't move; he wouldn't allow her a chance to escape. "Boyfriend?"

She laughed. "Uh, no." There was a combination of certainty and disbelief lacing the words. As if she couldn't believe he'd thought such a thing. "Parents. Home for the holidays."

Good, Cole thought. No boyfriend. Later, he'd examine why that pleased him so much. Right now, he would simply accept that he wanted her, and he wasn't about to let this end here.

There was no way in hell that Cole was allowing her to escape. And escape is what she intended. He was now clear that she'd started this little game, perhaps played it bold beyond her nature, because she'd known it could go nowhere—not with her parents waiting for her.

He reached for her coat as she stood up, calculating how he was going to deal with her intention to cut and run. She wanted him, but she didn't know how to deal with him outside a safety zone. And for him, that simply wasn't acceptable. He draped the coat behind her, allowing her to slide her arms inside while ensuring she remained facing him. The instant she was inside the coat, he grabbed the collar and pulled her body next to his.

She sucked in a breath and stared up at him. "What are you doing?"

"Making sure you don't forget me," he murmured, his voice low, laden with the desire coursing through his veins. "I don't plan to forget you."

"I can promise," she whispered. "I won't—"

He kissed her, pressed his lips to her soft, silky, warm mouth and drank her in. His tongue slipped past her teeth, explored with gentle strokes. She tasted like coffee and whiskey, like temptation and heaven. And when she sighed into his mouth, her tongue melting against his, he decided she felt like a witch because she'd damned sure cast one hell of a spell over him.

Slowly, he turned her to the corner, inched her into the area behind the jukebox. "Not here," she objected weakly. "Not now." The battle between the woman who wanted to let him take her to the bathroom and fuck her, here and now, and the woman who would never dare such a thing, was clear, and Cole wanted them both. Wanted to be the man who tore down her inhibitions. He wanted to be the man who found the real woman beneath the reserve.

"Now," he insisted, his hands caressing the sides of her full, high breasts, his fingers rubbing against her nipples, teasing them through the sheer fabric of her shirt.

Her breathing heavy, her hands covered his, while her back arched into him, silently welcoming him to pull her closer. An invitation he damned sure wasn't going to decline. Cole slid his hand over her tight little ass and molded her hips against his, fitting his cock into the heat of her body. He was hard, thick, raging with the need to be inside her. And he could damn near taste her desire in the air.

Her fingers spread across his chest, as if she wanted to explore his body but did not dare. When he was through with her she'd dare to do that and a hell of a lot more.

"What if I said I could make you come and no one would ever know?"

She offered no objection, just disbelief. "That's impossible."

Cole drew back, fixed her in a steady stare that said he wasn't going to back down. He'd heard the quaver in her voice, the sound of fear and excitement mixed together. "I love a good challenge, sweetheart." He pressed her against the wall, using his knees to urge her legs apart. "That's it, baby." He watched her expression as he traced a path up her thigh, then slid his hand along the seam of her jeans to caress her clit. She bit her lip, fought a moan.

The thrill of conquest burned through his veins, drew his balls tight, thickened his groin. He wanted her pleasure, wanted her aroused to the point of no return. And she was close, so close to completely letting go. Or so he thought.

Abruptly, her phone rang again and she squeezed her eyes shut. "Oh God. My parents." Her hands pressed against his shoulders, more firmly this time. "I can't believe I'm doing this."

Cole's gut clenched in disappointment over the sudden shift in her mood. And as much as he burned to run his hands over her hips and feel her softness nuzzled against his rock-hard cock, he sensed pushing her now would send her running for the hills, and that wasn't where he wanted her. In his bed was where he wanted her. If not tonight, later would do. It was time to ensure the game advanced to round two.

"I have to go," she repeated. Gone was the sensual, sexy woman of seconds before, her primness fast returning.

"One last kiss," he said, sliding his hands into the silky strands of her hair and brushing his lips over hers. "I'll be here tomorrow night," he said. "Same time." He released her, didn't give her time to say good-bye. "I'd really like it if you were here, too."

She inhaled, pulling her coat around her. "I . . . might. . . . I'll think about it."

Knowing he could do nothing more than hope she really did think about it, rather than running scared, he cast her a lingering inspection and then inclined his head. "Happy Thanksgiving, Holly." He turned away then, ready to find a cold shower, which he hoped like hell he wouldn't be repeating tomorrow night.

"Wait!" she called after him.

He turned to her and she stared at him as if she wasn't sure what she wanted to say. Then she said, "Happy Thanksgiving."

Between now and the next evening, she could certainly talk herself out of seeing him again, but right now, in this moment, she wasn't willing to turn him down. He smiled, satisfaction rumbling through him.

Chapter Two

Upon arriving home from the bar the night before, Holly had been greeted at the door by her parents, who were eager to tuck her into Grandma Reddy's cottage for her monthlong writing sabbatical. There had been hugs and kisses, and promises of peace and quiet to help her meet her deadline. They hadn't mentioned their hanky-panky in the pantry, and Holly certainly hadn't mentioned the naughty encounter in the bar.

But Cole wasn't so easily dismissed. Holly's bed had seen far more action last night than any bed she'd graced in a good long while. Too bad it was all fictional. Well, fictional, except for a little self-satisfaction. After all, the man had left her near orgasm, and needing release. A girl had to do what she had to do. Orgasm hadn't been hard to achieve either, with a plethora of hot images filling the fantasy cinema in her mind. Cole holding her, kissing her. Touching her nipples. Oh yes, touching her nipples. She remembered all too well how he'd stroked them with his fingers. How he pressed that hard body of his close to hers, his hips nuzzled against hers, his thick erection pressed against her stomach. She could only imagine what it would be like to have that hot, hard man inside her. And so she imagined it, over and over.

Holly sighed and rested her elbows on the wooden kitchenette counter, ignoring the notebook computer in front of her. The decadent acts of pleasure that the imaginary version of Cole had performed on her had been far-reaching and spectacular, and had occupied her evening with anything *but* sleep. The last time Holly had glanced at the clock, it had been four a.m., and that had been a good thirty minutes after she'd thrown a blanket over the display so she would stop watching the minutes click by.

Still in her pj's and slipper socks, Holly fidgeted with one of the red-and-white floral place mats, rather than with her keyboard. Her gaze lingered on the fireplace only a few feet away with its crackling red-and-blue flames—far easier on the eyes than the white page of a nearly blank document.

With a frustrated grumble, Holly shoved her hands through her already rumpled hair, and murmured, "What is your problem?" But she knew the answer, the reason for her distraction—at least for today's lack of production. She had no excuse for the many other unproductive days. Cole's kiss, his touch, his invitation to see him again tonight—all were wreaking havoc on her mind.

A knock sounded on the door, saving her from the reality of the keyboard. Her mother poked her head in the door. "Hey, sweetie," she said. "I'm not interrupting some great creative moment, am I?"

Holly snorted as she waved her mom inside. "I don't even remember what a creative moment feels like." She slumped against the cushion tied to the chair's back.

Margaret stepped inside, holding a large Tupperware container in her hands. "You just got here. Give it time." The wind caught the door and flung it wide open. The winter elements charged through the opening. "You could always hop on Dad's snowmobile and hit the trails out back. That'll clear your head."

Holly rushed forward to yank the door shut, the cold bite of winter slicing through her thin tank top. She'd enjoyed the miles of country trails surrounding the house in her youth. Her Texas blood was just too thin for that now. "No to the snowmobile. I'm so out of practice, I'd probably skid right into the iced-over duck pond." She hugged herself as she turned to her mother, teeth chattering. "Good gosh, it's cold out there."

"Record-breaking cold this year is the word on the television." Her mother disposed of the Tupperware on the countertop and then removed her gloves and her hat, and shook out her long silver hair. Smiling, she opened the container on the counter and displayed the scrumptious, chocolate-pecan bread inside. "I brought you some motivation."

"Oh my God, you didn't! I *love* that stuff. I'm going to gain ten pounds on this trip, I can tell already."

"Brought the lemon butter you love, too," Margaret bragged, slicing the bread and retrieving two plates from the overhead counter. "Let's go sit and chat. I've missed my oldest daughter."

Holly reclaimed her chair, happily accepting her plate. After spreading the slice with lemon butter, she took a bite. She shut her eyes in pure delight. "Oh yeah. Perfect." Before last night she might have called it better than sex. Laughter bubbled from Margaret's throat. "I'd put all of Grandma's recipes together for the family, but no one but me cooks. I guess cooking for one doesn't make much sense."

"Don't start with the marriage-settling-down talk, Mom," Holly admonished, "because right now, finishing this book is the only thing on my mind." And having the orgasm with Cole she'd missed the night before.

"I worry about you down there in Texas all alone," Margaret stated.

"I have high standards," Holly commented, patting her mom's hand. "Grandma and Grandpa were so happy. You and Dad are *obviously* happy." She couldn't resist teasing. "You can't even check a pie without him by your side. And here I wondered what you two would do with all your time after retirement." After two decades of teaching at the nearby college, they'd both retired this past August.

"Oh good gosh, Holly," Margaret said, blushing like a schoolgirl. "Please don't say anything to the rest of the kids. I didn't mean for that to happen. I . . . well." She waved her hands a bit helplessly. "Your father has just been so darned . . . feisty."

Holly's lips quivered with a hint of a smile as she held back laughter. "A little 'Viva Viagra,' as the commercials say, Mom?"

"Holly!" she exclaimed. "Stop that. And why must you assume Viagra is involved? Give your mom some credit, will you?" She managed a serious look all of two seconds before they both exploded into a good minute of laughter. Margaret wiped her watering eyes. "I cannot believe I am having this conversation with my daughter."

"Your thirty-year-old daughter," Holly reminded her. "I'm way past little girl and more than a little pleased to see you and Dad happy."

Margaret grew serious. "Your father was hurting after Grandma died. But we stumbled onto love letters that Grandpa had sent Grandma and read them all together. It sparked something in us." She shrugged. "Or maybe it was the wish I made on Grandma's ruby. She always said it was magical."

"Ruby?" Holly's brows dipped. "The ruby that Grandpa gave Grandma?"

"Yes," Margaret said, pushing to her feet and walking to the mantel where the brilliant four-inch stone rested on a gold stand, still in the place Grandma had kept it. She turned to Holly, holding it in her hands, the fire crackling behind her. "Do you remember the story behind the gift?"

Holly shook her head. "I just remember it was special."

"Special, indeed," Margaret agreed, sitting down beside Holly and placing the ring in its cradle in the center of the table. "And so very romantic."

"It's lovely," Holly said, and since romance was in short supply for her right now, she figured she might as well live vicariously through her grandparents. She propped her elbows on the table and slid her chin to her hands. "Tell me the story, Mom."

A sad smile touched Margaret's lips. "Grandpa was drafted to war before they were able to marry. He gave Grandma the ruby on Christmas day as a sign of his love, promising it held the magic of love and would ensure his return. He came home and they lived fifty happy years together."

Holly sighed. "Now that's what I call romance."

"Isn't it?" her mother asked, agreeing. "Grandma cherished

that stone as if it held a piece of your Grandfather's heart. She believed it held the magic of love, you know. That if you held it and made a wish, it would come true." Her mother smiled mischievously. "And now someone else is going to get to experience all that magic."

"What do you mean?"

"Come Christmas, it will be gifted to someone, as it was to her."

Holly's eyes went wide. "That's why her will was so specific about us being together this Christmas?"

"Yes," Margaret agreed. "That's when Grandma wants the big announcement made—the fate of the stone."

"Surely she would leave it to Dad," Holly commented.

"Grandma was a romantic," Margaret reminded her. "She will want it to go to someone who will see it as special, the way she did. Your father would cherish it because it was hers, not because of its magic."

Holly tightened her grip on her mug. "Oh please, say it's not me, Mom, because we both know how the others will react." In her youth, her goal of law school had meant responsibility, as had her role as oldest sibling and frequent babysitter—a duty that had often kept her from dating and socializing. "They always think I get special treatment as the oldest. I don't want to deal with that. If my name is in that envelope, please change it. Say someone else gets the stone. Say Dad gets it."

"You were kids. Of course they accused you of getting extra attention because you were in charge. We'd never have managed the university's demands without your help. We asked a lot of you, and you never complained."

"I saved the complaints for my friends," Holly quickly offered, not willing to be made into some sort of angel. "But I complained, Mom."

Margaret waved that off. "My point is—if a little magic, or romance, or whatever you might call it, comes your way, you're deserving, Holly."

"I don't want it," Holly stated, shaking her head. Her mother started to wave off her words yet again, and Holly added, "I'm serious, Mom. I don't want it."

"It's not your decision," she stated firmly, pushing to her feet to carry her plate to the kitchen. "The recipient of Grandma's gift will be revealed on Christmas morning." She set her dishes in the sink. "Why not enjoy the ruby until then? Maybe it will bring you luck." She smiled mischievously. "Or romance."

Half an hour later, Margaret had bundled up and left Holly to her deadline woes. After throwing some wood on the fire, Holly curled into her chair in front of her computer and took a bite of her sinfully delicious bread, thinking of another sinfully delicious distraction—Cole. Her mother didn't understand, of course, that the last thing Holly needed, with a deadline fast approaching, was romance. But then, her mother did have one important point— Holly needed some raw, emotional energy to fill her pages. She'd attacked life with a structured plan: a certain GPA to achieve, a certain college to attend, a legal career—and a man who would fit the model that felt appropriate to her life.

All that planning and none of it had made her happy. Which left Holly with a need to discover who she really was, besides a writer. Much like the heroine, Tabitha Moore, in her work in progress. A by-the-books attorney and control freak, Tabitha is forced into hiding by a deadly killer; then she finds herself in close quarters with a mysteriously sexy stranger, Luke Sterling, a renegade FBI agent. Despite her better judgment, Tabitha begins an erotic, dangerous ride with the agent. Yep. That was the plan. If only the pages would fill themselves with brilliance.

In her mind, Holly was Tabitha; their personalities were alike. She smiled. Cole was her renegade, a man who didn't fit the conventions of the world she'd built for herself. Interesting . . .

Seeing Cole again would be research. Work. A good way to feed her creative juices. She bit her bottom lip. Did she dare do this? Did she dare see Cole again? There would be nothing to pull her away from him this time, no family commitment. No job to get to the next morning. Nothing to keep her from finding out if he was really as good as her midnight fantasies conjured him to be. And that's what this had to be about—work mixed with a one-night fantasy—something she didn't indulge in.

And why not? Why didn't she ever indulge in fun fantasies? She wasn't an attorney working around the clock to become a partner, worried about fitting into their perfect mold. She didn't even want to fit into the mold she'd formed *for herself* way back when.

Holly made her decision. Cole was exciting, and both her book and her body were in desperate need of some excitement. She grimaced. Of course, there was a strong possibility that Cole wouldn't live up to her dreams. Her track record of failed relationships was pretty darned rock solid. But even the slight chance that Cole would be different . . . well, that chance had her reaching for the ruby.

Holly held the ruby in her palm and made a wish. *Please let this be a smart choice.* Okay. Boring wish. Not a fantasy worth wishing. She refocused. *Please let Cole be as sinfully good in bed as my fantasies—*

please let him be that good. Laughter bubbled from Holly's lips. Right. Like the ruby could decide his prowess. No. The pleasure would have to be all about the man. And Holly was going to enjoy demanding full disclosure.

COLE LOUNGED AT THE BAR of The Tavern, wearing a facade of languid disinterest, a cup of black coffee in front of him, no interest in alcohol tonight. He'd much rather get drunk on Holly. If Holly showed.

· Lord only knew he'd spent the better part of the day trying to convince himself not to come tonight—Holly was a distraction he couldn't afford right now, not with one business being sold and a bed-and-breakfast business to launch. But she was in his blood, and on his mind. There was no shutting off the fierceness of his reaction to meeting her.

Clearly, he'd ignored his physical needs for far too long—it was the only explanation for the wicked distraction she'd created in him. Not a difficult task, considering he'd long been without a woman—by choice, not necessity.

The female population of Haven outnumbered the males two to one. The single females three to one. In other words, the women were on the hunt, willing to surrender to a man's every desire in order to garner a ring on their finger. To a visiting male, that sounded like fucking heaven. To Cole, it was the one little piece of hell in the town he loved. He and his brothers were on every single woman's "to do" and "shackle at the altar" lists. Thanks, but no thanks.

He'd never felt inclined to marriage. Nothing against it. His parents had been damned happy, and he'd grown up better for it. But it just wasn't his thing. Never met a woman he could wake up with more than a few times without feeling suffocated. At thirty-four, he didn't see that changing.

But with the sale of the family business to a larger Manchester operation—his brothers were closing the last local jobs—his work demands had leaned toward bookkeeping and transition issues, and lots of them. All he could manage was a trip to work or to his own bed, alone. Luckily, they'd snagged a large enough sum for the contracting business to allow Cole and his brothers to redirect their efforts to their new endeavor, the remodeling of a large, local home into a bed-and-breakfast. The three of them could focus on one project, instead of chasing their tails between Haven and Manchester to pay the bills. Now *that* was going to be heaven.

The bartender motioned to Cole's mug, asking if he needed a refill. Cole waved him away. He didn't want coffee. He wanted a long, deep drink of Holly. Sexy, funny, prim little Holly. He was going to enjoy the challenge of sliding past the reserve he'd sensed in her.

Cole began conjuring a wicked fantasy about just that when his brother Jacob, the baby of the bunch at twenty-five, and almost ten years Cole's junior, appeared by his side.

"Did hell freeze over or what?" Jacob asked, surprise in his voice, a pool cue in hand.

Damn. The last thing Cole needed was Jacob panting over his shoulder when Holly arrived. "Speaking of hell," Cole commented. "What the *hell* are you talking about?"

"You're not working," Jacob explained. "If I didn't know better, sometimes I'd think you had a love affair with your desk." His gaze drifted to the coffee cup. "All work and no play seems to have you a bit confused, big brother. That's not beer."

Cole reached for his cup and gave Jacob a mock toast. "They ran out of beer mugs." He took a drink.

To say that Cole and Jacob were complete opposites would be an understatement. Jacob lived bold and wild, while Cole was reserved and controlled. Even Jacob's light brown hair was a little too long, his actions, a bit too spontaneous. Cole preferred a balance between work and play, which required more thoughtful actions. The same way he'd thought out every little place he wanted to kiss Holly.

That was exactly why he had to get rid of Jacob. "Leaving soon?"

"Why?" Jacob perked up. "Got a hot date I can steal from you?"

"Seriously," Cole said. "When are you leaving?" On another occasion, with a different woman, sharing a beer with his brother, he might just jump on the familiar challenge. But not now, not with Holly—not a chance. She was his.

"Ryder's home on leave," Jacob stated of his old school bud, a Navy SEAL who showed up from time to time, always unannounced. Ryder was an expert at punching Jacob's buttons.

"How much you down?" Cole asked, making it clear to Jacob that he knew he was getting his butt kicked.

"Two hundred," Jacob admitted grimly. "But it's still early."

"Plenty of time to lose more," Cole added sarcastically. For the most part, he respected his brother's unwillingness to back away from a challenge. But he also believed there were calculated times of retreat, and this would be one of them. "I'd tell you to stop before you bleed any more, but I know it would be wasted breath."

A cold blast of air rushed through the room as The Tavern door swung open, followed immediately by a blast of hot fire in his blood as he spotted Holly. So did every other man in the room—heads turned. His brother's head turned.

Possessiveness purred within him, precluding a downright growl. She had that sexy schoolteacher vibe that made a man want to crawl under her desk and make her scream—to prove he was the only man who could.

Yanking off her hat, she surveyed the bar, shaking free her long, silky blond hair a moment before her gaze caught on Cole. Instant awareness coiled low in his stomach. Jacob let out a low whistle. "I think I just found my Christmas present."

As if she could hear his words across the distance, over the sound of Elvis's "White Christmas" on the jukebox, her gaze snapped to the left, to Jacob. She remained still, perfectly still, and Cole sensed her unease.

"Oh yeah," Jacob said, studying her too intently for Cole. "I am definitely going to need an introduction."

"Not a chance in hell," Cole ground out between clenched teeth. "This one is off-limits, so back off."

He would have said more, but, without warning, Holly launched herself into motion as she darted in the direction of the ladies' room. Clearly, she was not happy he wasn't alone.

"Damn," Cole muttered under his breath, fearful she would change her mind about seeing him again. And he was aware there was a back door by the restrooms. If she bolted, he might not find her again. For reasons he didn't try to understand, that didn't sit well.

Cole pushed off the bar, ready for the pursuit, but paused to cast his brother a warning. "Ryder can only beat you and take your money if you keep playing."

He didn't wait for an answer, though Jacob replied with some sort of defensive mumbling that Cole decisively tuned out. He was already walking toward the restrooms, ready to move to Plan B. Jacob wasn't going anywhere soon, and he wanted Holly all to himself. Now, he just had to convince her that was a good idea.

His pulse kicked up a beat as he entered the narrow hallway leading to the restrooms and scrubbed his jaw, contemplating how Holly might react to finding him standing outside the door. And contemplated some more. Minutes passed and Holly didn't appear. Had she left? Damn it to hell. This was not how he had this night planned.

Voices sounded in the hallway—one of which was Jacob's, and—holy hell—Abe! Great. Jacob loved fucking with his head. Add his other brother to the mix, and it became ball-busting brotherly love. The kind he could do without tonight.

Suddenly, the doorknob to the restroom jiggled and Holly appeared in the doorway, her long silky hair cascading down her shoulders, a single stall and sink as her backdrop. Desire twisted in his gut, just as it had the night before.

"Cole?" Shock registered on her face at the sight of him there, waiting for her.

If she was shocked now, she'd be ten times more so when his two brothers invaded the tiny hallway. Cole's mind raced; the voices were growing louder. He stepped forward, his hands sliding under her coat, the warmth of her body seeping through the long sweater dress she wore.

Her lush pink lips parted in a gasp as he shuffled her into the restroom. "What are you doing?"

"Saving you from a family reunion with my brothers," he told her, kicking the door shut behind him.

She was flustered by his unexpected behavior. Her pretty, pale cheeks were flushed. Her hands rested on his chest, ready to shove him, yet she attacked with words, not actions. "Whatever the reason, it's not okay. You bullied me into a restroom without asking permission. And you're in the women's restroom!"

He arched a brow, amused, turned on. That damned prim quality she exuded was downright hot. "Without asking permission?" he inquired, watching her flush deepen. "I'll ask next time."

She pursed her pretty lips, not at all pleased with his rebuttal. "There won't be a next time!" she countered. "I'm leaving." She dropped her hands, tried to sidestep him.

Voices sounded—his brothers. Then the sound of the back door.

"His truck's still here," Jacob said clearly. "Maybe he left with that woman."

Cole tightened his hands on her waist. "That's them," he told her. "Do you really want to be seen walking out of here with me? Because I can promise you, it will amuse my brothers, among others. It's a small town. Gossip is king." He let go of her, but stayed close, again giving her a choice.

A frustrated sound slid from her lips. "Yes," she said. "I know that all too well. I grew up here."

His interest piqued, Cole would have probed for more information, but she wasn't done voicing her distress just yet. Panic brushed her features, laced her voice. "I don't want my parents embarrassed by this," she said, her hands fluttering in the air with the words and causing her scarf to slide off her shoulders to the ground.

Cole bent down to pick it up at the same moment that she did, their hands colliding in an electric charge of instant sexual awareness. They were facing each other, knees brushing, hands touching. Their eyes locked, lingered, burned with smoldering attraction. Her lips parted, as her chest rose with an inhaled breath—an invitation to kiss her that he barely resisted.

Instead, Cole slid the scarf around her neck and held on to it, resisting the urge to pull her closer. "I just want you to myself, Holly. Not a part of the circus of my brothers' well-intended fun." The familiar sound of their voices gave him pause, and he motioned to the hall. "Listen."

She strained her ears along with him. His brothers' voices were growing more distant. "They're leaving, for now." He took her hand and helped her to her feet.

"Oh, thank goodness," she whispered. "Now if we can dodge any other attention."

He was still holding her hand. "I'm parked out back," he told her. "Come with me. Another bar, a restaurant, anywhere you want. Just not here."

She hesitated. "I don't know. I . . . This isn't going how I planned this."

"Few things go as planned," he commented.

"Actually—"

He cut her off by pulling her close and pressing his lips to hers, swallowing her gasp as his tongue slid into the deep, warm recesses of her mouth and caressed. It was a short, sensual play of his tongue along hers before he pulled back and said, "Planning is overrated, Holly. Don't plan. Don't think. Just say yes."

She blinked up at him, her chest heaving slightly. He could sense the kiss had rattled her, aroused her. Shook her to the core. Well, she wasn't the only one. Holly had him twisted in knots. He wanted her. Had to have her on a primal level that reached beyond simple lust. It burned clear to his soul. "Just say yes, Holly."

She swallowed and shook her head. "Yes."

Chapter Three

Holly followed Cole down the hallway, his big hand swallowing her smaller one, her heart racing a million miles an hour. Good Lord, the man could kiss. It was almost embarrassing how well he kissed. Or rather, how Holly reacted to his kiss. She was wet. Wet! When in her life had one kiss damned near brought her to orgasm? Every inch of her body was aware of this man. And it both scared the heck out of her and excited her at the same time. Holly liked it, too. Liked this edgy, daring, sexy feeling Cole created in her.

And he was right. Planning was overrated. She'd certainly never planned to end up in that restroom like she did, but had she not—she might never have been kissed like that.

She wanted more of those kisses, which meant leaving was good. And unlike Thanksgiving evening, tonight the place was bustling with people; Haven's wagging tongues were piled into

The Tavern in force and she wanted no part of them. No witnesses. No connection beyond the night. No tomorrow or judgment.

With a hard shove, Cole pushed against a wicked wind to open the exit door. Snow fluttered furiously around them.

They stepped outside, where the cold air battered their bodies, a violent contrast to the heat they'd generated in that restroom.

Holly huddled deeper into her long, cashmere black coat, shivering violently, her gloves and hat still tucked in the bag hanging over her shoulder. Clearly, her decision-making where wardrobe was concerned was far too rooted in Texas living, because, suddenly, her dress, tights, and winter boots felt about as appropriate as a bikini. The cold cut a path up her skirt and chilled her to the bone. One didn't dress to impress a date in this weather. One dressed to stay warm. An old lesson she was relearning the hard way.

Protectively, Cole pulled her close, under his shoulder, so his big body blocked the wintry elements from attacking her, without concern for the absence of his coat, which he'd apparently left behind.

"You need your coat!" she yelled against the wind. The navy, long-sleeved tee and jeans he wore were barely enough to be called decent in these temperatures. The man must really want to avoid his brothers, but then, she had sisters, and could appreciate where he was coming from. She could love them and want to beat them within an inch of their lives, all in one beautiful, twisted moment.

Cole pointed to the far corner of the parking lot where a black pickup truck set in a secluded corner, one of the three vehicles parked in the rear of the building. "I'm over there."

Holly nodded as a gust of wind darned near turned her to ice, and she eagerly melted farther under the shelter of Cole's arm, which was draped around her shoulders. They couldn't get to his truck fast enough to suit Holly, and when he clicked the lock and held the driver's door open, she eagerly scooted inside. She couldn't see through the ice and snow on the windows; they would need to defrost to travel. Holly barely had time to slide her purse to the floorboard, let alone contemplate seating arrangements, before Cole had closed them inside the cabin, started the truck, and cranked up the heat. The next thing she knew, he was reaching for her.

"Come here," Cole ordered in a low, masculine voice that danced along her nerve endings almost as erotically as his muscular leg that was now aligned with hers. He opened her coat, merging their bodies beneath it. "I'll keep you warm until the heater kicks into gear." He grabbed her cold hand and brought it to his lips. His eyes locked with hers. "You're freezing." He covered her hand with his own to warm it.

Freezing? He thought she was freezing? Was he crazy? Holly was feeling the melting-butter effect he had on her all over again.

"You're the one without the coat," she managed hoarsely.

"I've lived in the cold all my life," he replied, obviously assuming she had not. "I'm used to it. But then, you mentioned growing up here."

She nodded. "Yes, but I've been in Texas a long time. I'd be in shorts right now if I were still there."

He arched a brow. "Texas. That's a long way from home."

"Yes," she said, biting back the urge to say more. He had said no thinking, no planning. And that felt right. It felt like the fantasy she'd burned for. "A long way from home."

A penetrating stare followed—he sent her a deep probing look that said he was trying to read her and, indeed, had. She saw the moment he registered the reason she'd avoided giving out personal details—the moment he knew she sought anonymous pleasure. He showed no reaction to that conclusion, but she doubted he'd complain.

He began rubbing her hand again, warming it a second before he reached out and tested the air flowing from the vent. "It's already getting warm." He tilted it more in her direction. "Can you feel that?"

"Yes," she confirmed. "Thank you. I feel it." Or rather him. She felt him. And he was making her hot. He had a raw, masculine presence that oozed power and control. The kind that attorneys learned to convey in law school, yet Cole possessed the authority naturally, wore it like a second skin. She bit her bottom lip, her gaze dropping to where the fingers of her free hand splayed wide against the wall of his amazingly broad chest. Cole raised his hand and covered hers, holding her palm where it rested, as if he didn't want her to stop touching him. His finger slid beneath her chin, lifting her eyes to his as he pinned her in a potent stare. The dull glow of a not-so-distant streetlight illuminated the dark passion in his eyes, and the sexual tension in the cabin suddenly grew thick, heavy, and delicious.

"I wasn't sure you'd show tonight," he said, the soft rumble of his voice dancing along her nerves in a sensuous tango.

Words escaped Holly, nerves clamoring inside her. Was he telling her he knew she was acting out of character? She didn't know. Probably. Yes. He must know. He touched her with cool confidence that said he knew his way around a woman's body, kissed her like a man who would dare her to take risks. Carried himself like pure, sinful masculinity. He knew she was out of her element.

Good gosh, she could barely breathe—let alone think—from the desire this man stirred in her. It frightened and excited her to imagine this powerful, gorgeous man on top of her, inside her, touching her. She was wet and aching. Needy.

Willing herself past her inhibitions, she acted on the desire to touch his cheek, reaching out for the rough stubble that felt erotic beneath her fingers. "I couldn't seem to help myself," she admitted finally in a raspy voice that she barely recognized as her own.

"I like that you couldn't help yourself." He kissed her knuckles and opened her palm, his lips brushing the sensitive flesh with ridiculously sensual impact. And his eyes, those dark emotive eyes, held hers. They reached inside her, touched her, *moved* her.

And for just a moment, she wondered if she had made a mistake. She'd had a few "vanilla" lovers, a few disappointments. But something told her there was nothing "vanilla" about Cole and his demands. Would she be able to handle him? Would she know what to do?

But then, he said, "I'd kiss you, but I'm not sure I will ever stop if I do," and his expression held such dire need, a confession of need that matched her own, that Holly threw aside inhibitions and fears.

For once in her life, she wanted to be daring. She wanted to know that feeling of completely uninhibited freedom that she'd tried so many times to create on paper, from nothing but pure imagination. And this man was the one to teach her that. On some level, she sensed this particular man could give her a freedom she'd never experienced before. That with him, she would explore her fantasies rather than simply wish them to life. And she wanted that—it fulfilled a need she'd long burned to fulfill.

Desire spiked with her newfound resolve, and she whispered, "I don't want you to stop," and slid her hand to his face and pressed her lips to his.

ONE TOUCH OF HOLLY'S LIPS on his and Cole was ramrod hard, his cock pulsing with white-hot desire. Her lips were soft, her touch innocent, yet oh-so-seductive. And the kiss, the kiss was laced with a promise that she was his, soft and willing. She trusted him enough to reach beyond her obvious reservations and give herself to him. He found this realization provocative, arousing. He wanted nothing more than to press Holly against the seat, spread her legs wide, and find his way inside her, but even more, he wanted to be worthy of the woman's gift—a part of herself no other had experienced.

Cole knew women, and Holly wasn't a one-night-stand kind of woman. Whatever had led her to this place tonight, needing to explore beyond her comfort zone, it didn't matter—what mattered was that she'd chosen him. And he planned to take damned good care of her. Slowly, he would guide her into confident territory, where she could explore her wants and needs.

Cole slipped his tongue past her lips, into the wet, warm recesses of her mouth, seducing her with his kiss, making love to her with his mouth. She rewarded him with a soft moan, a sensual sound that coiled in his gut and damned near undid his willpower. He could no sooner stop kissing her in that moment than he could stop breathing.

Deepening the kiss, he tasted her, his cock pulsing with the sweet honey flavor of her lips. She responded to the kiss with fervent need, clinging to him, offering him more of that sexy moaning that licked at his cock and tightened his balls.

Wisps of her silky hair tickled his cheek; the smell of her, the sweet aroused female scent, beckoned to him. He was hungry for her, starving—so he kissed her passionately. His hands slid under her coat to surround her slender waist, then brushed the bottom of her full breasts. She arched forward, melting into him as if she couldn't help herself, encouraging him. Cole caressed upward, thumbed her hard, plump nipples. He wanted more of her. Naked.

The coat had to go, he decided, and he didn't ask permission. He tore his lips from hers and slid it off her shoulders. Holly shrugged it away, urgency in her actions. The minute the barrier was removed, Cole wrapped his arms around her, and she willingly leaned into him. She was tiny, delicate, and unbelievably sexy.

He dipped his head, nuzzled her neck, and inhaled deeply. "You smell like vanilla and sugar," he murmured, sliding her hair to the side to nibble her neck.

She shivered and pressed her body along his length, soft against hard, her fingers latching behind his neck. Telling him she wanted *more* as much as he did.

In a fluid motion, Cole slid across the seat, lifted her, and pulled her onto his lap. With quick handwork, he slid her dress up her long, lean thighs until it was at her hips. The V of her body settled snugly across his groin, her black tights the only barrier between him and the slick wet heat of her core. He palmed her ass, pressed her hips against his erection. Cole ground his teeth against the throbbing demand of his cock, as she taunted him with how near he was to the ultimate satisfaction of being inside her.

Possessively, hungrily, he funneled his fingers into the silky blond strands of her hair and brought her lips to his. "I warned you I'd never stop kissing you and I don't plan to," he told her, a moment before his mouth slanted over hers in hard demand. It was a kiss to claim her, a kiss of domination, a kiss that said tonight she was *his*. She answered by giving herself to him, her tongue reaching for his, her hands moving over his shoulders like brilliant fire that shot molten heat straight to his cock.

He arched his hips into her, pressed her down against the bulge in his jeans. Rocked with her. Filled his hands with her breasts and thumbed the laces at the embroidered bodice of her dress, engaged by their path straight to her waist. He envisioned ripping those laces away and pulling them wide, exposing her lush breasts with his hands and mouth. And probably scare the hell out of her, he reminded himself, settling for a long, deep kiss before forcefully tearing his lips from hers. "Holly."

Dark, sexy lashes fluttered before she managed to fix a heavy-lidded stare on him. Her lips were gorgeous, plump and full from his kisses. "Yes," she finally whispered.

His lips curved with decadent pleasure. "I am coming to like that word." He gently fingered the laces, and they unraveled downward slowly, exposing a thin line of skin, his cock twitching with anticipation of seeing her. But he kept his eyes on hers.

"Open your dress for me, Holly," he ordered, releasing her, pressing his fists into the seat, giving her the power, and demanding, silently, that she act.

Shock registered in her face, and she bit her bottom lip; her hands rested on his upper thighs. "What?" she asked nervously.

"Open your dress and free your breasts," he ordered. "I want to see you, Holly."

Instant uncertainty filled her lovely face. "Here?"

"Here."

Her gaze went to the side windows, where snow fell with far too much fury to allow them to stay there much longer. "I don't know if I—"

He drew her mouth to his, their breath mingling with the carnal temptation to taste each other. But he held back, challenging her instead. "Let yourself reach beyond your usual limits, Holly." His teeth scraped her bottom lip. "Don't you want to experience pleasure without limits?"

She inhaled a shaky breath and then brushed her lips across his, tasted him with a sexy slide of her tongue before leaning back and reaching for her laces. Satisfaction rolled within him as he watched her part the material and display the silky fabric of a sheer black bra. High and full, her breasts overflowed the tiny piece of sexy fabric. The truck was toasty warm now, but he was on fire because of Holly.

"Unhook it," he ordered, his dick thick, aching to be inside her. "Let me see your nipples."

She did as he ordered, unsnapping the front clasp, which thrust those perky, pink nipples in the air as she shrugged the straps off her shoulders.

"You're beautiful," he said, filling his hands with her breasts and tilting his head to suckle one tight little peak into his mouth.

Gasping, she arched her back, clinging to him, her hand sliding through his hair as he licked, kissed, nipped. Panting, she started to rock her hips against the hard line of his dick, the friction damned near making him come in his pants. But this time was for her, and only her. It would be one orgasm in a series of many.

"Take what you need, baby," he said, gently pressing his cheek to hers as he savored her. Cole took his time touching her, finding out what pleased her, what got her hot. He wanted to know every way to touch her, every way to make her cry out in pleasure. And she was close to release now, so very close she was unable to kiss him, her warm breath tickling his cheek.

"Oh," she gasped. "Oh . . . I . . ." She buried her head in his neck, her hair in his face, but he didn't care. He loved it. Loved every fucking minute of her pleasure.

"Come for me, Holly," he whispered, his hands, his entire body, moving with her, working for her ultimate satisfaction. She gasped and tensed, and Cole ran his hand up her body, holding her as she shuddered with a sudden release. Caressed her as she came down, as her body relaxed.

But there was no relaxing for Holly. She tensed again, her face buried in his neck. "I can't believe I . . . I . . ." Abruptly, she pushed away from him, cut her gaze to his chest, and tried to pull her dress together. "I have to go."

No fucking way was he about to let her dart away, not without a fight. "Stop, Holly," he ordered. "Stop doing this to yourself. Watching you come like that was amazing. All it did was make me want you more." He touched her cheek. "No limits, remember?"

She studied him, assessing his words, and slowly her expression softened. But just when he thought he had her interest again, voices sounded in the distance. Instantly, she flew into motion, scrambling off his lap, and fumbling with her dress.

"No one is parked close enough to—"

A knock pounded on the bed of the truck, a warning that someone was approaching.

"Fuck!" The word ripped from his throat because he knew who was knocking. *Jacob!*

"Oh my God," Holly bit out between her teeth, tugging on her coat. "I can't believe I let this happen."

She slid across the seat and shoved open the door. Cole reached for her, but she managed to evade his grasp, and jumped out of the truck.

"Thanks," she said, wind and snow whipping wildly around her. "Or whatever I'm supposed to say under these circumstances." She shoved the door shut.

Cole pounded the steering wheel, and then realized he didn't even know her full name. He jerked his door open, and ice pelted down on his skin, snow instantly clinging to his shirt.

"Holly!" he called, noting she was already halfway to The Tavern. He started to pursue, but he drew up short when he realized it wasn't Jacob standing there, hands in a leather bomber jacket, but Abe, with his truck running a few feet away, as if he was in a hurry.

"Sorry, man," Abe offered, motioning to Holly. He wasn't an instigator, not one to show up unannounced, without Jacob by his side, prodding him. "But Jacob broke his damned leg."

"What? How?"

"Some bastard hit his wife, so Jacob intervened. Managed to land a foot on some ice in the process."

Ouch. "How bad?"

"Bad," Abe said. "Real bad. Thought you'd want to follow us to the hospital."

There was no question—he was following. He might want to beat Jacob's ass now and then, but Jacob was his baby brother. Cole shook his head. Before he turned back to his truck, Cole quirked a brow. "Did he at least pop the bastard a good one before he went down?"

Abe laughed. "Yeah," he said. "Popped him a nice shiner. But you know Jacob. He's looking at possible surgery, and he's worried about the woman having repercussions from his actions. He's pretty freaked out."

"That's our boy," Cole said, referring to the way Jacob was always fighting for the underdog. More than once, it had gotten him in trouble but always with good intentions. And no real man hit a woman. "Tell him I'll call the sheriff."

Abe nodded and Cole slid into his truck and yanked the door shut. Instantly, the sweet scent of her flared his nostrils. *Holly.* Regret ground through his nerve endings, pulsed in his cock. Turned out, he'd become a one-night stand after all. One that had finished with far too little of a good thing. And he couldn't be happy about that. No matter how fantasy-worthy this truck had now become.

Chapter Four

Three days after her hot interlude with a sexy stranger, Holly sat at Betty's Diner, her laptop in front of her. Surprisingly, she'd managed to put words on a few pages. Her cottage writing escape had become home of the "ruby wish" and subsequent fantasy man, thus a distraction. Which pretty much defeated the purpose of coming home for the holidays this early.

She couldn't seem to get anything done there for replaying that night with Cole. The kissing, the touching, how he removed her dress. She plopped her elbow on the table and rested her chin on her hand. God. The dress. And then the rash escape out of complete mortification that, once she'd recovered from her embarrassment, left her wondering what might have happened had she stayed.

"Get you more hot cocoa before I leave for the night, sweetie?"

Holly glanced up at Jean, the fiftysomething waitress who'd worked at the diner since Holly was a teen. "No, thanks, Jean."

"How's the next best seller coming?" she asked. "You sure been working hard. And here I thought you got to sit in you pj's and eat bonbons."

Holly grinned at that. "I admit to working in my share of sleepwear, but I've yet to eat a bonbon. Though I've heard they're quite yummy." She made a mental note to tell her mom to cool the bragging, and hug her for being proud enough to do it. Mom had made sure everyone she'd ever met in this lifetime knew when Holly had made the *USA Today* list.

Jean snickered. "Well," she said, hands on her robust hips, accented by a tightly tied white apron, "I can't produce bonbons, but we got plenty of pie and ice cream in the back if you decide you want some. Carol and Susan will be here until ten."

Holly glanced at her watch. It was eight now. She hated writing with a time limit. Damn. She shook off that counterproductive thought and focused on Jean, offering her a genuine smile. "Have a good night and thanks for letting me hog your table so long." It was true that small towns had negatives, like gossip gabbers, but it also came with lots of friendly faces, a warmer feeling in general that had been too easily missed on previous quick visits home. "It's nice to be home."

"You can hog my table any day," she said. "Come back tomorrow."

Behind Holly, the bell on the door chimed as it had many times since her arrival. She ignored any curiosity about new customers now as she had every other newcomer's entrance, avoiding distractions. Cole was enough to distract her focus on writing. She didn't need more.

"I probably will," Holly said. "I've gotten more done these past few hours than I have in a week."

"Good," she said. "Glad we could help." She reached in her apron and pulled out a book. "There is a little favor if I could ask?" She slid the book onto the table where Holly could see it was a copy of *Deadly Suspicions* by Holly Rivers, her pen name, which she'd chosen to avoid an accusation of distraction at the law firm while she was still there. Jean grinned. "Me and the girls were wondering if you could autograph our books. I mean how often can you say you knew a bestselling author when they were in braces and pigtails?"

"Of course," Holly said, blushing. She picked up a pen, scribbling a personalized note in the inside cover before handing it to Jean. "And for the record, I *never* wore pigtails any more than I eat bonbons." Carol, one of the other waitresses, a redheaded fireball who kept all the customers—and Betty—in line, slid a couple copies of the book onto the table. "I'll leave them here. No rush."

Holly laughed. "You got it, Carol. And actually, I'll take a cup of coffee after all." She had to make the most of these last two hours.

"Make that two," came a deep familiar male voice just before Cole slid into the seat across from her. Holly's eyes went wide, her heart thrumming wildly in her chest.

"Anything for one of the Wiley boys," Carol said, and rushed away.

"I better go, now that trouble has arrived," Jean said, teasing Cole, clearly familiar with him.

"Hey now," Cole said, giving Jean a sexy, one-dimple smile that would have set any woman's heart racing. "You'll give Holly the wrong idea. Because I *know* you must be referring to Jacob and Abe."

Jean chuckled, the light in her eyes saying that Cole's appeal reached across the age-groups. "'Cause you ain't got a lick of trouble in you, do you now, boy?"

"Not a lick," Cole replied mischievously, cutting Holly a sideways look.

Holly blushed at his little innuendo and the unbidden erotic images it evoked, but Jean didn't seem to notice. She chuckled a bit more. "I believe that about as easily as I believe fish can fly."

"Some fish can fly," Holly said instinctively, fumbling for anything to divert her mind from the memory of her naked breasts in Cole's hands. She'd always been the family encyclopedia, the keeper of important catalog information, which had served her nicely in the legal field as well.

"She has a point," Cole said, resting his forearms on the table and speaking to Holly. "I'm the nice, responsible brother of the three, and she knows that."

Jean shook her head. "I'll tell you all the gossip about him tomorrow," Jean promised Holly. "I'm out of here for now. You kids have a good night."

Cole's expression lit with amusement as he waved good-naturedly to Jean and then fixed a penetrating stare on Holly. He leaned forward and lowered his voice to a near whisper. "Wonder if that gossip will include a sexy encounter in the front seat of my truck three nights ago?"

Panic rose in her, but she quickly noted the amusement in his eyes and dismissed it, trying not to get lost in the depths of those chocolate brown eyes—with little amber and copper speckles that reminded her of autumn. Feigning more chagrin than she felt, she said, "You are not the 'nice' one you claim to be for even bringing that up."

"Because you'd rather pretend it never happened, right?" he pointedly challenged.

"That's right," she said, not backing down one bit. "I want to pretend it didn't happen. I wasn't supposed to ever see you again."

He arched a brow. "Is that so?"

She almost swallowed her tongue at that question but managed to charge forward. "Yes. It's so. And we both know you know it. Don't pretend otherwise."

"But here I am," he said softly. "What are you going to do with me?"

Holly leaned back against the leather of the booth, and tried to portray her calm and collected courtroom persona. But as she crossed her arms in front of her chest and the glittery Santa shirt her mother had insisted she wear that day, and now regretted immensely, she was anything but. She was in uncharted territory. The men she'd been with in the past might have been merely "vanilla sex" competent, but at least she knew what to do with them. This one, she did not. At least not outside her fantasies, definitely not in flesh and blood. She'd never acted as brazenly as she had with Cole. What was she going to do with him? There were lots of things she *wanted* to do with him. Like lick him in all kinds of places, but that wasn't going to happen.

He arched a brow that said, *Feel free to throw out suggestions if you are having trouble narrowing the options. Or I could suggest a few possibilities myself.* His eyes twinkled with sexy mischief. "You could start—"

Carol reappeared at that moment, and Holly wanted to scream. She could start how? Start by kissing him all over? By getting up and dragging him to the restroom and finally feeling what it was like to have that man inside her? To——

"How's Jacob doing?" Carol asked, filling the two coffee cups she'd brought to the table with the pot she held. "I heard from Katie over at the salon, he got in some fight at The Tavern Friday night, defending some woman from a wife beater, and broke his leg."

"Jacob is doing a fine job of defying doctor's orders to stay in bed and has irritated me every opportunity he gets. So he's pretty much back to his normal self, with the addition of a cast and bigger-than-usual attitude."

Carol chuckled. "He was a hero from what I hear," she told him. "Helped that poor woman. So cut the boy some slack. I'll give you some pie to take to him. That coconut kind he likes so much. Let me know if you two need anything more."

"I'll see that he gets it," he said. She walked away and he refocused on Holly. "And there you have the gossip circuit of a small town. She found out in the salon. But now *you* know. That's why my brother came to the truck the other night; otherwise they would not have. Some fun over a beer inside the tavern is one thing. They know appropriate boundaries."

Holly now felt bad for thinking the worst of his brothers the night before. "I'm sorry. I thought. . . ." She pushed her computer aside, welcoming him for the first time since he sat down. She should be writing, but she wasn't going to try now. The diner would close soon anyway. "Did Jacob at least get one good jab in before he went down?"

A slow smile turned up the corners of his mouth. "That's the exact question I asked when I found out."

She smiled. "You did?"

He nodded.

"And?" she prodded. "Did he?"

"He did," Cole said. "But the woman went right back to her husband. Jacob's feeling like he did it all for nothing."

Holly poured cream into her coffee and stopped a moment. "That's not true," she said. "Tell him it's not true. What he did told her there are people out there that will help. Maybe it will become the tiny chip in her husband's persona of intimidation that makes her less afraid to act. Sheriff Jack was involved, I assume? He's never been one to look the other way. He'll stay on the guy."

"Sheriff Jack is the reason Jacob isn't charged with assault. This kid he scrapped with is new in town. The sheriff promised the guy he'd take off his badge and punch him himself if he ever heard of him hitting a woman again. That pretty much discouraged him from filing charges." He studied her a moment. "You know this town as if you grew up around here. And if the staff here is any indicator, it seems folks know you, too."

Part of her clamored with the warning to stop the talking, to avoid getting personal, but she found herself answering anyway. "As I mentioned, I grew up here, yes. Went to school with Sheriff Jack. His dad pulled me out of more than a ditch or two in his day as sheriff." She shook her head. "That was when I first had my driver's license and it was not pretty. I wasn't so good at navigating in the snow."

Amusement flickered across his face. "And now? Are you good in the snow now?"

"Judging from the slipping and sliding I was doing coming over here, no," she said, and laughed, amused at herself. "I'm out of practice, for sure. Other than a short visit here or there, I've been gone ten years. Around my area of the country, these past ten years, snow is a fable."

"Where would that be?"

"Houston, Texas. Law school and then a law firm."

He picked up the book. "And then writer?"

"Yes. And finally doing it full-time, which has me nervous as heck. I can't seem to put words on the page. That's why I came home. I thought a change of scenery might help me through the terror of failure."

Glancing at the book and then at her, he said, "I think the part here that says '*USA Today* bestselling author' guarantees you've succeeded."

"One time on a list does not make a career," she said drily, and shifted the conversation away from anything that reminded her of the deadline fast approaching. "What about you? I know you weren't here before that because I've never heard of the Wiley brothers. And clearly everyone else has. How'd you end up here?"

"I came to town about two years after you left from the sounds of it." He slid back into the seat and stretched one long leg parallel to the table, his back against the wall, one arm lazily draped on the seat. Casual, easygoing. "My mom and dad—both gone now— retired from corporate living in upstate New York. Dad and I had always talked about opening a business together, and it seemed the right time. I was twenty-five, four years out of college, working for a big-city contractor. There wasn't a local operation in Haven, so it seemed a perfect fit. And where we went, my brothers tended to follow."

She curled her jean-clad legs onto the seat and angled herself toward him. "I have two sisters and a younger brother who I adore, but I don't think I could work with any of them." She lifted her cup and mock-toasted him. "You're a better man than I." She sighed and set her cup back down. "Though I'm looking forward to seeing them when they get here. I just have to get my work done first." She glanced at her watch. "They're closing here soon." Holly sighed. "And my parents' place is proving a distraction that's not working." She laughed, feeling a bit awkward about what that distraction truly was. "I guess this town will never be big enough for a Starbucks. I would've torn through some pages with a good White Mocha in hand."

"I have a nice, quiet den with a fireplace," he said. "Come home with me, Holly." A smile touched his lips. "Use me for my work space."

She laughed despite the nerves fluttering in her stomach. She shut her computer. "No. That's not a good idea." It was time to go far, far away from Cole Wiley. Before she did something she would regret later. It was too late for fantasy. She couldn't be the wild fantasy girl, free of inhibitions when she was Big Sis Holly Reddy, home for the holidays.

He sat up, fixed all his attention on her so she felt couldn't breathe. "No," she said, answering before he could ask again. "You'll distract me."

"I'll try not to."

"It won't work."

He laughed. "Good. I don't want it to. But the truth is, I have piles of paperwork waiting for me, with deadlines of my own. I'd still be working, but I was seeing double and had to take a break." He arched a brow at her. "So you see? We both have to work. We'll hole up by the fire and motivate each other to get our work done."

She laughed, and slid her computer into her briefcase. "You think we'll motivate each other to work." It wasn't a question. Nothing about being with this man was going to motivate her to work. More like, motivate her to get naked and scream an "Oh God!" two or three or ten times.

Mischief and mayhem lurked in the depths of those brown eyes as he said, "I'm a firm believer in reward programs."

Heat spiraled in her core. "Rewards," she repeated, her tongue thick with the word.

"Rewards," he assured her. "Would you like me to offer a few examples? Say, you complete five pages, so I—"

Holly's heart jackknifed as Carol approached the table. "No. No!" she cut him off. "No need for examples."

"Here you go," Carol said, setting the bag on the table. "A big piece of pie for Jacob." She pulled out her pad of paper. "You ready to order, Cole?"

He glanced up at Carol. "This will do it," he said, reaching in his pocket and tossing money on the table. "Just needed a little caffeine and it's back to work for me."

Carol made a *tsk* sound. "You're always working." She motioned to Holly. "You should try and make him relax a little."

Cole arched a brow, all sexy and playful, silently challenging her to do that and more.

Holly laughed nervously. "I'll get on that," she said. "Right after I write another three hundred pages."

Carol rolled her eyes. "What am I going to do with you two?" she asked before she scurried away as another customer called to her.

"The real question," Cole said, "is what are you going to do with me?"

Rip your clothes off. Lick every inch of delicious muscle. Holly shoved those naughty little thoughts away and finished packing her bag.

"Say good night is what I'm going to do," she said, but she wanted a push, a reason to do the naughty, not the nice. "So good night."

He studied her a moment, and she could feel him sizing her up, gauging her position. "I'll walk you to your car," he said finally. "You can follow me home."

There was her push. Holly's heart exploded in her ears, and she made one last-ditch attempt to convince herself to say no. The time for fantasy had passed. It was time to focus on the here and now. But the rewards Cole had mentioned . . . perhaps the rewards would be motivational. She would type five pages, she'd have an orgasm. Another five pages, it was his turn. Oh yes, she liked that. It might be highly productive.

"I have to get my work done," she stated. "This isn't negotiable."

A smile tugged on his lips. "Work first. Rewards later."

She inclined her head, satisfied he understood. Holly shoved her bag over her shoulder. "What are you waiting for?" she asked. "I thought you had a lot of work to do?"

One sexy dimple greeted her as he pushed to his feet. His big, delicious body towered so near her, she shivered with excitement. Because soon, that big, delicious body was going to be her reward. For the first time since arriving home, she couldn't wait to start writing.

Chapter Five

Not ten minutes after leaving the diner, with butterflies in her stomach, Holly stood in the foyer of Cole's home as he followed her inside. The ranch-style home sat only a few miles from her parents' place, and from what she could tell, it was cozy in its own right. Four stairs led from the tiled walkway of the entrance to a sunken living room. Decorated in warm browns, the overstuffed chairs and an amazingly comfy-looking couch sat before a massive rock fireplace. A big masculine desk framed the corner to the right of the hearth, with a notebook computer in the center, along with an open binder and files. If this was where they were working, it certainly was inviting.

The door shut behind her, and Cole stepped down the hallway to join her. Holly eagerly returned her attention to Cole, watching as he set the bag with her computer on the ground—he'd insisted on carrying it inside for her. Without question, he was as much a gentleman as he was a sinful diversion, one that she was no longer going to deny herself. Though she barely recognized the woman she'd been in the front seat of that truck, wild and wanton, unforgiving in her demand for pleasure, she had found that freedom alluring. If any man could awaken that side of her, Cole was that man.

She would have thought she'd be scared right now, afraid she wouldn't know how to respond to Cole or live up to his expectations. But she remembered that moment in the truck, when she'd felt embarrassed, and how amazingly wonderful he'd been. So far it seemed that, with Cole, there was no right or wrong to pleasure. There was simply pleasure. That was a trend she wholeheartedly hoped would continue.

Holly watched as Cole shrugged out of his jacket with a delicious flex of muscle and hung it on the rack beside him. Anticipation thrummed through her veins as he eased her coat from her shoulders. The coolness of the room shimmered over her skin, a contrast to the heat Cole generated within her. Her nipples tightened, her breasts grew heavy. Would Cole touch her now? Would he kiss her?

The answer came after he'd hung her coat up. His hands settled on her light blue, long-sleeved sweater, his hips framing her backside without actually touching. The urge to lean back and feel that long, hard body pressed close was almost too much for her to resist.

"Welcome to my home, Holly," he whispered near her ear, his mouth nuzzling her neck for a moment before he stepped away. Her body vibrated with dissatisfaction at the loss of his nearness, and she turned to face him, finding him still close, so very close—

he towered over her, his ruggedly male presence stealing her breath. Their eyes locked, the sexual tension between them riveting. One dark brow lifted in challenge. "Shall we get to work so we can earn those rewards?"

Work. Right. Work. Her book. "Yes. Yes, let's do that," she said softly, thinking about the rewards with ever-growing interest.

He retrieved her bag from the ground and motioned her forward. "Will the couch work or do you need a table?"

"The couch works great," Holly said as she walked down the few short stairs. "I love the sunken living room."

"My dad and I built my place," he said, setting her bag down on the oversize, square coffee table. "Then about two years later, we built the one next door for my brothers to share."

More and more, she liked this man. His way with people. His way with family. His way with her, for that matter.

"Sounds like you're all very close," she said appreciatively. She wondered about his mom and dad, but didn't ask.

He shook his head. "Yeah. We are. Losing my dad was rough. He had a heart attack a year ago." He pulled open the iron fireplace curtains. "Mom died of cancer a year before that. Honestly, I don't think my dad wanted to live without her." He shoved some wood into the fireplace, arranging kindling and logs.

"My grandmother died this past summer," she said. "Same kind of thing. My grandfather went and she was ready to go with him."

Dusting his hands off, Cole reached for a long lighter, and paused with a thoughtful look. "Hard to imagine that kind of love." He flicked the lighter to life. "But my parents certainly had it."

Pondering the concept of love, Holly typed in her password on her computer, while Cole finished setting the fire. Flames flickered, rich with shades of blue and red, and she lost herself in thought, wondering about that kind of love. She'd never yearned for love. Never felt incomplete without it. But lately, she had been empty inside in an unfamiliar way and assumed it was the seclusion of writing.

Suddenly, Holly blinked and brought Cole into focus, realizing that he was sitting on the edge of the hearth, watching her.

"It'll be warm soon," he said, tilting his head slightly, studying her. "Penny for your thoughts."

Holly glanced at his corner desk and back at him. "Wondering what you're working on?" she asked, and silently added, *And when you are going to kiss me*. "Looks like you have quite a stack of papers."

"Oh," he said, weariness slipping into his expression. "Yes. A never-ending pile, it seems. We just sold the family business to a Manchester firm, and they want every job we've ever done logged in a spreadsheet."

"Wow," she said. "That's a big step."

He nodded his agreement. "But not a big decision. I was ready. Most of our work was in Manchester, despite our efforts to find enough here in town, which had been our plan. The drive back and forth was killing profits and time." He ran his hands down his powerful thighs. "Once I finish this spreadsheet, we're done. We move on."

Disappointment jabbed at Holly. Was he leaving Haven right when she was thinking of returning? Not that she really thought she would return. In fact, most likely she would not. But still. She wanted to know. "What will you do now?"

"What I intended in the first place," he commented. "We're already working on that. We bought a house a few miles away to convert to a bed-and-breakfast. With all three of us focused on making it a success, we hope it will be one of several ventures in the future. Three brothers, three operations—that's the goal. But, of course, only after we master success with the first one."

"That sounds wonderful," she said sincerely. "And daring. Leaving behind an established business."

"Like leaving a law career to write novels?" he inquired.

Her stomach twisted a little at that comparison. "Yes. Exactly. I just made the big leap recently, and apparently I have performance anxiety." She laughed, but not with humor. "It's scared me into writer's block."

His brows dipped. "If you were successful enough to write full-time, why be nervous now?"

It was a question that she'd explored over the past few days and had come to a conclusion, one she was surprisingly comfortable sharing with Cole. "It's all I have now. The only source of income. I can't fail. . . ." The vulnerability of starting that sentence and finishing it with the reality of her situation, twisted her in knots.

Cole pushed off the hearth then, and Holly's heart raced as he moved closer. Cole knelt beside her, the coffee table and his body enclosing her against the couch. He reached out and brushed hair from her eyes, the barely there touch charging her with awareness.

"You won't fail, Holly." His expression filled with tenderness rather than lust, desire rather than demand. "You won't. In fact, I won't let you. How long are you here for?"

"A month."

"How many pages a day do you have to write to get the book done?"

"Including time off for the holiday, twenty good pages."

"How many have you written today?"

"Ten."

"Were they good?"

She nodded. "Yes," she said. "Yes, I think they were." Which was a miracle in and of itself.

He leaned closer, dipping his head, his breath a warm rush of tantalizing promise. She could almost taste his kiss, and he hadn't even touched her yet. "You need ten more pages," he repeated.

"Good pages," she whispered, thinking more about his mouth than about the keyboard begging for her fingers.

His lips brushed hers and she shivered. "I want you, Holly," he confessed, a moment before his tongue caressed past her teeth and drew her into a spellbinding kiss. She melted into the connection like warm chocolate near a hot flame. It was a long, sensuous kiss, a kiss of passion, a kiss of promise.

When he pulled back, Holly wanted to hold him, to tell him to keep going. But he framed her face with his big hands, held the control with that gentle touch, as he might hold a key.

"Ten more until I can do that again," he murmured. "Ten pages until I strip every inch of your clothing off and feel you next to me. That's torture, Holly." He kissed her forehead. "So get to work before I explode into flames." And then he was gone, pushing to his feet and leaving her feeling cold. The kind of cold no fire could warm. Only he could. Only Cole.

Holly watched as he settled those long, powerful legs behind his desk, and she drew a deep breath, her nostrils still alive with the fresh male scent of him. He flipped the desk light on and glanced her way. Their eyes connected, and they shared a smile. And then Holly went to work. Ready to finish those ten pages, to reach her career goals. Cole was right. She would not fail. Failure was not an option.

Holly had been punishing herself for not reaching page count, depriving herself of any form of pleasure, and it had paralyzed her. There was a lesson in all of this, no matter what happened with Cole. And thanks to Cole, she realized now that success and pleasure were best served in combination. She'd start with her part, the success, the page count. Then, move on to the part with him—the pleasure.

Hours after initiating their work challenge, Cole sat back in his chair and watched Holly diligently typing, deep in concentration. The faces she made, smiling or frowning, were adorable, as if she were living out the scenes on her pages.

He wondered at how a trip to grab coffee and stretch his legs had turned into Holly being here with him. He didn't invite women to his home, and he told himself he'd done so with Holly because she came with no strings attached; she wasn't in town to stay. Come the end of the holiday season, she would be gone. He didn't want or need the complications of a small-town romance, especially not when he was in the middle of a major life change in starting a new business.

But none of that explained why he felt so right sitting with her in front of the fireplace. Why the silence between them was comfortable rather than awkward. Why he could look at her for long spells of time without losing interest and it had nothing to do with the lust she'd stirred within him.

Lust that pulsed through his veins at rocket speed as she did a languid stretch before turning her attention on him. A barely there, shy smile tugged on her pretty pink mouth and told a silent story—in a mere two hours, she was done with her ten pages. And he was more than ready to offer her the reward.

As if confirming his observations, she pushed to her feet, her jeans cradling a lush ass the way, he vowed, his hips would be, sometime before this night was over. She crossed the room toward him, and he had no qualms about openly admiring the natural sway of her feminine curves as she sashayed toward him.

"All done, I take it?" he asked, leaning back in the leather desk chair, exploring the nuances of what made Holly, Holly—what made her so damn addictive.

"I am," she confirmed, easing around the desk to perch beside him on the edge of the wooden surface. "But now that I've finished my ten pages, I have a confession to make."

"Confession?" he inquired, his interest piqued.

"That's right," she said, sliding along the edge of the desk and scooting to sit directly in front of him.

Cole's gaze slid over her legs and he contemplated the moment he would inch them apart and find his way inside her. "Tell me," he urged, returning his attention to her face.

"I was afraid you'd be a distraction I couldn't afford," she admitted. "So when I went to The Tavern to meet you, I planned on one hot night, nothing more. No names. No tomorrows."

"And now?"

"Your idea of work for reward has thus far proven to be far more motivational than it has been a distraction." Her tone turned to teasing flirtation. "Of course, I have yet to find out if the reward is as good as the promise."

Cole slid his chair closer, his hands settling on her knees. "I can assure you, Holly, that the reward will most definitely be worth the work." His palms caressed a path up her legs, thumbs brushing her inner thighs to the fiery hot V of her body. She flushed and sucked in a tiny breath. Her responsiveness pleased him, and he'd barely gotten started. His hands tracked a path back to her knees. Slowly, he inched them apart.

"Are you ready for me?"

He reached down and tugged one of her boots off, setting her foot on his thigh. She had on pink polka-dot socks.

Holly laughed. "I didn't plan on showing my socks to anyone today."

Cole gave her a steamy look. "I can't wait to see what other surprises you have for me."

Cole discarded her other boot and set her foot on his thigh, his hands traveling down her calves as he pulled the socks off to reveal equally pink toenail polish. He smiled. She clearly liked pink. It fit her. A lovely, pink, passion flower yet to bloom. That was his job and he was going to enjoy every last minute of it.

"Anything else pink?" he questioned.

"Guess you'll have to wait and see," she joked back.

"Show me, Holly."

Chapter Six

*S*how me, Holly.

Holly's heart thundered in her ears as she replayed his words in her head. With any other man, she'd refuse to be completely naked and exposed, afraid of the vulnerability. But she trusted Cole, illogical as it might be since the man was a virtual stranger.

Nervous anticipation raged wildly within her, but not as severely as her desire for this man. She slid off the desk, bringing herself eye level with Cole's rich brown stare—a connection that touched her inside and out. She didn't remember ever looking into a man's eyes and feeling the sensations Cole created inside her. She coveted this man—or at least her body did—yearned for him in a way that downright shook her to the core. His hands nestling beneath her sweater, resting on her bare skin, and warming her, offered incentive to move forward, to feel more of his touch.

Reaching to the hem of her top, she pulled it over her head and exposed her turquoise blue bra. The rawness of his male hunger sent a shiver of excitement through her that thundered to a powerful halt between her legs. The look on his face said he wanted her. Watching her undress turned him on.

Aroused, empowered by this knowledge, Holly unsnapped her jeans and slid the zipper down. Cole leaned back in his chair again, allowing her room to shimmy the denim over her hips. She left the panties on. They matched her bra.

"No pink," she said, running her hands over the top of her bra, trying to forget reserve and simply act out her fantasies.

Powerful sensuality poured from his eyes as he leaned forward again and reached for her—positioning her between his legs, his hands shackling her hips.

"Take it off," he urged, his voice low, husky, his expression drawn with lust and desire. "Take it all off."

He clearly didn't care about pink or blue at this point. Gone was the laughter of moments before, replaced by something darker, richly passionate. And it both aroused and frightened her. This was the part where she feared she couldn't keep up, where she wouldn't know what to do. Or she'd look stupid doing it. But she wanted more of this darker Cole. Much more. She decided she would grant his wish, yield to his demand, as one might jump off a cliff into a body of crystal clear water. To get to the destination, there could be no slow, thoughtful tumble over the edge.

Holly unhooked her bra, tossing it aside, freeing her breasts. Cole's instant, ravishing inspection pebbled her nipples into tight balls. It was all she could do to stop herself from reaching up and touching them, to ease the throb of need. But she hesitated, suddenly back on the edge of that cliff again, her instinctive reserve something she couldn't seem to let go of.

But Cole didn't give the reserve time to take root. His hands settled on her hips, positioning her as she was before, between his strong thighs. His tongue quickly lapped at one sensitive nipple. Holly moaned with the sudden, unexpected pleasure, her hands sliding into his hair as he repeated the act on the other nipple.

He pressed her hands back to her breasts, melding the soft flesh with both of their hands. Then he spread her fingers, teased her nipples with his fingers and hers, before lowering his head. With her fingers still framing the stiff peaks, he licked and teased. It was an erotic sharing of her pleasure that had her dripping wet, her core clenching with desire, with unfulfilled need.

She reached for his shirt and tugged, shoving it up the wall of his muscular chest. He yanked it over his head and tossed it aside. His mouth lowered, slanting over hers in a hungry kiss.

Her fingers curled in the soft, dark hair of his chest, traveling along the solid muscle. She wanted to know what the rest of him was like. What they would feel like, skin against skin.

"I need you inside me," she whispered hoarsely.

He pulled back for a flash of a moment, stared at her, searched her face. Then, with a low growl, Cole reached for the silk at her hips and dragged it down. Her hands settled on his powerful shoulders, steadying herself, as she kicked the panties aside. A moment later he lifted her back onto the desk, where he spread her legs and put one on each arm of his chair. Her hands settled against the wood behind her, thrusting her breasts high in the air. She was naked, on display—he was still partially clothed. She wanted him naked, wanted him on top of her, inside her. But his warm palms branded her thighs, easing upward as they had before she'd undressed, and she forgot everything but the moment.

Urgency built within her as he caressed a path higher and higher, until finally, she was rewarded with the sweet bliss of his thumb gently stroking her nub. Pleasure jolted her, her lashes heavy as his fingers stroked a path along the slick, wet folds of her core. Two long fingers slid inside her and stroked the inner wall of her body in just the right spot. Her core clenched with each stroke of his fingers, each flick of her clit. With expert hands, he had her on the edge already. She was pumping against his palm, his fingers— lost, so very lost. She was sprawled out naked on top of the desk and didn't care. Her hips thrust against the expert manipulation of his hands. She could feel the edge of release curling inside her, almost taste the moment it would snap. She just needed one more stroke of those fingers in that exact spot. One more, one more. One . . . She shook with release, tumbled over, and jerked with the intensity. His fingers stroked her to completion, softer with each passing second. But she could still feel that deep thrum of need.

His hands scooped her back, pulled her to a sitting position. She knew when his mouth closed down on hers with a hard hunger that he'd sacrificed his pleasure for hers. Her palm curved around the hard bulge of his cock pressing against his jeans.

Breathlessly, she said, "This is what I want. You. You inside me. I can barely think I want that so badly."

"Hey, Cole," came a male voice from outside the front door, followed by knocking. "Open up, man." Then another muffled male voice.

"Holy crap," Cole said, grabbing his shirt and shoving it over Holly's head. "That would be my brothers. Again."

Holly scrambled to shove her arms into the sleeves, heart racing with panic. She crossed her arms in front of her body. "This can't be happening."

He laced his hands into her hair, brushed his lips over hers. "I'm sorry. I'll get rid of them. Don't run away like you did last time."

She scoffed at that. "I didn't run away. I—"

A fist beat on the door. "Cole, man. It's cold. I'm going to use my key."

"Wait, Jacob, damn it," Cole yelled, staring back down at Holly. "Promise me you won't bolt. I won't let them inside. I promise. They mean well."

"I understand what siblings can be like," she said. "The joy . . . and the downright torture, which this is, by the way." His eyes softened, lips lifting slightly a moment before he kissed her forehead. It was a sweet gesture, one that had that frightening, run-for-the-hills, can't-get-enough-of-it relationship kind of feeling to it.

He turned toward the door, and Holly hugged herself, noting the stealthy male grace in his every step despite his quickened pace. It was beginning to look like she'd never find out what it was like to have that man fully to herself.

Cole grabbed his jacket and zipped the front before disappearing down the hall and then outside. The muffled conversation was loud enough for her to hear bits and pieces. Something about a Christmas tree. They'd brought him a tree!

Holly snagged her jeans and shoved her legs inside. Wiggled her hips to pull them on. The front door opened and shut, Cole appearing in the hallway alone.

She didn't give him time to speak. "I heard," she said. "They brought you a tree. I have to go. I'm hurrying." She bent down to pick up her socks.

"They're putting it in the garage," he said, crossing the room.

Holly straightened as he reached her side. "No!" She pointed to the door. "Go get them. Tell them to bring it inside. I'm leaving."

She bent down and grabbed her socks and sat down in the chair. Cole knelt beside her. "Holly, I'm sorry about this. Abe ran into one of our mother's close friends, and she talked a lot about Mom and how she would be worried about us. How she would roll over in her grave if she found out her boys hadn't had a tree since she'd passed. So Abe rounded up Jacob and we now have a tree."

Holly's heart squeezed with that news and she touched his cheek. "I think the tree is a great thing," she said. "And I wouldn't dream of ruining that for you." Even in her mode of panic, Holly could see this was part of Abe's healing process.

"Then stay," Cole insisted. "Help us decorate it. It needs a woman's touch."

Holly's heart swelled. How had a wild night of fantasy sex turned into decorating a Christmas tree with his family? "I . . . I don't know. I . . . What about your brothers?"

He grabbed her hand and kissed her palm, peered at her with a plea in those chocolate brown eyes. "Stay, Holly. Help us decorate the tree, and then later"—he grinned—"I'll wrap you up and put you under the tree."

She laughed. "Wrap me in what?"

He wiggled an eyebrow. "Me."

TWO HOURS LATER, LAUGHTER FOLLOWED Holly into Cole's kitchen of shiny black-and-gray granite. Cole had gone for firewood while his brothers playfully argued over who deserved the honor of placing the topper on the tree. Smiling at the silliness of Cole's brothers, she thought of her own siblings with longing. Another week, and Rachel, the middle sister, would be the first to arrive home. Rachel was now a big-time advertising executive in New York City, which felt worlds away from Texas. Holly couldn't wait to give her a big hug and hear what was happening in her life.

Warmed by that thought, Holly filled her glass with ice and Coca-Cola and crossed to the door. But then she hesitated when she heard her name, knowing she shouldn't eavesdrop, but finding it impossible not to.

"I like Holly," Abe said. "Cole must, too, since he never brings his women home."

Jacob snorted. "Holly's going to go back to Houston. She's safe. Not that Holly isn't cool and all. I'm just saying. You know how Cole is."

How Cole is. Holly swallowed hard against the discomfort the words caused. She inhaled deeply and tried to understand why that bothered her. She'd not come here with the expectation of anything but a hot escape with Cole. It shouldn't surprise her that he would see her in the same way—a hot holiday escape that ended when she went back home. Her gut twisted a little. But Cole was no longer a nameless one-night stand. And she had never been simply an out-of-town girl leaving soon. She was thinking of moving home.

She turned back to the counter and set her glass on top, holding the cold surface with a steely grip. What was she doing? If she moved back here, things could be awkward with her and Cole. If she didn't—painful to leave. She didn't want to feel like her long-term decisions were influenced by a fantasy, and she feared that was where this was headed. She needed to talk to him, to figure this out.

Cole's voice sounded on the other side of the door a minute before he was suddenly there in the kitchen with her, leaving her no time to analyze her feelings or get a grip on them. Holly turned as he closed in on her; his legs framed hers, his arms outstretched to hold the cabinet on either side of her.

"Hey," he said as if they hadn't seen each other five minutes ago and she wasn't standing in *his* kitchen.

Holly found herself laughing, the coil of tension inside her fading quickly. "Hey."

He wiggled his brows. "I hear you're using me for my body?"

She grinned at the repeated words she'd spoken a few minutes ago to his brother Jacob. "I like your tree, too," she teased, feeling lighter by the moment. Cole was just so damn good at making her forget to be stressed—even when she should be. He was easy to be with. *Easy to have fun with,* she thought, as she added, "And it's a good thing." She lowered her voice to a whisper. "Because I can't even manage to get your pants off."

He laughed and kissed her, stepping closer so that the hard proof of his arousal pressed against her stomach. "Don't I know it," he murmured against her neck, and nibbled her ear. "I can't wait until we're alone."

Her hands sculpted his muscular back. He felt good. He smelled good. Like warm cinnamon and spice. "Me neither." Maybe tonight should be where she stopped this thing with Cole.

She didn't know what her next move should be. Didn't want to think about it at this very moment. But she did want to enjoy what time they had. She played with the dark strands of his hair. "Don't rush your brothers off because of me. They seem really into the tree thing."

He studied her, his expression suddenly serious. "I'm glad you're here, Holly." The sincerity took her off guard, warmed her inside out, and Holly knew in that moment that she was in trouble. She couldn't seem to get him into his bedroom, and if she wasn't careful, soon she might not get him out of her heart. Which made the idea of being daring, of reaching beyond her limits all the more appealing. Better to keep this in perspective—this was a fantasy, a fling. An erotic adventure.

"I'm glad I'm here, too," she said, sliding her hand down the front of his pants and stroking his cock. "Let me show you how glad." He thickened beneath her touch, and she felt the high of that power to please, to tease. She'd never been so bold, and she was beginning to like it. She went up on her toes and nipped his lips, while one finger tracked the ridge of his erection. "You like that, yes?"

"Holly," he whispered. "If you don't stop now—"

She smiled. "I might make you come?" she challenged, her body caressing a path down his until she was on her knees before him. Her hands settled on his hips as she tilted her chin, staring up at him. "Do you want to come, Cole?" She had his zipper down by the time she'd finished the question, her hand freeing the thick, hot length of his cock.

"Yes, baby," he said roughly. "I want to come. Take me in your mouth."

She wrapped the width of him in one hand, a ball of liquid pooling at the tip of the head. Holly stared up at him and licked it free. He moaned and grabbed the counter.

"Shhh," she warned. "Your brothers might hear."

"I really don't give a damn right about now, Holly," he said. "They know when to get lost, and if they don't, I'll kick their asses." His eyes heated, his cock pulsed. "Suck me, sweetheart. Suck me, now."

The idea that they could be discovered was surprisingly arousing. But she wasn't ready to give him what he wanted, not yet. She licked him instead, lapped at the silky head of his erection with long, languid strokes of her tongue, and found herself moaning when the salty taste of his arousal touched her lips. The muscles in her womb clenched and tightened.

She stared up at him, watching him watch her. The raw, animalistic hunger in his expression drove her wild. Teasing him was torture, and she could wait no longer. Holly drew him into her mouth, sucking him deep, and wrapped one hand around his stellar, tight ass. She wanted all of him, wanted him as hot as she felt. He pumped his hips, low guttural sounds escaping his mouth as he worked against her, pulsing and throbbing in her mouth. She could feel the tension in him, the need for release. He was damned near shaking and so was she. She'd never had a man come in her mouth and she wanted that now, wanted to taste his release, feel that power, that control. She licked and sucked, urging him onward. *Give it to me,* she thought. *Give it to me.* As if he heard her silent demand, he tensed and then shook, his cock spasming against her lips. Suddenly, her body clenched, tightened. Disbelieving, she realized she was coming, and with each pulse of her own body, she sucked him harder, deeper, took his pleasure with her own. Drank in every last drop of his release and then slowly, delicately licked the head of his still-thick erection and stared up at him.

"Now we can go finish the tree," she whispered.

HOLLY SNUGGLED INTO THE BURST of warmth surrounding her, her lashes fluttering as she came awake to find herself in Cole's strong arms. He lifted her from the couch where she remotely remembered curling under a blanket and listening to him and his brothers talk about holidays of the past.

"Where are we going?" she asked, her arms wrapping around his neck, noting the absence of his brothers, who had clearly departed while she slept.

"Not far," he said, settling her down on a blanket in front of the fire a moment before he pushed to his feet and started undressing. In a blink, Holly shook off the haze of sleep, her mouth watering. Finally, she had Cole to herself, all of him. She was instantly wide awake, enthralled by every inch of his exposed skin. The tree twinkled behind him, casting rainbows of color on the taut, gorgeous muscles he wasted no time displaying—first he removed his shirt, exposing broad shoulders, a tapered waist, and a six-pack of rock-hard abdominals that damned near made her orgasm just looking at them. Then, one piece after the other, his clothing disappeared.

In only seconds, he stood gloriously naked before her, his cock jutting forward in an impressive arousal. She was on her knees in an instant, crawling toward him, not about to wait for him to come to her, desire driving her to be the aggressor. Her body gushed just thinking about taking him in her mouth, and this time she would have no mercy. She would make him beg for satisfaction before it was over.

Holly settled at his feet, and caressed up his powerful calves and then wrapped the base of his cock with her palm. He moaned and stiffened, the lines of his face harsh, primitive, laden with the urgent anticipation she'd hoped to invite. She'd given her share of blow jobs in her college years, compliments of a boyfriend who favored his pleasure over hers. And she'd found that the process of mastering it, much like a craft, was enticing though not quite enjoyable. Never had she wanted to take a man in her mouth for the sheer pleasure of it—until now. Until Cole. She was like a new woman with Cole. Daring. Willing to explore and eager to use her newfound sexuality to lead an encounter. With a seductive glance upward, she pinned him in a stare and licked the liquid bead pooling at the tip of his arousal, her free hand skimming an amazingly tight ass.

"You like that?" she asked, her lips lingering near his cock.

"Yes."

She licked the head again.

"Holly," Cole murmured, her name etched with the burn of his desire, his fingers pressed to her head, in her hair, urging her onward as she did a slow swirl of her tongue around the head of his cock.

"Do it, Holly. Take me."

"Not yet," she said, lapping at him. She wanted more than his orgasm. She wanted all of him; she wanted him wild, a ball of sexual tension unleashed with explosive pleasure.

So, she restrained herself, restrained him, maintained a facade of leisure as she licked up and down his length.

With long, languid strokes of her tongue, she teased them both until finally, inch by inch, she drew his cock into her mouth, taking him deeply. He was hot and hard and, like before, she tasted, with satisfaction, the salty, taut need building within him.

Slowly, she began to pump his rod with her hand, suckling him and laving him with her tongue. Harder, she pulled on him; deeper, she took him—yes . . . she wanted him deeper. His cock expanded, thickened. What she couldn't manage with her mouth, she covered with a tight wrap of her palm. His muscles strained; the sinewy lines of well-defined male perfection flexed as pleasure stole away his control.

"Harder, baby," he panted. "Deeper." She smiled against his cock, and gave him what he wanted, working him with her hand and mouth. The slow rock of his hips was no longer contained, turning to all-out thrusts; his hands settled more firmly in her hair. He was on the edge, rushing over into release. She drew him deeper, and he tensed a moment before shuddering to release. She worked her mouth around him, lapped up every last moment of the reward, and then slowly brought him down.

But there was no time to revel in her success, her power over this amazing man. Cole swiftly shifted the power, claiming control. One moment he was standing, the next, on his knees in front of her, his eyes smoldering with the promise of a bounty of sinful delights. He lowered her to the blanket, framing her body with his, the fire beside them crackling with hot embers.

He whispered her name against her lips, "Holly." And she shivered with the passion-etched word. Shivered with the caress of his lips across her jaw, down her neck.

With sensual, tender hands, and nimble lips, he displayed a remarkable flair for finding every sensitive spot on her body. Demonstrating how sinful his lips could be in the most delightfully unexpected places, his tongue traced her wrist, the bend of her arm, the line of her spine clear to her backside.

She was lost, barely aware of the moment he slid a condom in place. Barely aware of her own name for the tenderness of his lovemaking.

And when he settled the pulsing thickness of his arousal between her legs, she held her breath as she waited to finally feel him inside her. He teased her, gliding his thick, hard length back and forth along the slick wet heat of the V of her body, stroking her with sensation but denying her the reward of release.

With a nip of his teeth on her lips, he pulled back to capture her in a fiery stare that implored her to look at him as he entered her. Only when he seemed confident he had her attention, did he slide that sinfully hard cock past her sensitive flesh. He hesitated a moment, taunting them both with what was to come, and then thrust hard. Holly gasped as he sunk deep, a kaleidoscope of sensations exploding in her body, followed by a sigh of satisfaction. A sigh he swallowed with a kiss, his lips slanting over hers with tenderness that turned to wild need. Soon they were in a frenzied rush of lovemaking—primal, red-hot. They moved together, faster, rougher, ravenous.

Cole grabbed one of her legs and pulled it over his shoulder. Holly quickly aided him, sliding the other one over his shoulder as well. He leaned forward and pinched her nipples; her womb spasmed around his cock. Passion ripped across his features as he grabbed her legs for leverage and, raising up on his knees, thrust into her with newfound force. Each thrust shot pleasure through her body, and the sight of his sweat-glistened body straining as he thrust that thick, hard cock inside her was complete bliss.

"Yes," she murmured as the build of pressure began; she gave in to the need to shut her eyes as she arched into him. She wanted more of that spot, to tell him so. *More.* More. Did she dare say it? It was something she'd never done before, but she needed this so damned bad. She needed . . . "Yes. Yes. Harder. Harder, Cole."

He groaned and pushed her legs to her chest, curling her inward and thrusting fast and hard. The explosion of pleasure came fast, without warning, and a cry lodged in Holly's throat. Cole pumped again and again, and then grunted with a hard lunge, sinking deep, and spilling his pleasure inside her. They clung to each other, riding out the last waves of release until slowly he eased her legs down and slid between them. They lay like that for long moments, his head buried in her neck, bodies melded together.

Minutes later, Cole rolled over and settled her under his arm, her head nestled on his chest. She felt remarkably content in a way she'd never felt with a man. A wonderful lover, a fire, a Christmas tree. What more could a girl desire?

Thinking of the tree reminded her of the tree topper. She'd fallen asleep without seeing it. She rolled onto her stomach to stare up at the tree. Cole immediately rolled to his side, wrapping his arm around her and nuzzling her neck and distracting her from the tree.

"What's wrong, baby?" he murmured.

The endearment, though easily spoken by a man to a woman, felt intimate and special. "I wanted to see . . ." She blinked up at the tree topper. "It's a ruby angel," she whispered. What were the odds of a ruby wish *and* a ruby angel? How odd. She almost laughed, wondering if Grandma Reddy was up to mischief from above.

Cole rolled to his stomach and lifted onto his elbows to study the tree. "My parents bought that angel their first Christmas together, forty years ago." His voice took on a distant, thoughtful tone—a mixture of happy and sad faded in and out of the words. "My mother was very romantic about it. She had to have that angel on the tree for luck. One year when I was a teen, I remember finding her crying in the attic. She thought it was lost. We tore the house apart."

"Where was it?"

He chuckled and cut her a sideways look. "A hatbox in the closet where she'd put it so it would be safe."

Holly smiled and stared up at the angel, thinking of the ruby Grandpa had given Grandma. Of the love both rubies represented. "It's beautiful," she whispered.

Cole pulled her close, so they lay facing each other, heads on the pillows he'd brought for them. "You're beautiful."

"Thank you," she said, and she might have blushed, if not for the solemn quality she sensed in him.

She could see he was the pillar in his family. But even pillars had weak spots. She sensed that in his effort to appear strong for his brothers, he'd never properly faced his loss and dealt with his own sorrow. He was hurting.

She thought about her grandmother, but decided not to share her loss. Or even how her father had coped with losing his parents. She didn't want to diminish the importance of Cole and his family.

Holly reached out and touched his cheek. "Healing takes time."

His chest expanded with the words, as if he was surprised she understood what he was feeling. He pulled her hand to his mouth and kissed it, thanking her without words. His arms wrapped around her and pulled her close, curling her next to his body. And Holly knew that at least for this one night, she was his pillar.

Chapter Seven

The room was cold, the fire long ago having died, but he was warm. Cole woke to a soft feminine scent. He blinked awake, light spraying through a nearby window. Soft hair tickled his nose as he looked down at Holly curled to his side.

He waited for that feeling that usually came at this point. The one that expanded in his chest and told him it was time to say good-bye. But it didn't come. He shook himself inwardly, reached for that familiar comfortable feeling, but instead found something else, something beyond comfortable, something that bordered on fulfillment.

Holly shivered and snuggled closer to him, the stiff peaks of her nipples brushing his chest as she lifted her head and stared up at him with sleepy sky blue eyes.

"I'm once again reminded that I'm not in Texas anymore." Her teeth chattered. "I'm cold."

And he was hard, his dick as stiff as a steel rod, and this wasn't a case of morning wood. This was about Holly. About wanting her almost to the point of need. About how she seemed to fit him in every way and understand him—see through his barriers to his struggle over the loss of his parents. Hell. She even seemed to "get" his brothers.

A growing sense of peace formed in him, and he rolled her over, slid on top of her. "I'll keep you warm," he vowed as he felt her body melding to his in all the right places, her arms wrapping around his neck.

"You better," she said. "Because you can't be inviting a Texas girl into your home and freezing her to death. It's not right."

Texas girl. She was leaving. He felt a surprising jolt of discomfort that he didn't like. He kissed her, preferring the sweet taste of her instant desire, rather than thoughts of her departure. Deciding he'd get over whatever he was feeling for Holly, he'd make sure he did. He'd keep her close, get his fill of her. Work her out of his system. Fuck her until he could fuck no more. Starting now, he decided. Cole slipped his hand between her thighs, caressed the silky heat of her lips, and entered her.

He pressed to the deepest recesses of her body, and Holly sighed in that sweet, satisfied way that reached inside him and twisted him inside out. Unexpected possessiveness flared within him with the fierceness of a wildfire. He never wanted her to make that sound for another man. The realization drew him up short, and he buried his face in her neck. A memory of his father talking about his courtship of their mother replayed in his head: *When all the female wonders of the world fade in her presence, you'll know she's the one.* Cole had laughed at that, certain that the many varieties of women would always be far more appealing than one woman. But then, he had never met Holly.

NEARLY TEN O'CLOCK ON SATURDAY morning, more than a week after Holly had helped decorate Cole's tree, Holly sat at Cole's island counter, computer in front of her, wearing only his T-shirt. Only a few feet away, despite the ultra-macho facade he presented to the rest of the world, Cole made an adorably sexy effort to cook breakfast. No cereal and Pop-Tarts today, he'd said.

"Damn," he mumbled, displeased with something happening inside the skillet that he was tending. He wore blue plaid pajama bottoms that hugged his nice, tight backside in all the right places. He cut her a look over his shoulder, the flex of muscle rippling beneath a white tee. "Sorry, babe, but your over-easy eggs just became scrambled."

"Even better," she promised, smiling to herself. She loved everything about this man, she realized in that moment. It was insane. Crazy insane. She'd never loved all the little particulars about a man. But that was before Cole. The way he moved, the way he smiled that one-dimple smile. The way he hummed as he shaved and sang Garth Brooks in the shower. She knew these things because they'd become inseparable, with a few exceptions. Holly would lunch with her parents, then spend a few hours at the cottage writing.

Later, she'd meet Cole at his place for dinner and more writing, with a delicious reward to follow. His creative sexual expertise was quite remarkable, and despite her silent daily vow that this night would be the night she'd return home, she never did.

Thus far, they'd kept their relationship, or whatever it was, under wraps. At first, that had been fine. But her feelings were changing, her desire for nothing more than a quick fling fading, replaced by a longing for something more that she could no longer ignore. And unless she was completely off base, he felt the same way. She just wished she could be sure.

Regardless, sooner or later, she had to tell Cole she was think-ing of moving home. *Sooner,* she thought. Because she wasn't going to be driven away by a love affair gone bad. But she also didn't want him thinking she'd moved back to Haven in some kind of desperate stalker mode. Right. She had to tell him. Tell him now.

She drew a breath. Small talk to lead into the subject, she de-cided. "I thought you said you couldn't cook," Holly teased, peek-ing over the counter to admire his tight tush and biting her lip in appreciation.

He eyed her over his shoulder. "Scrambled eggs and bacon don't count as cooking."

"And if I said I scramble eggs about as well as I fix a car, what would you say?" she asked.

Cole chuckled and cast her another quick look. "I like takeout, and as for the car, that's what brothers are for. In this case—Abe."

"Your brothers might be a pain some days, but you're lucky to have your siblings nearby," Holly said. Being around Cole and his brothers had made her wish her siblings were closer. But now even moving back home wouldn't make that happen, since the Reddy siblings had all left Haven. "And as for the cooking," she added. "I do make a mean box of Kraft mac and cheese. Add a little Texas salsa and it's gourmet, baby."

Cole's cell phone rang a moment before it vibrated across the countertop beside Holly. "Can you see if that's Abe?" he asked, lifting the pan to pour the eggs onto a plate. She knew he didn't want to miss the call. He'd been trying to reach Abe about some survey on the property they were buying; the meeting was being moved to later that day.

Holly's chest tightened with the request. They were feeling like a couple. She'd never felt like a couple. Never wanted to be a couple. She grabbed the phone and scanned the screen. "It's him," she said.

"Can you answer it?" Smoke poured from the pan as he ran water over it. Bacon crackled on the stove with the need for attention. "Tell him to hold on."

Another moment of surprise washed over her before she punched the answer button. "Hi, Abe," she said, trying to sound cool and collected when she was wondering what judgment Abe would make about her answering Cole's phone. "It's Holly. Cole's cooking and—"

"Wait a minute," Abe said, his tone clipped. "Did you say that *my* brother—as in Cole Wiley—is cooking? What *the hell* are you doing to him, Holly?"

He sounded so serious, Holly faltered, unsure what to say. Before she could formulate a response, Cole cursed, and Holly's gaze jerked in his direction. He was holding his hand where he'd burned it, his jaw clenched in obvious pain.

"Oh crap," she said, followed by, "Hold on," into the phone, as she jumped off the bar stool to go to Cole's aid. Then to Cole, "Are you okay? How bad is it?"

"I'll live," he grumbled, turning on the water and shoving his hand under. "Burns like a bitch, though."

Holly flipped the heat off the bacon, the phone still at her ear. "Abe?"

"I'm here," he said. "And that's what I was trying to tell you. Cole's a menace in the kitchen," he added, obviously overhearing the entire mess. "A downright danger. Always has been. Get him the hell out of there before he burns it down."

Holly's chest filled with barely contained laughter because it appeared so true, but now wasn't the time to jest with Cole. Still, it was quite comical that with the steely tough exterior and firm resolve Cole radiated, a kitchen skillet had him grumbling in pain.

"I will," she vowed to Abe. "I'll get right on that."

Cole surveyed his wound as she watched and, with a grimace, he shoved his hand back under the water. "Tell Abe the meeting is pushed back to four o'clock."

She started to repeat the message. "Cole says—"

"I'll be there," Abe said. "But do your womanly, kiss-the-wound-and-make-it-better thing and have him call me back. We've got trouble with that guy who Jacob scrabbled with at the bar. He came up to us at a gas station last night and tried to start something. I held Jacob back, but I was damned tempted to pop the guy myself."

Holly cast Cole a concerned look. "Yes, okay. I'll make sure." She ended the call and set the phone aside.

"Once I sign the final papers on the bed-and-breakfast, I want you to come see the place," Cole said as Holly grabbed a towel and filled it with ice.

It pleased Holly that Cole wanted her to see the bed-and-breakfast. "I'd love that." She stepped to his side at the sink and turned off the water. "Wrap this around your hand and call Abe back. You're going to want to talk to him."

He ignored the ice and studied her. "What's that look you're giving me? What's up?"

She sighed. "That guy who Jacob tussled with at The Tavern tried to pick a fight with Abe and Jacob last night at some gas station."

"That son of a bitch," he said, ignoring the towel, the burn apparently forgotten as he reached for the phone. He dialed Abe and then glanced at the towel. He leaned over and kissed her forehead. "Thank you."

She tried to hand him the towel again, but Abe answered and Cole launched into conversation, towel forgotten again as he paced and talked. Holly sighed and set the towel down, shoving a hand through her sleep-rumpled hair, before digging in to try and save breakfast. By the time Cole hung up the phone, she'd concluded it was a hopeless effort. The eggs were watery and the bacon burned and greasy.

Cole set his phone back down, hands on his lean hips, his lips a thin, hard line. He was clearly not happy. "You're meeting Sheriff Jack today about those research questions, right?"

"Yes," she confirmed. "This afternoon. Hopefully, before my sister gets in. She's already on the road. Should be here by dinner."

"Good," he said, his tone firm, decisive. "I'll ride along. We can get some food on the way. I want to talk to the sheriff before this situation with Jacob gets any more out of hand."

She shook what felt like cobwebs from her head. "Wait. You've spent a week-plus hiding me away in your house, and now suddenly you decide we're going public? You think you might want to ask me?"

A dark challenge flickered across his handsome features. "You have a problem with people knowing we're dating?"

That drew her up short. "What? Dating? Are we dating? Is that what this is?"

He picked her up and set her on the counter, gently but firmly, nudging her legs apart to step between them. "You got a problem with that?" he challenged, his deep-chocolate eyes daring her to answer wrong. "Because I have to tell you, Holly. I'm done pretending this is nothing. And if you think I'm letting you hide me away any longer, you're wrong."

"Me?!" she demanded. "You're the one who hasn't suggested leaving the house."

"Because you have a gossip phobia," he countered.

"I don't!" she said. "I didn't want to get caught in your truck with my dress up to my waist. I thought you—"

His hands slid to her face, an impassioned look etching his features. "You thought wrong." His eyes searched hers. "Holly. I'm not letting you go back to Houston without finding out why you make me so crazy."

Her heart squeezed and she struggled to form words. "I make you crazy?"

"Yeah, baby," he said, pressing his forehead to hers. "You make me over-the-top crazy."

Sweet wonder slid through her. "You make me crazy, too," she whispered.

She smiled inside and out. This big, gorgeous, wonderful man was crazy about her. And she was crazy about him.

Still. The moving-home situation twisted in her gut. "Cole." She bit her lip, a bit nervous. Pressing her hands on his chest, she leaned back. "I need to tell you one thing."

He tensed, a muscle in his jaw jumping. "There's someone back in Houston."

"No!" she said, her hand brushing his cheek. "Nothing like that. I just . . . well . . . I came home for the holidays thinking of moving back to Haven. No one knows. I didn't want to be pressured to make a decision. But I need you to understand that if we don't work out, well . . . I won't be tucking tail and running back to Houston. Stay or go, I'm deciding based on what is right for me."

His eyes darkened, dilated. "Fair enough. As long as you know I plan to influence your decision." His palms pressed her T-shirt up her legs. "Starting now." He nibbled her ear. "I'm going to eat you for breakfast. Then you can take me to lunch." He went down on his knees, inched her legs farther apart, and then, with a gentle repositioning, he lifted one leg, and then the other, over his shoulders.

He leaned into her, his breath warm as it feathered her clit. "I'm going to taste you now, Holly." His eyes held hers, and he lowered his head, watching her as he suckled her sensitive nub into his mouth.

Holly gasped at the intimate contact and waves of pleasure shimmered through her limbs. Suddenly, he was licking her, exploring her with a firm, confident tongue that quickly built sensation into writhing desperation.

"Cole," she panted, asking for that untouchable, unbelievable place that only orgasm could deliver.

"Easy, baby," he murmured, brushing two fingers across her cleft before penetrating her, curving his fingers just right.

Holly arched into the feel of it, cried out when his lips and fingers worked together, worked her into a place of pure oblivion. There was no inhibition, no holding back the soft moans that floated heedlessly from her lips.

Tension tightened her stomach, her hips, the wave of pleasure rushing at her, release quivering around his fingers, into his mouth.

Any other time, with any other man, she'd have turned away, tried to hide her pleasure. But not with Cole. It didn't matter that he was watching her, that he seemed to see straight to her soul. Not anymore. He made her crazy and she liked it. Maybe, she even loved it. Maybe she loved him.

Chapter Eight

Several hours after the flipping, life-changing conversation he'd had with Holly in his kitchen, Cole was still shaking, scared in his boots as they exited the sheriff's office, his arm protectively wrapped around her shoulders. But this was the best damned scared he'd ever felt in his life. A raw, share-everything-you-are, good and bad, as in total emotional and physical disclosure. It was flipping terrifying. And exhilarating. He didn't care if he'd known Holly two weeks or twenty years, she was the "one" for him. He knew it down to the very core of his existence.

An icy gravel mixture crunched beneath Cole's feet as they stopped next to Holly's sensible rental car, and he pulled her into his arms. She'd told him she'd bought a BMW to celebrate her first, big, courtroom victory. He wanted to celebrate her next victory with her, and judging from what he'd read in the pages of her book, she was headed toward another one.

Holly slid her arms under his coat, her soft, warm body pressed close. Her cute, pointed chin tilted upward, her cheeks glowing rosy red from the wind. "Sounds like the sheriff is going to take care of Jacob's little problem."

Turned out the other kid had a petty theft and family violence record that made the sheriff none too happy about having him in town. He didn't plan to allow him to stay. "I hope he gets on it before Jacob does it for him."

Holly settled her hand over his heart. "Jacob has that cast. That should be a deterrent."

Cole sniffed at that. "You've been around Jacob enough to know he's not detoured by much."

Reluctantly, she agreed. "That is true."

"Did Sheriff Jack answer all of your questions for the book?"

"Oh yes," she said. "Exactly what I needed to finish up this chapter that I'm working on." She shifted the conversation, casting him a shy look. "I know I said I couldn't come out tonight because my sister's arriving, but can I change my mind? Come out late, after everyone's in bed?"

Was she kidding? "Hell yes, you can change your mind," he said as strands of her long, blond hair fluttered out from beneath her woven pink hat and tickled his chin. He slid his hand around her waist, brushing the curve of her hip. "You clearly don't get it yet, Holly, but you will. You will. As far as I'm concerned, you belong in my bed. Tonight. Every night."

She blushed, her lashes fluttering. "Cole."

He slid a finger under her chin, leveled her in a steady gaze. "In case you didn't catch on," he said, "we had lunch in one of the most popular restaurants in the town and turned plenty of heads. I picked that place for a reason—to tell everyone, including you, *especially* you, this is the real deal." He held his breath, not sure what to expect from her or how she would respond. "You're it for me, baby. You're mine. I don't plan on letting you go."

She bit her lip in a shy moment before turning to seductive play. "I like this possessive-caveman Cole Wiley. It makes me hot." She pushed to her toes and nipped his lip. "Make sure you bring him to bed tonight."

"Sweetheart," he murmured. His hands caressed up her rib cage, and brushed the swell of her lush breasts. "He'll be ready, willing, and waiting." He patted her ass and reluctantly released her, yanking open her car door. "I better run before I miss my meeting."

Her hands settled on the top of the door before she climbed inside. "Call me after you finish your survey. I want to talk to you about Christmas."

His brows dipped. Was this the part where she shut him out? "What about it?"

"About us . . ." she hesitated, those pink cheeks smudged pinker, the adorable shyness returning. He loved the way she could be sexy, hot, and aggressive one minute, and prim and proper the next. "I was thinking," she said, trying again. "Well. You know. Us together, for Christmas. Our families, maybe. If you think we might?"

A grin of pure appreciation filled his face. He leaned over the door and kissed her. "Yes. No maybe about it. Christmas together is perfect. You're perfect."

He left her sitting there with a big, gorgeous smile lighting up her lovely features. And as he climbed into his pickup truck, Cole decided that life was good. It was damned good.

AN HOUR AFTER LEAVING COLE back at the sheriff's office, Holly sat
at Grandma Reddy's kitchen table, her laptop in front of her, still
grinning to herself like some silly schoolgirl over the way things
were going with her and Cole. She thought of his statement *"you're
mine"* and grinned some more. For the independent woman she
considered herself, Cole's caveman routine should be stifling. But it
wasn't. It was hot. It was amazingly hot. Maybe because Cole had
already proven he had a softer side, the one who'd read her work
the night before when she'd been stuck on a plot point and then
helped her think her way out of the corner she'd written herself
into. She smiled and started writing, sliding quickly into a zone
where the words flew onto the page.

Abruptly though, her fingers froze over the keyboard when a
commotion outside jerked her out of the scene she was writing.
Voices. Banging. What the heck?

Both concerned and irritated at being pulled away from her
work, Holly rushed to the door and shoved her arms into her coat,
her feet into the snow boots her father had given her several days
before. Standing on the porch, she saw a group of men drilling a
hole nearby on the property. What?

She dug her phone out of her pocket and tried to call her parents but received no answer. Surely they would have told her if
there was something going on today before they left for the
airport.

Holly stomped down the stairs and made it all of a few steps
before she froze. *Cole?* She blinked. Surely that wasn't Cole standing there, talking with three other men. A few steps away from

them, several other guys were taking some sort of measurement. On her parents' property. What was going on?

Her stomach lurched, and her hand pressed against it, as another truck—a familiar truck—pulled up and a moment later, Abe crossed toward Cole. She had a bad feeling about this. Really bad.

Holly launched into action, praying this gut-wrenching feeling that twisted and turned with every step was for nothing. Cole seemed to sense her approach, his gaze lifting, seeking, and settling on Holly. His handsome, chiseled features flashed with surprise a moment before his long, lean legs began eating up the distance between them.

She could barely breathe for the cold air and fear eating away at her lungs as she stopped in front of him. "What are you doing here?" she asked. "Who are those men? I thought you were doing some inspection on the property you're buying. What's going on, Cole?"

With a grim set to his jaw, Cole stepped closer, tried to touch her. She jerked away. Her attention shifted over Cole's shoulder to where Abe stood gaping at the two of them. The implications of him being there weren't missed on Holly. She knew that Abe was supposed to meet Cole for the property inspection.

She ground her teeth and cast him an accusing glare. "What are you doing here? What is Abe doing here?"

"Holly," he pleaded.

She squeezed her eyes shut, his lack of explanation the only answer she needed. "Oh God. This can't be happening." Slowly, she opened her eyes and forced out the question burning a fast-deepening hole in her gut. "This is the property you're buying, isn't it?"

"I didn't know. I——"

It was true! "You're buying my family home?!" She exploded with a combination of panic and anger. Her hands went to the side of her head, fingers in her hair. She was coming home to Haven, and home didn't exist. Had her parents' retirement put them in financial distress? Were they ashamed to ask for help? She flung her arms out to her sides. "How could you not tell me that?! How?"

He held his hands up. "I didn't know, Holly. I didn't know. Your last name isn't even Reddy. How would I know?"

"My last name *is* Reddy!" she yelled, fully aware that the other men, Abe included, were staring at them, jaws to the ground. Well, let them stare. She hoped their eyes popped out and their ears fried. She balled her fists by her sides, and added, "It's been Reddy every damned day of my life!"

Helplessly, he shook his head. "Your book. I thought——"

"My God, Cole. It's a small town. I can hardly pee without a report being sent home to my parents. You want me to believe that everyone but you, the man who has been fucking me nightly, knows my real name?"

She didn't ever use the F-word. She didn't. But she was hurting, panicked. Shaking.

"Get off!" She pointed. "Get off the property, now. It's not for sale. I'll take care of whatever financial mess my parents are in. You won't steal this property from them. You can't."

Cole jerked back as if slapped, his jaw setting in a steely hard line, a solemn expression in his dark eyes. "It's not like that, Holly," he said, his voice low now, as tight as a rubber band ready to pop. "And I can't believe you'd think that of me. Your parents want to travel. They're *excited* about selling."

Of course, they *said* that. Who admitted having financial difficulties?! She drew in a hard-earned breath. "Leave, Cole," she whispered. "Go away and don't ever come back."

She turned on her heels and raced toward the door, expecting him to follow. But she reached the stairs, reached the door, and Cole wasn't there. She wrapped her hand around the doorknob and knew he was still standing where she'd left him and it hurt. She shoved open the door and went inside, leaned on the wooden surface and waited for the knock that didn't come. A stinging sensation bit at the back of her eyes. She didn't want to cry. She refused to cry over Cole Wiley, a man who'd obviously been manipulating and using her in some way.

She squeezed her eyes shut. Damn, damn, damn. She was crying.

As excited as Holly was about seeing her sister Rachel, and as hard and long as she hugged her, it was torture to bite her tongue through the happy homecoming and not pull her parents aside. It was, after all, only an hour after she'd wiped her tears from her confrontation with Cole. She'd pulled herself together, after being instructed to bring the ruby to the main house, and now Holly sat next to Rachel in the family living room. She watched as her mother placed the stone on the mantel and announced that the ruby's destiny would be disclosed Christmas morning.

"Grandma left a sealed letter with instructions," Margaret explained. "She wanted us all here when it's opened."

"Well, of course, it's going to Holly," Rachel said, casting her a sideways look. "The oldest. The golden child who did no wrong."

Holly snipped that idea immediately, not about to carry the

added weight of this childhood argument at a time like this—with their family home on the line. "The golden child, as in the babysitter, diaper changer, the one who got in trouble for everything you guys did. You sound like Mason now. Please."

Rachel narrowed her eyes on Holly and laughed. "God, I've missed arguing with you."

Holly found herself smiling despite the stress weighing on her shoulders. "I've missed arguing with you, too."

"Whatever the destiny of the ruby," Margaret said, "Grandma found a way to make it special for the entire family." The family story of the ruby followed—including Grandma Reddy's belief that it held the magic of love—and Holly fought back a wave of emotion. The ruby wish had started her down the path that had led to Cole, and looking at the whimsical expression on Rachel's lovely, heart-shaped face, she was headed to the same place.

"So all I have to do is wish for a big, hunky guy, and he'll come calling?" Rachel joked. She shoved a wave of dark hair behind her ear and bit her lip. "I think I'll wish for someone tall—at least six foot three, broad shoulders, a six-pack, and blue eyes." She sighed. "Yeah. That would be nice."

Holly scoffed at that before she could stop herself. "Careful what you wish for," she said, thinking of her own wish. "You might get it."

Rachel and Margaret both stared at Holly. Rachel arched a dark brow. "Something you need to talk about, sis?"

"What?" she asked. "No. I'm just uptight about my deadlines. I need to get back to work." She hugged Rachel. "I want to hear all about that big-time advertising career of yours before you leave. Love ya, sweetie. Glad you're home."

Holly stood up and tried to sound nonchalant. "Mom, that contractor who came today left some paperwork he said you needed, if you want to walk over to the cottage with me to get it?"

Her mother's face froze. "Contractor?"

"Cole Wiley," Holly said. "He went over everything with me in detail."

"Yes," Margaret said. "I'll be right over."

The doorbell rang and before anyone had a chance to respond it was open. Buzzy, the nosy neighbor next door, sounded off as she let herself in. "Hello, everyone!" Holly's eyes met her mother's and in silent, mutual agreement, they made a path for the door. Neither of them wanted to deal with Buzzy's questions right now. Poor Rachel would just have to deal with the joy of a welcome home, Nosy Buzzy style.

FIVE MINUTES LATER, HOLLY'S MOTHER sat across from her at Grandma Reddy's kitchen table.

"Is this about money, Mom?" Holly asked. "Has retirement put you in a bad spot?"

"No!" she said, looking appalled. "Of course not. The house is paid for. We want the money to travel. We want to live a little. And none of you are here. Why should we sit back and let life pass us by? We planned to tell everyone after the holidays. We thought it was best that way."

Holly pursed her lips. "Because you knew we'd be upset."

"We hope you'll all be excited for us. We're going to see the world, sweetheart. But yes, we worried that one, or all of you, would be upset, and we didn't want to upset the holiday festivities. We never intended for you to find out the way you did. That had to be a shock."

Her mom didn't know the half of it. Finding out that Cole was buying their property shook her in a way her mother couldn't begin to understand.

"You're sure this Cole Wiley isn't pressuring you in some way?"

Her mother laughed at that. "Oh, goodness no. If anything your father is pressuring him to finish up the paperwork."

Holly leaned back in the chair. Everything was spinning out of control, and she had to get it back to normal. Maybe Cole really hadn't known her last name. Maybe he was innocent of any wrongdoing. So why did she still feel so betrayed and angry at him?

THE NEXT MORNING, AFTER SPENDING an hour with the banker handling the house sale, Holly exited the shelter of the bank building to find herself smack in the middle of the beginning of a blizzard, the wind whipping big, white snowflakes around her. Holly hunkered down in her long, black coat, her best black suit far from adequate cover even with knee-high boots. She was lucky she'd thrown it in her bag at all. It had been a last-minute whim. Old habits were hard to break. A suit was still familiar territory she clung to like a security blanket. Too bad she hadn't chosen a pair of dress pants. But then, she hadn't figured she'd really need the darned thing at all.

She slid into her car and quickly flipped on the heater, her hands shaking. She tried to tell herself it was from the cold. Frozen and for what? Nothing. No. That was wrong. She now had the peace of mind of knowing her parents were not in financial distress, *and* she wasn't sitting at home wishing Cole would call so she could yell at him. She wanted to hit him. She also wanted to kiss him. She dropped her head to the steering wheel. How did everything get so out of control?

Cole had the control. He was about to take ownership of her home in Haven. And he had her heart. She felt completely vulnerable. And the wall all this had erected between her and Cole felt as if it reached clear to the sky. She felt her choices had been taken from her. If she wanted to come home, if she wanted her family home, she had to be with Cole. And didn't she want to be with Cole? She did. She wanted it as readily as she did her next breath.

"So what's the problem, Holly?" she murmured. "What's the problem?" Her stomach rolled with the answer. She was scared, she realized. And the longer she went without talking to Cole, the more frightened she became about the control he held over her life. And the more certain she was that she couldn't give someone that kind of power over her.

Holly started driving, determined to get a grip on herself and everything happening around her. Cole didn't dictate her actions, her future. He could own her house, but he didn't own her. Whatever happened, whatever choices she made, they were hers. She would take back control.

That resolve lasted all of ten minutes, until the weather and her car proved she was nowhere near having any control. One minute her hands were steady on the wheel, the next her tire blew, and she was wildly trying to steer the car in a straight path with no hope of actually doing so. Her car skidded and landed with two tires in a ditch. She sat there, in the middle of a storm, and burst into tears.

Sitting behind the wheel of his truck, Cole drove toward town, the radio announcer talking about yet more early-season bad weather. He didn't give a damn if a blizzard had rolled in. Let it snow. Let it sleet. He was going to get hammered. Absolutely flipping hammered, like he hadn't been in a damned decade. After damned near twenty-four hours, it was clear that Holly showing up to apologize was about as likely to happen as a heat wave in Alaska. Evidently, he'd been a fool for thinking she'd figure out he'd done nothing wrong and show up to kiss away the pain of her attack. He sniffed. *Fool*, he thought. *Nothing but a fool.*

With a grimace, Cole turned the corner leading to the main road and squinted past the windshield wipers. There was a car in the ditch to his left, and his heart froze.

"Fuck!" That was Holly's car. How long had she been there? Oh God. Had she been coming to see him the night before and gotten trapped? The worst-case scenarios flashed in his mind. She was injured, bleeding, freezing to death.

Feeling as if his heart would explode from his chest, he accelerated and U-turned near her location. He had his door open before the gear was fully in park, the wind gusting against him as he charged toward Holly and wrenched open her door.

She gasped. "Cole?"

He bent down, framed her face with his hands, checked for injuries.

"Are you hurt? Are you okay?" She stared up at him, silent, a look of shock registering in her face. "Damn it, Holly. Are you hurt?"

"No," she said. "No. My tire blew. I'm fine." Abruptly, she pushed him away, her eyes colder than the wind beating at his back. "I'm fine, Cole. Let go."

Grinding his teeth, he let her go, and leaned back on his heels. Now he had confirmation of where they stood. In the sewer. He pushed to his feet.

"Are your parents on the way?"

"They didn't answer. I called a tow truck."

"I'll take you home. They'll bring your car along later."

She hugged herself against the cold that his body was no longer blocking.

"No, I—"

"This isn't a negotiation."

Her chin lifted defiantly. "You can't make me leave."

"Try me," he said, his voice implacable.

He grabbed her hand and hauled her out of the car, and smack into his arms. "Don't make me throw you over my shoulder and carry you, Holly."

Her eyes went wide. "You wouldn't."

"You already think I'm some sort of monster," he ground out between his teeth, trying not to notice that damned vanilla scent of hers. "What do I really have to lose here besides keeping you from letting pride freeze you to death?"

She glared at him. "Fine. Let go of me." She shoved at his chest. "I'll get in the *damned truck!*" He released her and she started walking, almost slipping in the process. He reached for her, and she slapped him away. "Don't touch me!"

He dropped his hands and gave her an exaggerated wave to the truck. "Get in my side so you don't end up in the ditch, like your car." She didn't respond, but treaded the precariously icy ground with a bit more care than before. That made it easy for him to out-pace her and grab the door. She slid across the seat and didn't stop until she was plastered to the passenger door.

Cole slid inside the truck and didn't move. He sat there, absorbing the discomfort of the space between them. He didn't like it. He didn't like it one bit. And it was ending, one way or the other. Tonight.

Chapter Nine

The short ride to the cottage was full of stiff silence that only served to piss Cole off. And when she bolted out of the door the minute he pulled the truck to a stop, that was the last straw. He deserved more than a slammed door.

He managed to reach her door a second before she shut it, shoving it open and closing it behind him. She was facing the wall, hanging up her coat and suit jacket. She whirled to face him, surprise in her face. "Cole—"

He didn't give her time to say more. With two long strides, Cole pinned her against the wall, his legs enclosing hers. "You have no idea how pissed off I am at you."

"I know," she whispered hoarsely, squeezing her eyes shut. "I know. Cole, I—"

He kissed her. It was a hard, angry kiss, meant to punish her for distrusting him. The kiss of a starving man who desperately needed sustenance. And she gave back all that she got, her tongue lapping at his with fierce strokes, her body pressing against his. That primal caveman side of him that she brought out screamed with demand. He buried his face in her neck and inhaled the soft scent of her desire. His cock thickened, pulsed.

"Holly," he whispered by her ear. He wanted inside her where he belonged, where she knew he belonged. Wildness careened inside him. A wild desire to claim her.

And so his mission began, to claim his woman. His hands branded her hips, her breasts. She arched into the touch, moaned with pleasure. He savored the gentle touch of her fingers gliding through his hair, caressing his scalp. He shoved her skirt to her waist, wrapped his palm around the curve of her lush ass and wrapped her leg around his hip. Then, he fixed her in a heavy-lidded stare as he pressed his hips to her, his cock thick against her stomach.

"Cole," she gasped, her head resting against the wall, her cheeks flushed, her eyes heavy.

His gaze didn't waver as he reached up and ripped open her shirt, tiny buttons flying everywhere. He yanked the material of both bra cups down and exposed her nipples. Bent and licked them, then kissed her. She clung to him, her soft sounds of pleasure, of desperate need, driving him wild. Making him hot. He was so hot. And so was she. Writhing against him, she rocked her hips, soft sighs sliding from her throat.

He ripped her panty hose, and slid his fingers along her drenched lips. She shivered and moaned. Whimpered his name. He unzipped his pants, wasting no time sliding inside her, damned happy they'd had the birth control conversation because he wasn't sure he could have stopped himself from taking her here, now, at this moment.

Hot wet heat milked his cock as he sunk deep. That wild need to claim her was all his mind could manage, that and the anger at her because she'd pushed him away. A frenzied rush of punishing, erotic thrusts followed. It was the pulsing and pounding of two people trying to break through an emotional barrier with their bodies. A frenzied pumping that ended when her body claimed his, when her muscles spasmed around him and pulled a release from him so deep he could barely breathe.

Neither of them spoke, but the silence was rich with tension, with the barriers that passion could not erase. Cole pressed his head to hers and inhaled the moment, not sure if it would be the last between them. This hadn't been his intention when he'd followed her. They had to talk. He knew it and he had no doubt she did, too.

Anger started to burn all over again, anger over the way she'd shut him out. She'd let him inside her body, but not into her mind, not into her heart. He'd be damned if he was playing that game.

He picked her up and carried her to the bathroom, setting her on the counter and stepping away, feeling the disconnect of their bodies like a blast of cold air. He adjusted his pants and then grabbed a robe off the wall hanger and tossed it to her.

"Put it on," he said, his gaze flickering over her puckered nipples, his dick daring to throb again, as if he hadn't just been inside her. "We have to figure out what is going on between us, and believe me, if you don't get dressed, we won't figure out anything but how I can get back inside you anytime soon." He didn't hold back the truth. He didn't hold back one damned iota. The truth was, he was hurting. Holly, the only woman he'd ever opened up to, spoken to of the past, of his pain over losing his mother, had nothing but scorn and, apparently, sex to offer him.

She blushed and fumbled with the robe, and he didn't miss the slight shake of her hands, or the puckering of her nipples beneath the creamy silk of the robe. She hugged herself, and Cole leaned against the wall, crossing his arms over his chest, studying her.

"I need to understand what's going on, Holly."

THE BATHROOM WAS TINY, ESPECIALLY with Cole occupying most of it with his big sexy body. Holly wanted to slide off the counter and hug him so she could feel his arms around her again. But the implacable set of his jaw, along with the steely stare, said it was time for answers. And she wasn't sure she had them. She barely understood her own stupid behavior. It had been raw panic. Fear. A control thing that being with him again made her see as pathetically silly and unimportant.

"I feel like no matter what I say, I can't make this right," Holly finally admitted. "And that scares me almost as much as you do." She expected him to say something, but he didn't. She shifted a bit on the counter, tied the sash around her waist, pressed her hands to the surface beneath her. "When I thought you'd betrayed me, I was crushed. Then I found out you hadn't, but I couldn't seem to let go of how that betrayal felt."

"The one that wasn't real."

"But don't you see?" she pleaded. "It *felt* real. If I count on us and then we fall apart, what happens to me? And the family-home thing—I'd been thinking of moving home. For that, I need a foundation. I've always planned for things. I couldn't plan for any of this. I couldn't plan for you." Everything about the man had her crazy, out of her mind. Good Lord, she'd almost had crazy, wild sex with him in the front of his truck. "It's like a spinning ball, and I keep rolling faster. I can't even drive my damned car without needing you to rescue me."

His lips thinned, and he pushed off the wall. "I just realized something I was a fool to miss. I've taken the risk and made myself clear. I've told you, you're the real deal for me, Holly. I've said I want you in my bed, where we both know you want to be, too. But in my life? You don't even want me in your house. Not unless you can write me on your planner first. And baby, we both know that isn't how this thing with us is. It's all or nothing, and you just don't have it in you to give it all."

"I can. I will."

He moved toward the door, rigid, unwilling to listen. Helplessness overcame her but she knew she had to do something or he'd be gone. Holly jumped off the counter. She plastered her hand on the hard wall of his chest. "Don't go."

Cold eyes met hers, eyes that said he'd made up his mind. He was leaving. "I can't make this right, can I?" she whispered painfully.

"At the moment," he said, "it doesn't appear that way." He removed her hand from his chest. "I need to think, Holly, and I can't do that when I'm with you." He walked out of the room, and she followed, her stomach roiling, as she watched him open the front door and exit without looking back.

Holly resisted the urge to run after him. Words weren't enough to convince him she was past her temporary insanity. She had to find another way.

THREE DAYS LATER, COLE STOOD inside The Tavern with a beer in his hand, and an empty shot glass on the bar. He reached for his beer and swallowed a long slug. After all, he was celebrating. And somewhere up in Manchester, so were his brothers. They'd signed the papers, sold the company, yippee ki yay, and all that stuff. Tomorrow they'd seal the deal on Holly's family home. He'd talked to the Reddys that day. They were thrilled. His brothers were thrilled. Cole, well, he wanted another drink.

"Another, Joe," he yelled at the bartender, breaking through the jukebox tune of Garth Brooks's "Shameless," a reminder that did nothing to help his grisly mood. Joe arched his brow as if he considered denying him. Cole scowled. "Give me another damned shot, Joe."

Joe stalked the few steps dividing them and poured the liquor, his lips a thin, hard line. "Drinking away a woman, I take it." It wasn't a question, rather a well-versed bartender's expert assessment.

Cole scowled again and Joe said, "Thought so. Won't work." He turned and walked away.

Cole downed the tequila and vowed to make Joe a liar. What insanity had brought him to The Tavern of all damned places, he didn't know—the place where he'd first spiraled into the abyss, otherwise known as Holly.

He hadn't heard from her. Told himself it didn't matter. Told himself the ripping pain in his gut was nerves over the sale of the business. But he knew better; he knew it was her. He'd overwhelmed her, charged at her like everything else in his life. He got that. So he'd backed off, hoping space was the answer.

"You got an answer, all right." He grimaced, downing the rest of his beer. "Just not the answer you wanted."

He was about to order up another shot—Joe's scowls be damned, he'd take a cab home, even walk if he had to—when Joe appeared and poured him one on his own, then discreetly nodded toward the door. "That's the guy your brother two-stepped with." Contempt thickened in his face. "Up to his same no-good crap."

Cole turned to inspect the guy in question who was more punk kid than man. Tall but lanky, hair too long, jeans ripped, shirt hanging half over his belt—a style statement gone wrong. He looked more sixteen than twenty-one as the sheriff had pegged him.

In the corner, trapped by the kid, was a woman curled back against the wall, body tense, her face pale, eyes wide with fear. Suddenly, the kid jerked the woman by the hand and started charging toward the door with her in tow.

"Oh no," Cole said, downing his shot. "This shit's stopping here, tonight." Cole and Joe shared a look.

"I'll call the sheriff," Joe said.

Cole charged toward the door, a heartbroken man with adrenaline and tequila pumping through his blood. He pushed open The Tavern door about the time the punk kid reached his truck. Long strides led Cole behind the kid as he reeled back to slap his wife. Cole grabbed the kid and started walking back to the bar, him in tow, shouting, while bystanders hooted and hollered. The kid squirmed but he was the weaker of the two, no match for Cole. A fortysomething female opened the door for them. Cole gave her a short salute. "Thank you, ma'am."

Inside The Tavern, Cole rotated the kid around, then lifted him with two hands. Bingo, he hit his mark. The kid's belt hooked on a coatrack just low enough to leave his feet dangling.

The kid spat at Cole, spraying a disgusting mess all over his face before blustering a collection of curse words, some of which Cole doubted Webster's had yet to define. Somewhere in there was a promise to press charges. Grand. Just. Fucking. Grand.

Someone handed Cole a napkin, and he wiped his face off, sauntering back to the bar as Joe filled his glass. "Figure you'll need that one when the sheriff gets here."

"Can always count on you to tell it how it is, can't I, Joe?"

IN HER PARENTS' HOUSE, HOLLY sat at the kitchen table, talking with her sister and her mother about her brother, Mason, arriving the next day, but her mind was elsewhere. Because tonight was the night she was going for it—she was going to show Cole how much he meant to her.

She had everything all planned out perfectly. She'd called Abe and found out today the sale of their business had been made final. She knew the sale of the house was being finalized the next day, thanks to her mother. She had something planned for later that evening when Cole arrived home from Manchester; waiting in her car was a bottle of champagne, his favorite chocolate cake from the bakery up the road—the one he drooled over every time he passed it—and balloons. All to celebrate the sale of one business and the purchase of another.

But there was more. She'd given notice at her apartment in Houston. She had a sealed envelope with proof she was moving back to Haven at the risk of having no place to live—on the promise that Cole wanted her in his bed every night. If he still wanted her.

"What do you think, Holly?"

Holly blinked, realizing she wasn't paying attention. What had Rachel said? Something about a town skating party.

"When is it?" Holly asked.

"Tomorrow night," her mother inserted. "Your father and I will be gone for a little romantic dinner we've planned. It would be great if you kids could go out together. It's always quite a lovely event, dear. You'd enjoy it."

Holly smiled to herself, aware they'd be celebrating the sale of the house despite their arrangements to stay an extra month but allowing renovations to begin. The idea of her parents traveling and enjoying life had grown on her, once she'd set aside her own selfish need for stability. A house wasn't the basis for happiness. It was the people inside.

"It would be great if you could go," Rachel chimed in, peeling away the plastic wrapper on a candy cane. "I mean, I know you have that deadline and all, but it would be nice to have you along."

Holly sighed regretfully. "I need to stay focused right now, so I can be free the week of Christmas and enjoy you guys."

The phone rang and her mother crossed the kitchen to answer it and then returned almost instantly.

"Holly," she said. "It's for you."

Holly frowned, her heart lurching at the discomfort she noted on her mother's face. Holly crossed to her mother's side and reached for the phone, but Margaret held it tight, covering the receiver with her palm. Margaret eyed Rachel over Holly's shoulder. "Give us a minute, honey."

Rachel didn't ask questions. They all knew when to scoot, and when Mom wanted time alone with one of them, the others made a fast exit. Of course, Holly would have to deal with Rachel's questions later—much later, she hoped.

"What is it, Mom?" Holly asked.

"It's Abe Wiley. Is there anything I should know?"

She shook her head, bit her lip. Her nerves jangled wildly. Her cell was at the cottage. But why would Abe call her here?

"It's personal, Mom. Nothing to do with the house." Her mother didn't look satisfied, and judging from the way she clutched the phone, Holly wasn't getting it without offering up some answers. "I've been seeing his brother. That's why the house thing hit me so hard. I thought he knew who I was. I thought—" Holly touched her temples. "Mom. Something could be wrong. Abe wouldn't call me here if there wasn't."

Her mother handed her the phone. "We'll talk later."

Holly nodded and slid the phone to her ear. "Abe?"

"Holly," he said. "Cole had a run-in with that kid who was harassing Jacob. He's in jail, and Jacob and I are in Manchester. We're on our way, but can you—"

"I'm on my way," Holly said, handing her mom the phone. "I have to go." Her mother called after her, but Holly kept going. Cole needed her.

⸎

TEN MINUTES LATER, HOLLY SLAMMED her car door shut outside the sheriff's office and rushed to the door. She stepped inside, shivering in nothing but a pink sweater and jeans, and found herself staring straight into Cole's shocked expression.

"Holly?"

Her teeth chattered, the coldness seeming to reach to her bones. Or was that emotion? Either way, she couldn't control the shaking.

"I rushed over. I—"

"Good Lord, woman," he said, shrugging out of his coat and then pulling it around her shoulders, rescuing her even as she tried to rescue him and, damn, it felt good. "Where is your coat?"

His coat swallowed her whole, but it smelled like him—spicy, masculine, perfect. She didn't ever want to take it off.

"I didn't think to grab it," she said. He still held the coat lapels, his warmth encasing her with courage. The shivers started to subside. "I heard you were in jail. It's that guy that Jacob had issues with, isn't it?"

He nodded. "Yes," he said. "He was roughing up his wife again. I grabbed the guy and hung him up on a coatrack to wait for the sheriff to arrive."

Holly shook her head, clearing the cobwebs. Surely she didn't hear that right. "What do you mean, hung him on a coatrack?"

Cole never got the chance to answer. Sheriff Jack, who stood at least six foot three with broad, muscular shoulders, walked into the lobby and did it for him. "Stuck his belt over the notch, just like you would a coat." He tossed some paperwork on the desk, and Cole let go of the coat.

Sheriff Jack continued, "It was priceless. The best Christmas present you could have given me." He shook his head. "You're lucky he didn't press charges, though. Good thing the wife flexed some muscle and threatened the guy. You should have waited for me, and you damned well know it."

"I was waiting for you," Cole countered. "I just wanted to make sure he did, too."

The sheriff chuckled, and Holly couldn't help joining in herself. "About ten more minutes on that paperwork and we'll get you out of here," the sheriff said.

Holly found herself laughing and sitting down next to Cole. "I just can't imagine what that would have looked like."

Cole fixed his attention on her, his eyes a dark abyss, his lips a grim, hard line. Then abruptly, he pushed to his feet and grabbed her hand. A minute later, they were in a private office, with the door shut. "Holly, why are you here?" Apparently, he was done with small talk.

Holly struggled to secure the giant coat hanging heavily on her shoulders. But that weight was nothing compared to the weight of his confrontation. "I thought you needed me. I . . ."

He gave a slow, hard nod, his lips flattening. Then he reached for the door. She grabbed his arm, instant awareness between them, electricity darting up her arm.

"Cole. Please. If you walk out of this office, it will kill me. Maybe you didn't need me, but *I* need *you*, and I won't say that doesn't scare me. But being without you scares me more." Her heart sputtered and then raced wildly. "This isn't exactly how I planned this, but . . ."

The energy in the room shifted, but still he was stiff, unyielding. "You planned this?"

"Yes," she confessed. "Well, not this, now. Later. At your house. I was going to be waiting for you when you got home. I had a cake, and champagne, and . . . It was to celebrate. One business gone, another starting." He didn't so much as blink, and she started to ramble, nervous, afraid this was a mistake, a mess. "Then Abe called and I rushed over here, and all that went out the window. I mean, everything I'd planned . . . and see, I plan, Cole. It's me. I like that you make me more spontaneous—no, I love it. I—"

He kissed her, his arm sliding around her waist, his tongue coaxing her lips apart. Holly clung to him, reached on her toes and flung her arms around his neck.

A knock sounded on the door a moment before the sheriff said, "You're free to go, Cole."

Holly clung to him, tilting her chin up and letting him see into her soul. "No. No, you're not. Not this time."

A few days later at Cole's house, Holly and Cole lay naked on top of the bed, big fluffy goose-down blankets beneath them, and a fireplace crackling in the corner.

Holly had gone to the contract signing to support both her family and Cole's. They'd all agreed that they'd keep the bed-and-breakfast a secret until the time was right, and Cole had offered her parents a permanent room at the house, in between travels. After all, it would be Holly's home, too, as far as he was concerned, and every holiday could be spent there as if nothing had changed.

Holly scooped a bite of chocolate cake off the plate in front of her and sighed. "I love this cake. I love this room."

He took her plate and set it on the nightstand, and then pulled

her beneath him. "I love that it's our room now. So how much notice do I have to give you 'to plan for a proposal'?"

Holly smiled, feeling the hard proof of his arousal settle between her legs. "I'm quickly learning to enjoy your spontaneity. Go
with what feels right."

"*You* feel right to me," he said, brushing his lips over hers and
then sliding inside her, burying himself deep within the recesses of
her body.

She sighed with pleasure and wrapped her arms around his
neck. Right had never felt so good.

Hot for Santa

BY

CATHRYN FOX

Chapter One

'Twas two weeks before Christmas . . .

*N*ick Grant . . .
    God, just thinking about him made her wet.

Wet, wild, and wanton.

Seated at her mother's kitchen table, advertising executive Rachel Reddy briefly closed her eyes and allowed her mind to drift to Nick.

As her body flooded with warmth, it had her craving sex. Hard, carnal, unapologetic, handcuffed-to-the-bed-and-make-her-beg-for-it kind of sex. A far cry from the wham-bam, thank-you-ma'am drivel she was accustomed to, that's for sure.

Rachel wasn't sure if it was her client's killer smile, rock-hard physique, big, rugged hands, or hewn thigh muscles that had her mind conjuring up erotic fantasies about him. Or perhaps it was the way he took such painstaking care of his customers' needs at his sporting goods store that had her feeling feverish with lust. Either way, she wanted him. Up against the wall, down against a mattress, but mostly, between her legs.

She wasn't normally so lascivious, but something about a guy who paid such special attention to others led her to believe he'd take that same meticulous care with her naked, needy body. And that got to her in a way that made her sex throb like it had never throbbed before. Heat and desire prowled through her as she visualized herself held hostage to his bed, tortured and tormented by his deft hands and skillful ministration.

Yummy . . .

Rachel shivered in sensual delight, then worked diligently to redirect her thoughts. Here she was in Haven, New Hampshire, watching her mother mill about in the old homestead kitchen, which was so *not* the place to be fantasizing about a client; someone who'd simply hired her firm to create a professional advertising campaign for his new outerwear line.

Commanding herself to focus on something else, she drew her knees to her chest, wrapped her arms around her legs, and watched the wind whip light, fluffy snowflakes past the windowpane. As she contemplated what to wear to the town's annual outdoor skating party later that night, she caught sight of her father, Thomas Reddy, trudging down the long icy driveway with his trusty ax in hand, and his loyal Labrador retriever, Murphy, in tow. Thomas was off to help out Old Man Denby with his woodpile, no doubt. She smiled to herself, pleased at how some things never changed. She took a moment to think about Old Man Denby, his wife, Gracie, and their son, Travis—a man Rachel had always thought would one day be her brother-in-law. Unfortunately, things just hadn't worked out between Travis and Rachel's younger sister, Tori.

The old house creaked and groaned in distress as another huge gust battled the exterior, and Rachel hugged herself tighter, comforted by the warmth and coziness inside. It was an unusually cold day in Haven, blustery even—not a great day to be outdoors. She crinkled her nose in dismay and glanced at the ominous gray sky overhead. Perhaps she'd have to rethink the annual skating party that evening.

Her gaze wandered to her father's beaten-down snowmobile path. Even though she would love to head out, to stretch her legs on one of the cross-county ski trails, go sliding on the frozen duck pond, or take Murphy for a hike up to Grandma Reddy's cottage, she suspected it was a little too nippy for such extended exposure to the elements.

The falling temperatures might be keeping her—a lover of the great outdoors—inside, but Rachel really didn't mind, because she'd been back in the old homestead for the holidays for a couple of days now, and was feeling quite happy and content, despite the fact that she didn't have someone special to share the Christmas festivities with. Someone intelligent. Someone with integrity. Someone lip-smacking scrumptious.

Someone like Nick Grant.

Nick . . .

Rachel bit down on her bottom lip to suppress a moan as fantasies of Nick kept intruding upon her thoughts. Everything about him aroused her. Intrigued her. Heated her up in a way the hot, burning embers in the living room fireplace never could. Good Lord, drop her in a snowbank and her scorching body would likely melt a path around her. No need for sidewalk salt when she was thinking about Nick.

What the heck happened to her hard-fought battle to pull herself together and block Nick from her mind? Once again she quickly recognized that now was not the time or place for such scandalous thoughts. She'd wait until later tonight when she was nestled all snug in her bed, visions of sugarplums dancing in her head. And by sugarplums, she meant Nick.

Marshaling her libido for the time being, she ran her fingertips around her steaming mug of hot chocolate, and turned her attention to her mother, Margaret Reddy, who was bustling around the big farmhouse kitchen, cooking up a storm in celebration of the season. Her eyes were bright with laughter, anxious and excited to have all her children come together under one roof for the holidays.

Now that her mom and dad were retired from the university, and their children were all grown up and gone, Margaret had embraced the Christmas season wholeheartedly. It was the time of year for celebration and family. That, and it allowed her to show off her exceptional culinary skill, none of which Rachel had inherited, *thank you very much.*

Truthfully, it felt good to be home, to enjoy a home-cooked meal instead of Chinese takeout or nuked food that had intimately introduced itself to her hips. Not great for a girl who loved physical activity yet no longer seemed to have time for it. It also felt good to climb back into her favorite comfy sweats, and let her long curly hair down for a change. Back in New York she wouldn't be caught dead out in such an outfit, but here in Haven she could kick back in comfort because she didn't have to dress to impress.

Humming along off beat to a Bing Crosby Christmas tune drifting in from the dining room stereo, her mother plopped a tray of cookies onto the Santa place mat smack-dab in the middle of the long oaken table and wiped her hands on her gingham apron. Rachel pulled the warm sweet scent of fresh gingerbread into her lungs, letting the scent awaken her olfactory senses and bring back childhood memories.

She smiled and recalled her girlish dreams of moving to New York. She'd always envisioned herself living in a big, spacious apartment in the Village, a place where she'd make her mark in the business world, and find herself a knight in shining armor.

Of course, as a few of her friends had recently told her, and Meat Loaf had so eloquently put to music: *two out of three ain't bad.* Except it was bad, or at least the guys she attracted were bad. Bad with a capital B. Greedy, insensitive jerks who were merely concerned about their own needs. Men who wanted her at their beck and call, and who had no respect for her long hours or dedication to her job. Sure, it was fine for them to have professional careers, but if those needy New Yorkers were looking for a mother figure or expected a Susie Homemaker because she'd come from a small town in New Hampshire, they had another thought coming. Having grown up in a family with two scholarly parents, education, goals, and professional pursuits were most important to the four Reddy offspring.

Despite her ever-expanding hips, Rachel scooped a hot cookie from the tray and let out a long-suffering sigh, wondering why all the good guys were either taken or gay. She thought about her younger and only brother, Mason. He was definitely one of the good guys. Any woman would be lucky to have him, except he was happily playing for the other team and had been for quite some time now.

And then there was Nick . . .

Nick Grant, owner and CEO of Hilltop Gear. A gorgeous hunk of a guy who had been completely off-limits.

Until now.

Now that the campaign had been put to bed, so to speak, the only thing separating them were a few hundred miles. But that would soon be rectified when she went back to New York after the holidays. Then she'd see about putting something else, or rather *someone* else, to bed. Until then she planned on spending the next two weeks relaxing in the homestead while visions of Saint Nick danced in her head.

"So what's he like?"

Rachel shot her mother a glance in time to see her pull a new bag of sugar from the floor-to-ceiling pantry, a beautiful yet functional addition to the home that helped bring the country kitchen up-to-date. Rachel did a slow perusal of the room, noting that her parents had invested quite a bit of time and money into modernizing the old homestead. Everything from the new appliances, warm cranberry-colored walls, ivory-painted cupboards, and rich granite countertop had the kitchen looking like a real-estate show home. Not that her parents ever planned to put the place up for sale, however.

Rachel's glance roamed back to her mother, who was studying her, awaiting a response. "What's who like?" Rachel asked around a mouthful of warm gingerbread. Little pieces of cookie crumbs fell onto her white knit turtleneck sweater, and she concentrated on brushing them away while trying to feign innocence.

Margaret Reddy laughed, and Rachel knew the jig was up. *Busted.* Cripes, it's not like any of the Reddy offspring could ever get anything past their mother. Even into her retirement years, she was far too quick on her feet and far too astute for any of them.

"Come on, Rachel. You've got that look in your eyes again. The one you used to get when you were a little girl daydreaming about Prince Charming. So tell me, who is he?" Margaret wagged her finger and quickly slipped back into mother mode. "And don't talk with your mouth full."

Rachel swallowed, and took a sip of her hot chocolate, not really wanting to tell her mother about Nick—especially all the delicious ways she wanted him to take command of her body—but desperately wanting to talk about him just the same.

"He's just a guy who hired my firm for a job." Oh, but he wasn't just *any* guy. He was a guy who seemed to respect her as a professional, and with the way his eyes caressed her body in admiration, it was clear that he'd never forgotten she was a woman. He was sweet, funny, and thoughtful, the antithesis of the men she usually attracted.

Margaret narrowed her blue eyes and tucked a silver lock behind her ear. "And . . ." she prompted.

Rachel shrugged. "And, well, he's nice." Nice and hot with a panty-soaking smile that had her itching to shed her clothes, as well as her inhibitions.

With her eyes alive with curiosity, her mother questioned, "Nice, huh?"

"Yeah, nice."

"Does this guy have a name?"

"Nick," was all she offered. Once again, just thinking about him made her wet.

"So you've gone out?"

Rachel averted her gaze, suspecting her mother could read her every lusty thought. "I have strict rules about dating clients." But, of course, now that the ad was completed, technically Nick was no longer an *active* client. He was just a hot hunk of a guy ripe for the picking—providing he wasn't taken or gay. Rachel was pretty sure he wasn't. At least she hoped. But she still couldn't help wonder why a great guy like Nick was still single.

Her mother quirked a brow and probed, "Is he cute?"

Desire slammed into her and heat ambushed her sex as she conjured up memories of his roguish good looks and blatant masculinity. She steadied herself and strived for normalcy.

"Yeah, he's cute. . . ."

"And?"

Her tongue darted out to wet her lips. Without conscious thought her gaze wandered to the porch door. "And, well, he's . . . he's . . . he's . . ."

Out of her peripheral vision she caught her mother's curious glance. "He's what, Rachel?"

He's standing in the archway!

Rachel's pulse leaped, and she swallowed. Hard. Why the heck was Nick standing in her mother's doorway, under the mistletoe no less, looking like sex incarnate?

As though moving of its own accord, her finger pointed to the doorway. Margaret spun around, clasped her hands together in front of her chest, and let out a laugh of joy.

"Mason," she cried out, and made short work of the distance between them. Mason wrapped his arms around their mother and spun her in a circle. "You're early. I didn't expect you for two more days," Margaret added.

Always the smart-ass, Mason said, "Well, if you want me to go and come back later . . ." His green eyes glistened with laughter as he teased her, and her mother playfully swatted him in return.

Rachel sat in her chair with her jaw practically dangling on the floor as she looked past the festive reunion and kept her gaze locked on the gorgeous hunk leaning casually against the doorjamb. Nick's seductive blue eyes moved over her face with intimate recognition, and a half grin curled up his sensuous mouth. The wet snow covering his dark hair and broad shoulders like a thick coat of dander did little to diminish his masculine allure. In fact, it only added to it.

His movements were easy, lazy, and his gaze never left hers as he went to work on removing his jacket and hanging it on the coat-rack. He looked natural, comfy, and laid-back in his faded blue jeans that displayed athletic muscles, and a blue sweater that showed off a lean stomach and hard pectorals. His thigh-melting virility and killer smile stole her very next breath and Rachel found herself clenching her legs in response. The mere sight of him practically rendered her senseless.

She wet her lips and gripped her chair, feeling like she'd just been pumped full of aphrodisiacs as heat and need enveloped her. Sensual overload nearly fried her brain, and the gush of moisture between her legs hadn't gone unnoticed by her. Hands down, he was the hottest guy she'd ever had the pleasure of setting her eyes on.

At six foot four, Nick towered over her brother and could easily see Rachel huddled at the kitchen table, and could, undoubtedly, easily see the color blooming high on her cheeks as a mixture of arousal and surprise worked its way through her bloodstream.

Rachel swallowed and diligently fought to clear her lust-drunk brain.

Her efforts proved futile.

She stared at Nick, despite her attempt not to gawk. When he turned his attention to Margaret, to exchange a few pleasantries, it gave her a moment of reprieve from his mesmerizing baby blues. With her lascivious mind still focused on his rock-hard body, she was only half listening to the conversation, but her ears immediately perked up when her brother introduced Nick as his "partner" and informed them all that he would be spending the holidays with them.

Partner?

Shock weakened her limbs as understanding dawned in small increments. Nick was Mason's partner. Oh God. Rachel felt her blood drain to her feet.

Nick was gay!

"Rachel. Hello. Earth to Rachel," Mason said, and it suddenly occurred to her that Mason had asked her a question.

Jesus, she had no idea how long she'd been sitting there both stunned and distraught by that announcement. She slammed her mouth shut and took a quick second to regroup. For a moment, silence stretched on as everyone looked at her; then Rachel blinked her mind into focus and gathered her wits. Ignoring the erotic pulse of pleasure between her legs, she forced a smile, jumped from her seat, and advanced with purpose. She threw her arms around Mason and worked to sound casual. "Hey, baby bro, long time no see."

He polished his knuckles on her head and managed to knot her curls, an annoying little habit he'd kept from childhood. She scowled, suddenly annoyed that some things never changed.

"Hey, big sis. You're looking good."

His teasing words reminded her that she was dressed in her un-attractive, oversize sweatpants, looking like she'd just crawled out of bed, hardly the well-groomed, put-together Rachel that Nick was accustomed to seeing in New York. Not that it mattered. Not now. Not with Nick batting for the other team. Rachel bit back a frustrated groan.

Why, oh why, are all the good ones gay?

After she inched back, she went to work on finger-combing out the tangles as her mother herded them all to the kitchen table. "Come on, sit down and I'll make coffee to help warm you both up."

As she moved across the room, with Nick tight on her heels, his nearness made her breathless and rattled her beleaguered brain. She could feel his questioning eyes on her, as though waiting for her to greet him personally, or at least acknowledge their profes-sional relationship.

Nick took a seat at the head of the rectangular table, stretched his long legs out in front of himself, and cataloged the room. Ra-chel reclaimed her chair to his right and, needing a distraction, took a big gulp of her hot chocolate and swallowed loudly. Mason must have noticed the speculative way Nick was staring at her. Mason opened his mouth, as if he were about to make an introduction; then his eyes widened, like the sight of Rachel had triggered some-thing in his brain. He angled his head and smoothed down his chestnut hair as he questioned, "Oh hey, Rachel, maybe you already know Nick. Didn't your firm do a campaign for Hilltop Gear?"

Rachel arched a brow. "What makes you think that?"

"Because I'm working at Hilltop now."

Surprised at that announcement, her mind raced. So that's how they knew each other. Wait! Maybe they were simply business partners. It wasn't uncommon for any one of the siblings to bring home a friend during the holidays. Honestly, Rachel couldn't remember a Thanksgiving without a room full of people. She felt a moment of hope, but it was quickly squashed when it occurred to her that Nick had come home with Mason for two long weeks. Obviously, there had to be more going on between the two for them to want to spend such an extended period of time together, and share in such an intimate, family-oriented holiday.

Mason pulled off his gloves and scarf and shook away the snowflakes as his glance went from Rachel, to Nick, back to Rachel again. "I know I've only been with the store a short time, but I vaguely remember seeing an invoice. . . ."

Rachel caught the curious look on her mother's face, and could almost hear the wheels turn as she put two and two together. Damn it, the last thing she wanted was for her mother to figure out that Nick—her brother's boyfriend—and the guy she'd been crooning over were one and the same. And she sure as hell didn't want Mason to know.

Flustered, Rachel shook her head. "No," she bit out, sounding a little too throaty, especially since she was trying to present a calm and cool demeanor.

Nick was Mason's boyfriend . . . ?

She'd been so busy the last few months, finishing up Hilltop's account and then clearing her desk before the holidays that she hadn't had a moment to speak with Mason. Of course, it wasn't like she kept track of her brother's employment situation anyway. Especially since he went through jobs quicker than he went through boyfriends. If that was possible. Mason was brilliant in his own right and with his master's degree in business he was a valuable commodity in the professional world. But due to his intelligence, boredom came easily, leading him from one job to the next in search of fulfillment.

Mason shrugged and reached for a cookie. "I just thought you two might know each other."

Once again, Rachel shook her head adamantly, and Nick gifted her with a confused, yet somewhat amused look. "No, we've never met," she vowed.

"Well, then let me properly introduce you." She watched Mason's eyes light up when he glanced at Nick, and was pretty certain that her own face reflected that amorous look. "Nick, this is my big sister, Rachel. Rachel this is Nick, my new par—"

Just then, a knock came on the door and their neighbor Buzzy came rushing in. "Mason," she squealed. "I thought that was your car. I just wanted to pop in for a quick second to say hello."

"Buzzy," Mason said, and stood to give her a hug.

Thankful for the distraction—because Rachel so did not want to hear Mason reinforce the fact that the man she was crazy about was his newest partner—Rachel slunk back in her chair and prayed the ground would open up and swallow her whole.

Never met? What the hell?

As Mason chatted with Buzzy, Nick watched Rachel, studying her body language from where he sat at the head of the table. She must have felt the intensity of his gaze on her because she fidgeted restlessly, looking at everyone and everything except him.

He shot her a suspicious look and tried to sort through the turn of events. Now why on earth would Rachel blatantly lie about knowing him? What kind of game was she playing? He considered her odd behavior for a long moment then decided to play along for the time being. But he sure as hell planned on getting to the bottom of it before he went back to New York.

Honestly, when his brand-new business partner had invited him home for the holidays, Nick had no idea that Rachel Reddy from R&R Advertising was Mason's sister. Nick had only recently brought Mason on board as his account manager and clothing buyer, but the two had never really moved beyond a professional relationship, never shared personal information. It was only when Nick had mentioned in passing that he'd be spending the holidays alone, that Mason had opened his family home to him.

Growing up an only child with parents who fought constantly and only spared him a glance when they were angry, Nick had always longed for a big happy family during the holidays. Although he wasn't much of a drinker he knew he could always turn to his good buddy Jack Daniel's for a bit of comfort this holiday season. But even that left him feeling a little raw and a whole lot hollow come Christmas morning.

Sure, he could call on one of his many female acquaintances, but that only took the edge of loneliness off for so long. Besides, most of the women from his social circle would be off with their families, gathered around a huge tree exchanging gifts, love, and laughter. So when Mason dropped the invitation into his lap like a neatly packaged Christmas present, Nick jumped at the chance.

Although, at first he had been reluctant to go for the full two weeks. After all, Mason and the rest of his family would want time together. But Mason had insisted that the old homestead was always open to friends, and that the only true way to experience a Reddy holiday was by taking in every festivity, which started with a skating party at the town hall later that night. So in the end, he agreed and with the warm welcome Margaret had given him at the door, he knew he'd made a sound decision.

Nick couldn't deny that he was looking forward to being part of the big family, to soak up every functional and dysfunctional moment, and to bask in their quirks and eccentricities, if only for a couple of weeks.

And finding Rachel in the big old Reddy home was like the icing on a cake, or rather, the angel on top of the tree.

Speaking of angels . . .

In the office, Rachel was all businesslike, creative, proficient, and downright brilliant. Although he respected her unwavering professionalism, he couldn't help but noticing she was all woman. Even so, she'd always maintained a reserved demeanor with him, and showed no signs of an attraction, physical or otherwise.

Until now.

Nick was quickly learning that Rachel Reddy was a whole lot of contradictions, because something about the way her hungry gaze had just drunk him in when he darkened her doorway, told a different story altogether. It told him her needs and desires matched his and that the carnal attraction between them was mutual, powerful, and all consuming.

Those soft chocolate eyes of hers had roamed over him with heated interest, and the pretty pink blush coloring her cheeks alerted him to her womanly interests. Interests he'd be more than happy to ignite, explore, and sate, if given the chance.

Sure, she was attractive in the workplace, even with her hair tied back in a severe bun, and her sexy curves kept tamed beneath her no-nonsense, buttoned-to-the-neck business suits, but the difference in her appearance outside the office totally blew his mind. She was sexy, yes, but he had no idea just how breathtakingly beautiful she really was.

Seeing her kicking back in her loose-fitting white sweatpants, tightly knotted at the waist and rolled at the cuffs, had him feeling all peculiar inside. The damned pants were big enough for the two of them, but the way they rode low on her voluptuous hips somehow made them sexier than lacy lingerie. When dressed for comfort, Rachel oozed sensuality like no one else and that nearly shut down his mind.

Nick bit back a low growl of longing as his cock throbbed with interest. Christ, what he'd do to crawl into those oversize pants with her, tie an impenetrable knot and fasten them together so he could do wickedly delicious things to her for the remainder of the holidays.

Her white turtleneck sweater framed her beautiful face and hugged her sensuous body, accentuating her curvy breasts, feminine shoulders, and slim waist. Nick's throat dried, and his fingers itched to pull her close and shape the pattern of her body. Dark curly hair tumbled in loose waves down her back, and a few wispy strands brushing over her breasts made her look warm, cozy, rumpled, and inviting.

Sexy as hell.

Her full lush lips were damp and slightly parted. As his body beckoned hers, all he could think about was dragging her into his arms and kissing the hell out of her. Then he'd abandon her mouth, and with exquisite gentleness he'd kiss a path down her silky flesh and with the soft blade of his tongue, he'd tease open her other set of damp lips. He'd spend a long time between her legs, licking and sucking her pussy until she came all over him. Then he'd lap up every drop, and rehydrate himself with her cream.

With his blood pulsing hot, Nick worked to rein in his lust before he acted on his impulses. Still feeling slightly off kilter, he drew a shaky breath and smiled when Margaret brought him a mug of coffee.

Christ, what the hell was he doing? Now was so not the time to be fantasizing about Rachel. Censoring his thoughts, he exchanged a few words with Margaret, then inconspicuously shot Rachel a sidelong glance. As he studied her, she tucked her legs beneath her on the chair and it was then that he noticed her bare feet. His body thrummed and her sexy toes once again prompted his dick into action. As his cock stood half-mast, he shifted in his chair to alleviate the discomfort. Oh fuck. There was something about those bare feet of hers. He'd never had a foot fetish before, but then again he'd never set his eyes on Rachel's pretty painted toes before either. He briefly closed his eyes against the flood of southern heat.

As Mason, his mother, and their neighbor delved into animated conversation, getting caught up in one another's lives, Rachel dipped her head and cast him a sideways glance. She blinked quickly and shadowed her emotions, and he suspected she was completely unaware of her allure. When their gazes met and locked, a flash of passion raced through him and turned his entire world upside down. As her long dark hair fell forward it camouflaged her flushed cheeks, but did little to hide the interest in her eyes. By God, she was, undeniably, the most enticing combination of sweet and sexy that he'd ever had the pleasure of viewing. Lust and want, no . . . *need* sang through his veins.

He shifted, and the delicious scent of gingerbread, cloves, and cinnamon wafted before his face. He sifted through the different aromas until he found Rachel's. Inhaling deeply, Nick pulled her alluring scent into his lungs. The familiar, enticing mix of jasmine and vanilla seeped under his skin and bombarded his senses, wreaking havoc on his already overstimulated libido and making it harder and harder to regain his composure.

He took a sip of his coffee to drown out the moan crawling out of the depths of his throat. All dressed in white, Rachel might look like a treetop angel, but she sure as hell brought out the devil in him.

Truthfully, under the circumstances, Nick couldn't see that as a good thing. He'd hardly think Mason would find humor in Nick ravishing his sister and engaging in a frivolous holiday fling. Not only that, Nick's company, Hilltop Gear, had recently used her professional services, and because she did such a bang-up job, likely would again.

Which once again brought him back to the question, why the hell was she was pretending she didn't know him?

Chapter Two

Well, hell!

So much for relaxing at the homestead while visions of Saint Nick danced in her head. Now it would be two weeks of pure torture, with a libido that was ready to go off like a supernova every time Nick came near. Cripes, who was she kidding? He didn't even have to be near. Here she was in her bedroom—having excused herself from the joyous reunion—on a completely different level of the house and the distance did little to help diminish her desire for him.

Him, as in her brother's boyfriend! Bloody hell!

What the heck did those two see in each other anyway? Okay, okay, so she couldn't deny that Mason was a great guy, and Nick, well, Nick was everything a woman—or a man, apparently—would ever want in a partner. But seriously, they were completely different. Through their business dealings she'd come to learn that Nick was a lover of the great outdoors, like her, whereas Mason didn't have a "taste for it" as he always so poetically put it, and preferred to sit by the fireside sipping hot cocoa. Nick was determined, focused, and dedicated, choosing to spend his time and energy building a successful business. Mason, on the other hand, changed jobs like he changed his underwear. Honestly, Nick had more in common with her than her brother. But far be it for her to tell Mason, or even Nick, how to pick their partners.

A low groan sounded in Rachel's throat as she tossed her frilly purple accent pillow onto her bed and scrambled to her feet. She padded barefoot across the hardwood floor to her wide sill. After plunking herself down on her window seat, she looked out over the vast expanse of ice- and snow-covered land. Off in the distance she could see smoke coming from Grandma Reddy's cottage.

Perched on the cushioned nook, Rachel's thoughts raced to her big sister, Holly, who was currently huddled up in the quaint cabin completing her novel. Even though Rachel would love the company, something to distract her oversexed body from Nick, she didn't dare break Holly's focus.

As she watched the billowy gray cloud hover over the cottage, Rachel reflected on Grandma Reddy, with all her milk and cookies, crazy anecdotes and her precious ruby—a stone Grandpa had given her—that she'd always kept close. Rachel crossed her arms over her chest and hugged herself. Oh how she wished Grandma were still here with them all. She never failed to bring a smile to Rachel's face and lift her spirits. And speaking of spirits, even though Grandma wasn't with them this Christmas season, Rachel knew she'd be here in spirit, filling the house with all her warmth and love.

The sound of heavy footsteps climbing the stairs drew her attention and heralded someone's arrival. She sucked in a breath and sat up straight, waiting and listening. From the way the old floor moaned and groaned she could only surmise that it was Nick in all his muscular glory making his way to his room. Heck, she could only imagine how much she, too, would moan and groan if Nick was climbing over her.

The steps slowed outside her closed door, then picked up again, carrying Nick to the bedroom adjacent to hers—Mason's old bedroom. Rachel let out a breath she hadn't realized she was holding, then tiptoed quietly to her bed, threw herself onto her mattress, and sprawled out her limbs.

Her mind drifted, and the sudden image of Nick's rock-hard body on top of hers flashed through her mind. Visions of his hands pinning hers above her head while she handed her pleasures over to him had her body writhing and mewling in pure sensual bliss. His hot, wet lips on her skin, indulging in her body and doing the most delicious things to her mouth, her breasts, between her legs . . .

Her lids slipped shut, and before she even realized what she was doing, she dipped one hand inside the band of her sweats to stroke her throbbing pussy. She brushed her index finger over her engorged clit, bringing it out to play. Imagining it was Nick's hands caressing her sensitive nub, she slowly began to pick up the pace until her body practically vibrated. In no time at all, passion began at her core and moved onward and outward building a powerful, mind-numbing climax.

She wet her lips. "Mmmm, so good."

The sound of her own voice snapped her back to reality and had her lids flying open. As she sobered, her brain skidded to a halt and she berated herself for masturbating while fantasizing about her brother's partner.

Nick is Mason's partner. . . .

Annoyed and beyond sexually frustrated, she pulled her hand from her pants, jumped from the bed, and marched to her closet. It was time to put Nick Grant out of her mind once and for all. And there was only one surefire way to accomplish such a challenging mission.

She rifled through her clothes and searched for something appropriate to wear. Despite the cold weather, she planned to attend the annual skating party at the town hall, after all. Hadn't she said she needed more activity in her life? And, since maybe it really was time to give up on finding herself a good man, a man she could spend the rest of her life with, the party would be the perfect spot to find someone to help work out all her frustrations, sexual and otherwise. She wasn't into one-night stands, but under the circumstances, desperate times called for desperate measures.

After deciding on a pair of skinny jeans and warm Lopi sweater that Grandma Reddy had knitted for her a few years back, she dressed quickly and headed for the stairs.

She sauntered through the living room, taking a moment to rub her hands in front of the fire, and glance at the sparkling Christmas tree before heading to the kitchen. As she approached, she heard her mother and Buzzy chatting at the table.

"So he's Mason's boyfriend then?" Buzzy asked.

"At first I just assumed he was Mason's business partner, but I wonder if there is more between them. He's never brought a man home to stay with the family before, which makes me wonder if Nick is the 'one.'"

Rachel pulled a face, her mother's words simply confirming her own theory.

"You could always ask him, just to confirm."

"If I ever get him alone, I just might do that. And honestly it doesn't matter—he's welcome to spend the holidays here."

Buzzy lowered her voice. "Did you see the way Rachel was looking at him?"

On that note, Rachel cleared her throat to announce her arrival and walked toward the kitchen. She suspected her mother knew exactly who Nick was, and why Rachel had been ogling him. But she also knew her mother would never come right out and say it, especially after Rachel had blatantly lied about knowing him. Sure, her mother was curious and astute but she also had tact and consideration and would wait for Rachel to broach the subject.

Buzzy narrowed her beady hazel eyes and fluffed her short black hair as her jerky gaze peered through the doorway and swept over Rachel. Something about her short twitchy movements, and the way she was always pecking about reminded Rachel of a pigeon.

"Rachel, come sit with us," Buzzy said, and tapped the chair beside her.

It wasn't that Rachel disliked Buzzy. Not at all. She was an old family friend who lived down the road and visited frequently. Probably too frequently. But since she was all alone in that big old house, Margaret always welcomed her with a smile. Just like Margaret welcomed everyone. Rachel liked Buzzy well enough. What she didn't like was the way she lived vicariously through the Reddys. Which was a nice way of saying that she was as nosy as hell, and the last thing Rachel wanted was to explain to her again why she'd yet to find herself a man in New York.

Not wanting to appear rude, Rachel rushed in and dropped a kiss onto Buzzy's cheek.

Buzzy smiled up at her. "Rachel, sit, let's talk more about the men in New York."

Rachel stifled a groan. "We'll talk more later. Right now I'm running late for the annual skating party." Rachel pulled on her parka, hat, mittens and boots, then grabbed her skates from the back porch and headed out the door.

"Don't forget your dad and I are going out to dinner tonight, Rachel, and won't be home until late," her mother called out after her.

When Rachel stepped outside, the wind slapped her in the face, stinging almost as much as Mason's shocking announcement. The winter sun was low on the horizon, and snow and ice crunched beneath her feet as she tracked around her Honda and cut down the winding lane. Since the town hall wasn't too far, she decided to walk. Maybe the cool air would help clear her head as well as her libido.

After only a few minutes down the road, she began to rethink her skinny jeans. Not only were her legs cold and stiff, jutting out beneath her like two frozen Popsicle sticks, the way the seam kept rubbing against her sensitive clit had her mind straying back to Nick again. Her sex fluttered and pulsed, and fueled her desires. Working diligently to ignore the erotic sensations, she pulled in an icy breath and, with determined strides, trekked on.

Five minutes later, she stepped into the town hall and soaked up the heat. She stood still for a moment, letting her body thaw as people milled about eating cookies and sipping hot drinks from Styrofoam cups. Sparkling colored lights adorned the room and glistened on the corner tree, blinking in a nonsequential pattern. After she'd gained feeling back into her extremities, Rachel grabbed herself a hot toddy, and let her glance move over the crowd, taking in all the familiar faces. From across the room she waved to Misty and Josh, high school sweethearts who were having their first child. Misty rubbed her protruding stomach and Rachel wondered how she was going to explain that "little round belly" to the kids when she dressed as Mrs. Claus at the department store. Too many gingerbread cookies, perhaps? Heck, Rachel knew all about that. Playing the part of Santa and Mrs. Claus was something the two had done for years, although Misty might be better off switching roles with her husband this time around.

Once again her gaze surfed over the faces before settling on one. The town's bad boy. Luke Russo. Perfect.

As she took in his playboy demeanor, she warmed to the idea of giving up the search for a good guy. Now she just planned to settle for some good old-fashioned sex. And Luke was just the guy to help her work out a few frustrations. Again and again.

NIGHT HAD FALLEN AROUND THEM and the cool wind nipped at their flesh as Nick and Mason hustled down the long, winding lane. As his breath turned to fog in the chilly night air, Nick pulled his collar up against the bitter gusts, then jammed his hands into the pockets of his parka. Keeping pace with Mason, who looked like he was straight out of *GQ* in his cashmere peacoat, he turned the corner and headed down the main drag leading toward the town hall. Mason really did have great taste, which was why Nick was thrilled to have him as head buyer at the store.

Once again, Nick's thoughts raced to Rachel and he wondered if she'd be at the hall. A little over an hour ago he'd spotted her from his bedroom window, hastily making her way down the driveway in her big white parka, looking like the abominable snowman with a pair of skates draped over her shoulders. She really did have something for the color white, he mused. Although he wasn't opposed to it, he thought she'd be far better suited for pink. Jesus, just thinking about her pretty pink lips, both plump sets, had his body burning and begging him to answer the pull in his groin. He fisted his hands inside his coat, bit back a low growl of longing, and stared straight ahead.

Off in the distance he could hear laughter and see a crowd skating beneath the towering street lanterns. As he took in the festivities, a strange tingling moved through his blood and warmed his darkest corners. He swallowed down the lump in his throat and slowed his steps in an effort to take it all in.

The older children were speed skating around the rink like they were pumped up on sugar. Younger children were tucked in between their parents, learning to take their first strides on skates. Off in the corner, lovesick teenagers were lip-locked under clumps of mistletoe that were hung from every possible lamppost. Santa made his rounds, laughing joyously and handing out copious amounts of chocolate and candy canes. At least now Nick understood the sugar high.

Nick stood back in mute fascination and ached with a sense of longing as he observed the collection of merry people. An invisible band tightened around his heart, and he felt his knees go weak.

Christ, he knew he wanted this, but until this moment he really had no idea just how much he ached for it. He had always yearned to have a big loving family, but there was something so comforting and inviting about this particular gathering that it had him feeling all sentimental inside.

Realizing that Mason was well ahead of him, he picked up the pace and doubled his steps to catch up. As they moved closer to the group, it baffled him just how much he wanted to belong, to be a part of Haven's annual celebrations. To come together year after year and meet family and old friends. To share memories and laughter over cookies, cocoa, and candy canes. Chaos erupted inside him and he cleared his throat, rattled by the rush of emotions.

Just then he caught sight of the sheriff's Stetson bobbing like a buoy in a sea of people as he moved through the crowd, his head a foot above the rest, not at all unlike Nick's. Using his broad shoulders, the sheriff maneuvered his way through the masses and stepped in front of Mason to block his path. "Mason, my good man. Long time." He patted Mason on the back and then moved in for a hug.

"Too long." A wide smile split Mason's face as they embraced. Nick watched the exchange, taking in the way Mason's eyes lit up like a Christmas tree, and the way the two touched with intimate recognition. "I was hoping to run into you," Mason added, then turned to Nick. "Nick, this is Jack Roberts, a good friend of mine." Mason turned back to Jack. "Nick's staying with us for the holidays," he explained.

With his shoulders squared and his body tense, Jack turned to him, and they stood eye to eye. With an unwavering glare, Jack stared at Nick, his mouth set in a grim line as he sized him up. Intuitive intelligence told Nick the man was trying to decide if he was friend or foe. After a long thoughtful moment, Jack's body relaxed, obviously having decided that Nick posed no threat to his relationship with Mason. Jack thrust his hand out.

"Nice to meet you, Nick."

Apparently, as Mason had explained to Nick before, he didn't give off the right kind of vibes—whatever the hell that was—and no one in their right mind would ever mistake him for gay.

After shaking the sheriff's hand, Nick scanned the rink in search of Rachel. When he spotted her laughing and cavorting in the middle of the frozen pond with some local playboy, gripping a white Styrofoam cup like it was her lifeline, anger rose sure and swift, and possession like he'd never felt before raged through his blood and caught him off guard.

What the hell . . . ?

As his gaze lit on them, his mind raced. Okay, so he might not know her well, but he sure as hell knew her well enough to know that she didn't chase after playboys. Guys who'd use her up and toss her away like she was a disposable coffee cup, with no regard for her needs and desires. Rachel was bright and astute, and because of her profession, she had an excellent understanding of human nature. Which left Nick with one conclusion—she knew exactly what she was getting herself into. He paused to consider that a moment longer, and then suddenly understanding dawned. Fuck. If she was looking for a hot Christmas fling, he damned well wanted to be the guy to give it to her, not some asshole who cared nothing about her. At least he'd be gentle, caring, and considerate, and take the time to understand and satisfy all her needs.

The sheriff must have sensed his rising fury. Jack leaned into Mason, gestured with a nod toward Rachel, and spoke in quiet words. "What's gotten into her anyway? She never had the taste for guys like Luke before. You want me to do something about it?" He cracked his knuckles in anticipation. "Just say the word, Mason."

Mason looked past Jack's shoulder. "What the fuck——" He took one step toward her, but Nick stopped him.

"I got this."

"Forget it, Nick." Mason jabbed his thumb into his cashmere coat. "She's *my* sister——"

Nick put a placating hand on his friend's shoulder. "No, Mason, really, I got this. You two go get caught up, and I promise I'll make sure she gets home safely."

Mason was about to protest, but Jack spoke up. "I think Nick's the man for the job, Mason."

After Mason conceded, Nick and Jack exchanged a knowing look; then Nick carefully picked his way across the slippery ice. He shot a glance back over his shoulder to catch Mason staring at his sister, deep worry lines etched across his forehead, and it occurred to him just how protective Mason was of her, and how protective the sheriff was of her.

Just how protective *he* was of her.

He turned back around and focused on Rachel, and for the briefest of moments he could see uncertainty clouding her big dark eyes as she blinked up at Luke. Nick immediately got the sense that she was moving past her comfort zone. His gut clenched, and everything in him reached out to her.

Having learned early on in life—thanks to his volatile parents—to either mind his own business or use humor to defuse a situation, he stepped up to her and cupped her elbow, signaling his intent. "There you are."

She spun around, and her eyes dimmed with relief. He noted the play of emotions across her face and wondered what she was thinking and how she would react when he hauled her the hell out of there.

"Nick," she said breathlessly, and the scent of rum and eggnog on her breath hit him hard.

As his protective instincts came out full force, he conjured a smile, pulled her from Luke's tenuous grip, and, as expected, watched Luke steel himself. "Where do you think you're going, little lady?" Luke hauled her back into his arms.

Nick's gaze shifted and locked on Luke's and in a deceptively calm voice he said, "She's coming with me."

"Like hell." His voice grew loud, challenging, and the commotion quickly drew unwanted attention. Nick shot a glance around and scanned the spectators. Now was definitely not the time or place for this. He leaned into Luke and whispered into his ear. Luke's head jerked back with a start. Eyes wide, he held both hands up, palms out, and then he gave a quick nod of his head. "Sure thing. She's all yours."

Satisfied that Luke wasn't about to make an unwelcome scene, Nick put his mouth close to Rachel's ear. "Let's go."

Eagerness washed over Rachel's face, and she quickly nodded in acquiescence. "Where are we going?"

His gaze moved over her, taking in her ruddy nose and cheeks as well as her chattering teeth. A rush of tenderness overcame him. He softened his voice. "Home, Rachel. You've been out here too long. You're damned near frozen to death." He glanced at her feet. "Where are your boots?"

She pointed to the bench. He slipped his arm around her waist and ushered her across the ice. People bustled about as he cleared a spot for her on the wooden seat and sank to his knees in front of her.

Neither spoke as he leaned forward and went to work on removing her skates. She angled her head to watch and her fragrant hair brushed against the back of his neck. Her warm familiar scent curled around him and he drew it into his lungs. As his senses exploded, the enticing scent of jasmine worked its way through his veins and pooled in his groin. Goddamn, what the hell was the matter with him? He couldn't seem be around her without getting a raging hard-on.

He could feel her eyes on him, studying his every movement, and all he wanted to do was press his mouth to hers and kiss every inch of her body.

Just then someone tapped him on the shoulder. His muscles tightened in preparation, as he half expected to see Luke standing over him. He slanted his head, and saw a kid grinning like the Cheshire cat and pointing upward. Nick followed the direction and spotted a cluster of mistletoe hovering over Rachel's head.

"You gotta kiss her, mister," the kid yelled out, and started skating circles around them while chanting, "You gotta kiss her. You gotta kiss her." The kid's enthusiasm was contagious and despite himself he chuckled. Rachel quickly joined in, and it was the first time he heard her laugh, really laugh. Her entire face lit up and he became hyperaware of the way it affected him. "You gotta kiss her. . . ."

Just how many candy canes had the child eaten anyway? Nick slipped his hand around the boy's waist to still him. "Okay, okay, kid, I get it." The child shimmied out of his hold, snickered loudly, and skated off to torture some other unsuspecting soul. Nick glanced at Rachel to gauge her reactions, but she was already wetting her plump lips.

Instantly drunk with need, he felt all rational thought flee his mind like a group of mountain climbers facing an avalanche. "What was it that kid said again . . . ?" His voice was so dark and desirous he hardly recognized it.

"You gotta kiss her . . ." Rachel provided.

A jolt of sexual energy leaped between them and the hunger inside him consumed his every thought. When she inched forward, the invitation proved too powerful for him to deny. The sight of her parted lips shattered his resolve. He pressed his mouth to hers, let out a low groan, and drank in her sweetness. Goddamn, she tasted better than he'd ever imagined. And trust him, over the last few hours, he'd imagined. A lot.

Her body relaxed into him and she moaned against his burning mouth and probing tongue. Before they had time to finish what they started, someone bumped into them, knocking Rachel off the bench, and knocking some well-needed common sense into him.

She fell with a thud, her socked feet still draped over the bench. Sprawled out on her back, Rachel groaned, rubbed her head, and said, "Damn, that's going to hurt in the morning."

Nick pushed her boots on, jumped up, grabbed her hand, and hauled her to her feet. Their bodies collided, their groins bumped and he wondered if she could feel his rock-hard erection straining against his zipper. Needing desperately to lighten the mood, he said, "No more rum and eggnog for you."

Feigning insult she pumped her finger into his chest. Now how she made that gesture feel erotic, he'd never know. "Hey, mister, falling had nothing to do with the rum and eggnog, which I might add was very tasty. Maybe we should get another."

Rolling his eyes, he shook his head. "I think you've had enough."

She held up her mittened hand. "This is hardly too many."

Nick couldn't help but laugh when he looked at her mittens, unable to tell how many digits she was holding up.

A loud hiccup came out of nowhere, and she covered her mouth and chuckled. "I only had three, but I'm not much of a drinker," she confessed. "I don't really have a *taste for it.*"

He smiled when she used Mason's favorite expression. "*Nooo . . .*" He exaggerated that one word. "I never would have guessed."

She planted her hands on her hips and glared at him, but she couldn't keep the amusement from her voice. "Nick Grant, are you mocking me?"

He pointed to her. "You? I wouldn't dream of it, sweetheart."

She opened her mouth, to come back with some smart-ass comment no doubt, but he cut her off and caught her hand in his. "Come on, let's get you home."

The sound of the crowd dwindled at their backs as they made their way down the deserted road. A comfortable silence fell over them, and the clouds overhead peeled back to reveal a mosaic of glistening stars. Icy branches sparkled beneath the moonbeams and cast shadows on the ground below. It was cold and wintry, but a beautiful evening nonetheless.

After a long while, Rachel broke the silence. "What did you say to Luke?" she asked through clattering teeth.

He put his arm around her to help keep her warm body and shot her a playful grin. "I told him I was your gynecologist, and you were late for your herpes treatment."

She stopped dead in her tracks. Her mouth dropped open and her eyes widened, but he couldn't help noticing the admiration lingering beneath. "Ohmigod, you didn't?" she asked, her voice laced with both shock and humor.

"Yeah, I did." He suddenly recalled the doubt he'd spotted in her eyes and his smile dissolved. "What were you doing with that guy anyway? He doesn't seem like your type."

For the briefest of seconds she looked like she was about to tell him, but then she quickly steered the conversation away from herself, a habit he was becoming increasingly familiar with. "It's cold. We should hurry."

He sensed she was holding something back, but decided not to press. Once again, silence reigned as they continued their way back to the Reddy homestead. As he guided her around a slushy, halffrozen pothole, he felt her eyes on him again. He cast her a sidelong glance and arched a brow. "What?"

She looked worried. "What if he didn't believe you?"

Nick rolled one shoulder. "I guess I never thought that far ahead. Besides, something tells me he's not known for his intelligence."

She grinned and nodded in agreement. "You looked like you were itching to lick him like a dog."

He angled his head and laughed at her expression. "Uh, Rachel, I'm not really sure how to take that."

Her soft chuckle carried in the breeze and curled around him, doing the most delicious things to his libido. She whacked him playfully. "You know what I mean." Her eyes turned serious for a moment, and her voice dropped an octave. "Really, Nick, what would you have done?"

He grinned. "I guess I would have licked him like a dog." Although he'd much prefer to lick her like a cat and make her purr.

She pulled a face. "I'm just glad it never came to that. I really like the way you handled it." She threw her hands up in the air. "Even though come tomorrow morning the whole town is going to think I have herpes." She groaned but the amusement dancing in her eyes belied her emotions. "But better that than a fight."

"And here I always thought most women wanted big macho men who solved problems with their fists," he teased.

"I guess I'm not like most women."

"So I see." He let out a slow breath and it hung heavy in the air as he recalled all the frequent and sometimes violent parental fights he'd witnessed in his childhood. "It's Christmas, Rachel. I threw the guy some charity because the last thing I wanted to do was cause a commotion in front of all those children."

She stared at him for a long moment, then said in a quiet voice, "And I see you're not like most men." Respect flashed in her eyes as dark lashes blinked up at him. "You have a real strength of character, Nick." Something in her expression softened and touched him deep. He cleared his throat, shaken by the emotions she brought out in him

Flustered, he stopped and turned to her. "Look, you seemed like you were having second thoughts, like you'd gotten yourself into a situation that escalated beyond your control, so I stepped in to help out. No big deal, okay?"

She swallowed and her voice was so low, he had to strain to hear her. "I appreciate the way you considered the children's sensitivities. Most guys wouldn't." She dipped her head and studied her boots. "It never fails to astound me the way you're always so caring and considerate of everyone's needs."

He placed his hand under her chin and tipped her head until their eyes met. He winked at her. "For a girl I just met you sure seem to know an awful lot about me."

As though knowing exactly what he was getting at, her eyes widened and she moved half a foot away, stepping toward the narrow road. He saw the truck coming around the corner, its plow dropping as it approached. Nick grabbed for Rachel, but it was too little, too late. Cold, wet slush crashed down on her like a tsunami wave, leaving her standing there soaking wet and gasping for air.

Looking like a melting snowman, she lifted her arms out to her sides. "What . . . the . . . hell . . . ?" she muttered, her lips quickly turning an odd shade of blue.

"Jesus, Rachel." As her body began trembling from head to toe, Nick brushed the slop off her clothes, and opened his coat to her. He slipped his hand around her waist and splayed his fingers against the small of her back to offer his heat.

He shook his head and scoffed. "Now what makes me think that was Luke?" He anchored Rachel to him, cradling her body in his arms, and she relaxed into him. His muscles bunched in response, and his cock tightened to the point of pain. He pressed against her skin, his body registering every delicious detail of her sexy curves.

A pause and then, "Nick . . ." When she tilted her head, her eyes were dark, and full of urgent need.

"What?"

She wet her lips. "Thanks . . ." Her voice came out raspy, broken, and he wasn't exactly sure what she was thanking him for. Getting her away from Luke? Considering the children? Offering her his warmth? Or keeping it a secret that they knew each other?

Pleasure forked through him when he felt one of her hands snake around his waist. Hunger consumed him and, completely caught up in the moment, his eyes shifted downward to examine her lips. Her mouth slanted as she ran her thumb over his cheek and brushed away a drip of slush. The gesture warmed more than just his flesh. With his mouth hovering only inches from hers, all he could think about was ravishing her and taking full possession of her body. He ached to strip off her clothes, drive his cock deep inside her, and fuck her like he'd never fucked anyone before. His muscles bunched, his dick thickened, and common sense packed a bag and headed south.

She wet her blue-tinged lips. "Nick . . ."

Reality came crashing down at the sound of her shaky voice. Unease hit him and he sucked in a sharp breath in an effort to pull himself together. He stepped back, extricating himself, needing the distance to help bank his desire and push back the lust. As his passion slowly receded, his brain cleared and he paused to consider the ramifications of his actions.

Rachel had been drinking, and he would not take advantage of the situation. No matter how much his cock clamored for attention and screamed for release. Acting purely on his sexual urges would lump him with the likes of Luke. Besides, she was Mason's sister, and with his strong brotherly instincts, he knew he'd be crossing the line if they indulged in a wild sexual affair. What a way to repay a friend for opening his home to him over the holidays.

"Come on. We need to hurry home to get you out of these wet clothes and into something warm before you get hypothermia." Gorgeous brown eyes full of desire stared up at him and he rushed on, "I promised Mason I'd take care of you, so don't go and freeze to death on me now, or he'll kill me." He flashed his teeth, an attempt to bring a smile to her face.

His efforts backfired. At the mention of her brother, her eyes blinked back into focus, and desire immediately segued to dismay. He felt her retreat, both physically and emotionally. The quick change took him by surprise. He'd never seen anyone go from hot to cold so quickly. Was it the alcohol? Or was it something else entirely?

Ten minutes later, Nick guided Rachel through the porch and into the kitchen. Except for the embers glowing in the fireplace and the flickering tree lights in the living room, the place was dark and silent. He turned on the fluorescent kitchen light and glanced around. "Where is everyone?" he asked in a whisper, not wanting to wake her parents if they were upstairs asleep.

"Ro . . . man . . . tic . . . ," she chattered, and shook her wet mittens. "Din . . . ner."

The sight of her wet clothes and rosy cheeks propelled him into action. "We need to get you warm and we need to do it fast." Nick peeled off her mittens, and unzipped her jacket while she kicked off her boots. Once he had her sufficiently undressed, he pulled off his own outerwear and slipped his arm around her back. "Come on."

She could barely lift her legs as he ushered her up the creaky stairs and into her bedroom. After a quick scan of the room, he turned on the corner lamp and pulled down her blankets. "Strip down to your underwear," he commanded and began to shed his sweater.

Her eyes widened and moved over his face. "What . . . what are you doing?"

He pinned her with a glare and turned serious, professional. "This is what I do, Rachel. It's my business."

"This is what you do?" She gave him a perplexed frown. "You get naked with half-frozen women?"

"I sell gear and outerwear for all different types of activities, including mountain climbing," he said, stating the obvious to the woman who'd just completed a campaign for him and knew all about his business dealings. "Trust me, I know all about frostbite and the best ways to deal with it."

He pulled his sweater over his head and her eyes strayed to his chest. "Couldn't . . . couldn't I just have a warm bath?"

Jesus, she looked terrified. A few minutes ago her eyes were dark with desire, and now she was gawking at him like he had the plague. He shook his head in confusion. She really was a whole lot of contradictions.

"No, your skin will burn and you'll itch something fierce. This is the best way. Now, unless you want to lose dexterity in your extremities, I suggest you get undressed and use my body for heat."

He averted his gaze to give her privacy. Concentrating on his own clothes, he released his zipper and wondered if he was some kind of masochist. Having Rachel between the sheets was like dangling a lamb in front of a hungry lion. Temptation to the extreme. He just hoped—prayed—that the seriousness of the situation would help cut through the lust and keep him focused.

He pulled his pants off and tossed them over her rocking chair. When he glanced at Rachel, who now stood before him in her lacy bra and underwear, fire pitched through his blood and his cock damned near ripped a hole in his leggings.

She crinkled her nose, and questioned in a soft voice, "Are those women's tights?"

He cleared his throat and shed the rest of his clothes, taking care to keep his boxer shorts in place. "Yeah." Technically, they were women's Icebreaker Leggings, but he didn't bother to explain that he personally tried out every piece in his outerwear line before putting it on the shelves. The well-being of each and every customer, both male and female, was most important to him, and he refused to offer a product that he didn't back fully.

As he moved to the bed, he held open the blankets to her and lectured himself on keeping his cool and not taking advantage of the situation, despite the way his cock was clamoring for him to do just that. Not only was Rachel frozen to the bone, she'd been knocking back rum. Besides clouding her judgment, the rum also aided in decreasing her core body temperature, and he needed to warm her up and warm her up fast.

He patted the empty spot beside him. "You coming?"

Chapter Three

Y^{ou coming?}
    Oh God, she just might be.

Gathering every ounce of strength her frozen, yet needy body could muster, she dragged herself across the room and slipped between her warm flannel sheets. Even though she'd purposely put her back to Nick, she was still conscious of his every breath, his every movement. Her gaze fluttered about the room, drinking in the intimate ambience, the soft light, the comfy mattress, and the hot guy next to her. It made her feel warm, cozy, snug.

Horny.

Nick moved closer and she could feel the heat radiating off him. "Damn, you're like ice," he murmured.

Even the deep cadence of his voice made her wet. She bit down on her bottom lip hard enough to draw blood and forced herself to focus on something else. Nick was only in her bed to warm her. It was *not* a ploy to get her naked and make wild passionate love to her.

Unfortunately.

Nick was a man of strong character, a man with integrity, a man who was sweet, kind, and caring, and was only helping his partner's sister out in a time of need, she quickly reminded herself.

He draped his arm around her and pulled her in tight, her cold body sucking the heat from his. *Sucking* . . . Oh God, she did not want to think about sucking at a time like this.

She forced herself to divert her attention and concentrate on thawing her extremities. Trembling, she shimmied in closer and noted the huge difference in his body temperature. "Your body is so hot." She worked hard to sound casual, like she climbed between the sheets with her brother's boyfriends all the time. "I think I'll have to invest in a pair of those tights."

"I'll send you a few pairs," he offered, and rubbed his hand up and down her arm to smooth out her goose bumps. In one slick movement, he turned her to face him, grabbed her feet and placed them between his thighs. Her feet immediately began to warm but Nick damned near jumped off the bed. His eyes widened and he made a tortured face. "Sweet mother of God!" Rachel couldn't help but chuckle at his reactions.

"Sorry," she mumbled, then poked him in the chest and followed up with, "But this *was* your idea."

"Hey, be careful before that mouth of yours gets you into trouble." He gave her a playful wink. "I'm sure I can still find a snowbank out there with your name on it."

She relaxed into him, enjoying the easy comfort that had fallen over them. Silence descended upon the room and seconds turned into minutes as he worked his hands over her flesh.

His long strokes and callused palms scraped over her curves, as he slowly introduced himself to her body. He touched her with such gentle care that she could feel all her composure slipping away. Mesmerized by his soft caresses, her mind wandered and a surge of excitement raced through her as she once again pictured Nick between her legs, his tongue on her hot center, working her into a frenzy of lust until she climaxed all over him. Her body shook with urgent need and there wasn't a damned thing she could do to stifle the erotic whimper bubbling up from the depths of her throat.

Her sound of pure carnal delight seemed to have gained Nick's attention. His throat worked as he swallowed and the concern in his eyes became her undoing. "You okay?" His breath was hot on her neck when he spoke and the hypnotic tone of his voice brought on a shudder.

Shaken from her fantasies, her voice thinned to a low whisper. "I still can't seem to get blood flow back into my feet." When she wiggled her toes between his legs, he drew in a sharp breath and she forced herself to focus on something other than how close her feet were to his *private parts*—private parts she ached to touch, kiss, feel inside her.

Nick is Mason's partner. Nick is Mason's partner. She continued to repeat her new mantra until her brain cleared.

She watched him for a moment, his primal essence completely overwhelming her. "Nick."

"Yeah?" He propped his elbow up on his pillow and rested his head on his palm. Soft blue eyes met hers, and her stomach fluttered.

"How long have you known Mason?"

"A little over a month."

His raspy voice sent a barrage of erotic sensations through her body and his warm breath had her aching to taste the sweetness of his mouth. "He's a great guy."

"Yeah, he is. Even though he hadn't known me that long, he wouldn't condone my spending the holidays alone in New York."

She swallowed, guilt eating at her like a thousand hungry locusts for fantasizing about Mason's partner. "I wouldn't ever want to do anything to hurt him." And she wouldn't want Mason to hurt Nick either, but the way Mason was cozying up to Sheriff Jack at the town hall hadn't gone unnoticed by her. Obviously, Mason had a thing for tall, muscular men. Her brother really was a great guy, he just wasn't a long-term guy. She wondered if Nick knew that.

He gave her a perplexed look. "Me neither."

He brushed his hand down her side, his fingers coming perilously close to the outer edge of her breast. His intimate touch seeped under her skin and she fought the urge to squirm—right underneath him. Her nipples tightened in bliss and hunger prowled through her. She bit back a breathy moan and shivered. Almost violently.

Nick mistook her shiver. "Christ, girl, what am I going to do with you?"

Oh, she had a million possibilities. . . .

He pulled her in tighter. Heat and strength radiated off him as he offered his warmth and she nearly went out of her mind. Her sex throbbed when his hands raced over her flesh. His warm fingers burned everywhere he touched and deepened her desire for him. Her body practically convulsed when he ran his hands down her legs and cupped her feet.

He shifted his position and lowered himself on the mattress. He closed his palms around one foot, brought it to his mouth and exhaled. His warm breath sent heat charging to her pussy and she lubricated in response. Oh good God! The tang of her arousal saturated the room and she wondered if he smelled it. Mortified by her body's reactions, she squeezed her eyes shut, but when she felt something hot and wet against her toe—something that felt like a tongue—her lids sprung back open.

"Nick."

She spotted the thin sheen of sweat on his upper lip. He dragged in a huge breath, and for a fleeting moment need flashed in his eyes and she sensed something inside him give.

"Rachel . . ." The urgency in his voice surprised and excited her. He slid up her thighs and over her stomach until they came face-to-face. His nostrils flared, his jaw clenched. Shaky hands raced through her hair and rattled her passion-drenched mind. He tipped his head to look at her. His eyes were dark, intense. Carnal. Oh Lord, one minute he was warming her toes with tender concern, and the next he was climbing over her, looking completely wild and out of control. His mood changed without warning and she had no idea what brought the shift on; all she knew was that she felt equal measures of fear and excitement. "I can't quite seem to get you warm," he murmured, his lips hovering over hers.

She began panting, and her brand-new mantra drifted away like dust in the wind. "It . . . it could be dangerous, don't you think?"

"Yeah, I do." His blue eyes darkened, triggering a craving inside her. A craving only he could sate.

"That's not good." *Breathe, Rachel, breathe.* "Not good at all." Her gaze raced over his face, trying to read him.

His brow furrowed. "What should we do?"

A wave of passion overcame her, and her sex muscles undulated. Her pulse kicked up a notch and without conscious thought, she darted a tongue out in invitation. "Your lips. They're warm."

"You think I should put my mouth on you?"

Warmth spread out over her skin, and raw desire seared her insides as she pretended to mull it over for a second. "Under the circumstances, I don't think we have a choice." Dear God, she'd never been so bold before, so brazen. But there was something about Nick that brought out the vixen in her, making her feel wild, sexy . . . *naughty.*

"Where should I put my lips, Rachel?"

Her body flushed hotly and she grew impossibly slicker. She moistened her mouth and dragged her finger over her bottom lip. "Maybe you should start here. . . ."

No sooner did she get the words out than Nick's burning mouth came down hard. The soft blade of his tongue raced over her lips then slipped inside for a deeper exploration. His tongue thrashed against the sides of her mouth then tangled with hers. Her body moved under his and her heart pounded erratically as he pillaged her wanton mouth.

After a long moment he inched back and trailed kisses over her jaw. The delicate slide of his tongue turned her inside out. The pleasure was most exquisite.

So much for just *her* mouth getting her into trouble. His seemed to be doing a fine job all on its own.

He met her glance. "Are you warm yet?"

With her breasts heavy and achy, she shook her head. "Afraid not." Need made her voice husky.

"You think I should put my mouth somewhere else?" His warm breath wafted across her cheek. His gaze was dark, intense, tortured.

Blood pounded through her veins and since she was well past the point of vocalizing anything intelligent she simply nodded.

"Tell me where?" he demanded in a soft voice.

Rachel slid her hands over her body and gripped the cup of her lacy bra. In a silent message, she tugged, just enough to expose one distended nipple.

Nick's nostrils flared and he gave her a scalding look. "Do you think if I put my mouth on your nipple it will help warm you up?"

She wanted that so much she felt dizzy. Without bothering to mask her enthusiasm, she gave a quick nod and practically whimpered in delight.

His eyes dropped to her bare breast. "I suppose it's worth a try." His head descended and his tongue was on her in seconds, taking possession of her body and greedily drawing her hard nub into his mouth. Light gentle flicks turned into long, heated sucks. Her nipple tingled and tightened beneath his hot, wet mouth. Each velvet stroke brought her closer and closer to the precipice.

Rachel raced her hands through his hair, holding his mouth to her quivering body. A low moan cut through the room and she widened her legs as Nick continued to stoke the fire inside her.

When her body began pulsing, she whimpered for release. Her hands slid to Nick's shoulders and she gave a little push, her actions conveying without words exactly where she needed him.

"Still not warm?" As he breathed the words over her skin, it elicited a shudder from deep within.

She pinched her eyes shut and tossed her head from side to side.

"Do you need my mouth somewhere else, Rachel?" The dark desire in his tone had her lids springing back open.

"Nick . . ." she murmured.

"Tell me." He gripped the sides of her hips and the urgency in his voice touched something deep inside her. Bone-deep warmth flowed through her and tangled her emotions. "Tell me where you need my mouth."

She drew a deep breath but was unable to fill her lungs. Pushing on his shoulders, she guided him downward. "Here. I need you here, Nick," she murmured, shocked at her boldness and the sheer desperation in her voice.

His lashes fluttered against her skin as he slid down her body. She widened her legs even more, granting him full access to the hungry little spot that needed his undivided attention. He insinuated himself between her legs, pressed his nose to her silk panties and inhaled, pulling her aroused aroma into his lungs.

"Dear God," she whispered. When he blew a hot breath over her pussy, she let out a little gasp and began trembling from head to toe.

"Are you getting warmer, Rachel?"

"Yes, no, I don't know . . ." She bucked against him but he pressed his hand to her stomach and pinned her to the bed and in that instant it occurred to her just how much she liked being restrained.

He trailed his fingers over her stomach, her hips, and her thighs, taking the utmost care with her body. His touch was so painstakingly gentle it stirred feelings inside her and it suddenly occurred to her that if she spent one more second in his arms she was going to fall for him, and fall for him hard. As alarm bells jangled in the back of her head, she angled her head to see him.

Through the silk material of her panties, Nick pressed his lips to her clit and her body began to burn up. Flames licked at her thighs, sending heat to every nerve ending in her body. She gyrated against his mouth. "Oh my God, Nick. I'm burning up."

Her words seemed to trigger something inside him. His head came up with a snap and he pulled back as though he'd forgotten where he was, and what he was doing. His hasty retreat took her by surprise and his change of mood occurred so swiftly it left her stunned. His expression turned serious and dark stormy eyes met hers, like he was waging some sort of internal war.

As her brain struggled through the lust-filled haze, her heart raced and she knew she was in trouble. His touch, his kisses, and his gentleness worked some mysterious alchemy on her heart and soul. By small degrees, his body tightened.

Oh God, what had she gone and done?

Nick raced his fingers through his hair, pushing it off his face. His turbulent gaze took in her rumpled state as he, too, seemed to realize the mistake they'd just made. "I . . . uh . . . ." He appeared to be at a loss for words, so she came to his rescue and gave him a way out.

"Looks like I'm all warmed up now. Thanks for your help," she said, despite the fact that she needed him to continue as much as she needed him to stop.

He gave her a look she didn't understand, climbed from the

bed, and gathered his clothes. He tossed a long, lingering glance her way, before he turned around and disappeared into the hall. "Good night, Rachel."

As she watched him shut the door, her body thrummed and her mind worked to sort through the turn of events.

What the hell just happened?

Unfortunately, her brain was too far gone and her body too far lost in a haze of lust for her to make sense out of it tonight. All she knew was she needed to take the edge off before she splintered into a million tiny pieces.

It was her feet that did him in.

Soft, smooth, with manicured nails painted in the hottest shade of pink. Oh fuck, she was so damned sexy. So sexy he couldn't control his primal urges around her.

Nick shook his head in disgust and berated himself, hardly able to believe how far he'd let that go, how much of a selfish bastard he was. Sure, he ached to spend all night between her legs, licking and fingering her until she creamed in his mouth, over and over again, but under the circumstances ravishing her was hardly the honorable thing to do, no matter how much they both seemed to want that.

When her soft whisper had covered him like a blanket of lust, every logical reason he'd had not to forge full-force ahead and fuck her sweet little pussy suddenly seemed so irrelevant.

Oh Christ, hadn't he lectured himself on taking advantage of Rachel and the situation? He knew better than that. But there was just something so damned sweet and sexy about her that had him acting on impulse and going against his own best interests, *against her best interests.*

When the alcohol wore off and her body temperature returned to normal, her thoughts would clear. Then he had no idea how she'd react to his kisses. With her hot/cold behavior, it was anyone's guess.

Nick slipped into Mason's room, and tossed his clothes onto his bunk bed. It was then that he realized he'd left his leggings back in Rachel's room. Still in his boxer shorts, he spun around and backtracked down the hall. He stood outside the door and tapped lightly but when she didn't respond, he quietly inched it open in search of his belongings.

What he saw instead rocked him to his very core. Spread out on her bed, completely naked, Rachel ran her hands over her sensuous body. Her beautiful breasts with rosy red nipples swayed slightly as she writhed on the sheets. Lips wet and parted, a pink hue colored her cheeks and her dark hair tumbled over her shoulders in complete disarray.

The soft bedroom mewls coming from her mouth turned his legs to rubber, and his cock to granite. Her intoxicating voice whispered across his flesh like an intimate caress and awakened every nerve ending. Captivated by the sight before him, and bewitched by her dark desirous murmurs, Nick locked both knees to keep himself upright and stood stock-still, trying to remember how to breathe.

With the room seductively scented by her arousal, lamplight fell over her body, and the soft dark hair matted to her pussy glistened beneath the rays. His stomach tightened and pressure built in his body as his cock throbbed to drive into her drenched core and stay there for the rest of his vacation. He clenched his jaw to suppress a growl. Oh fuck, he should leave. The gentleman in him urged him to get the hell out of there, but the man in him demanded he stay put.

The man won out. Selfish bastard that he was.

His eyes fixed on the apex between her legs in time to see Rachel open her pretty pink lips and scrape her finger over her engorged clit. With her every sensual movement seducing him from across the room, she widened her legs and bent one at the knee, the position providing him with a clear view of her gorgeous cunt.

Lost in the heat of the moment, blood pulsed hot through his body and he was damned near close to shooting a load off in his boxer shorts just from watching her. As her pleasure mounted she made a sexy noise, brushed her nipple with her thumb, and pushed a finger high inside her pussy.

Sweet mother of God!

It was the most erotic thing he'd ever seen. Primitive desire raged inside him. Her breath came hard and ragged and her hips lifted from the bed. Using long, luxurious strokes, she eased her finger in and out of her hot tight center, in and out, picking up the pace as she chased an orgasm.

Keeping up the rhythm, she ground her clit against her palm, and it was all he could do not to walk over there and lend her a helping hand. But he didn't dare move and miss a second of her sexy solo act.

She shifted and rotated and pushed another finger inside to stretch herself open wider. Her breath caught on a gasp as lust stole every ounce of his strength. Her fingers plunged harder, deeper while she brushed her other hand over her engorged nipples.

Dizzy with want and overwhelmed with desire, Nick sagged against the doorway. The need to lose himself in her was so intense it rocked his world. Christ, it was almost frightening the way she affected him. His muscles were trembling, and he was sure he was going to go mad with want. Juices pearled on the tip of his crown and his cock spasmed to the point of pain. If he didn't soon rectify that big problem, he was either going to rupture an artery or spontaneously combust. Nothing good could come from either one of those.

Her lids fluttered, her head flew to the side tossing her long silky hair across her pillow, and she moaned without censure. A second later, a violent tremor wracked her body as she climaxed. Nick inhaled her rich sensual scent as she gave a whimper of relief. After a moment, she drew a calming breath and pulled her bedding to her shoulders.

With the utmost care, Nick backed out of her room and silently shut her door. Forgetting all about his leggings, he tiptoed quietly back to his room, ripped off his boxer shorts, and quickly went to work on abusing the hell out of his cock.

Chapter Four

Rachel awoke to bright sunshine streaming in through her window. She'd fallen into such a deep sleep last night after she'd finished what she and Nick had started, she hadn't had time to sort through her emotions or the intimacies the two had shared.

She took a moment to recall the desire flicking across Nick's face, the intensity in his gaze, the sensuous way he tended to every inch of her body, and the erotic way he'd paid homage to her mouth, her breasts, between her legs. . . .

Her pulse kicked up a notch and doubt whispered through her blood. Surely to God a man who was batting for the other team could never pleasure a woman like that.

Maybe she'd misread him. Maybe he wasn't gay at all. But if he wasn't, what had caused him to pull back so abruptly and flee from her room like he'd just made a colossal mistake? And why would Mason introduce him as his partner?

Rachel tossed her head to the side and it was then that she'd noticed Nick's leggings. Okay, the man wore women's tights. How could he *not* be gay?

She slipped from her bed, pulled on her housecoat, and gathered his underwear in her hand. She shook her head in bewilderment. Nick really was a confusing mix of seductive masculinity and tights-wearing femininity. His sexuality was a conundrum, for sure.

As she considered that a moment longer, she decided a little investigative research was in order. Sure, she could come right out and ask him if he was pitching or catching for the other team, but she really didn't want to risk offending him—or Mason.

She crept from her room and noticed that the house was already alive with activity. She could hear her parents, Mason, and Buzzy all laughing over breakfast. She stilled and strained her ears. As she deciphered the voices, she listened for Nick's rich, sensuous tone. Two small steps led her to the banister to peer over and she winced when the wooden floor creaked beneath her bare feet. Just then she heard the shower turn on and quickly concluded that it was Nick. With Nick in the shower and Mason downstairs it'd give her the perfect opportunity to snoop . . . er . . . investigate.

With Nick's tights in hand, Rachel tiptoed into Mason's childhood bedroom. The first thing she'd noticed was that only one of the bunk beds had been slept in. Either Mason and Nick had cuddled up together or Mason hadn't come home last night.

She spotted Nick's open suitcase and gave the contents a once-over. Besides another pair of tights and a woman's thermal pajama top, it looked like any man's suitcase. She checked off the list: pants, sweaters, shirts, boxer shorts. Despite the women's clothes, she still held a modicum of hope that she'd been mistaken about his sexuality.

She caught sight of Nick's shaving kit on the dresser. She nibbled her bottom lip and listened for a moment. After making sure the shower was still running, she peeked inside and found a bottle of shampoo. Pulling it out, she turned it over in her hands and read the label—restorative treatment to protect hair and fight dryness due to the elements. Then she discovered a bottle of hand cream—to prevent chapped and cracked skin. Okay, so he cared about his hair and hands. No big deal. Lots of guys used special hair- and hand-care products. Right? None that she knew right off the top of her head, but still . . .

She rooted around some more, examining the assortment of colognes, toothpaste, and toiletries, until she found a bottle of JB head lube. Damn. She frowned as her stomach plummeted. It was that tiny tube that stole her last vestige of hope.

It was the exact same *"head"* lube she'd seen at Mason's apartment in New York, but she'd never looked close enough to figure out which *head* it was used for, and she certainly wasn't about to now. One logical thought popped into her head. Nick and Mason had more in common than she realized. And not only did they share the same products, they likely shared the same . . . *everything.* Like her brother, Nick was about as straight as a circle.

Frowning, her mood darkened and a lump lodged in her throat as she tiptoed from the bedroom. With her back to the hall, she quietly pulled the door shut, turned around and ran smack-dab into a wall of muscle. Nick. Her glance panned his body, noting that he was standing before her in nothing but his towel, loosely knotted at the waist.

One little tug . . .

Her head jerked up with a start and she could feel her cheeks suffuse with color.

"Good morning, Rachel." His rich baritone brought on a shiver of longing.

Instantly aware of his close proximity and his rock-hard body, she grew slick between her legs. She tightened her robe, not wanting Nick to get a whiff of her heady arousal.

Concealing her emotions, she smoothed her hair back, gave a tight nod, and offered him a counterfeit smile. "Good morning. I . . . uh . . . I was just returning your tights."

A bead of water fell from his hair and landed on his well-defined chest. She practically salivated. Linking her fingers together, she bit the inside of her mouth and resisted the urge to track it—with the tip of her tongue.

Nick dipped his head and leaned close. His fresh soapy scent curled around her and nearly shut down her brain. His face was dark, solemn. His eyes were full of tenderness and concern and it did the weirdest things to her insides. He pitched his voice low and said, "I'm sorry about last night. I just want you to know I'm not that kind of guy. I'd never take adv—"

Her heart was pounding so hard she cold barely decipher his words. All she knew was that he was apologizing for the intimacies they'd shared. She held her hand up and cut him off. Christ, she was embarrassed enough by her behavior as it was. She was the one who asked him to use his mouth to warm her. She was the one who craved the feel of his lips on her skin, the one who practically threw herself at him.

Him, as in her brother's boyfriend.

She lowered her voice to match his. "No need to apologize. It shouldn't have happened." She scoffed and rushed on. "And believe me I know you're not that kind of guy. It must have been the alcohol, or the cold numbing my better judgment."

He blew a long, slow, tortured breath. "You must understand that Mason is—"

"Mason never needs to know." Another round of guilt ate at her when she thought of Mason. Gathering every ounce of strength she possessed, she pushed back the heat inside her and presented a calm, cool exterior. She sidestepped Nick. "Now, if you'll excuse me. The sunshine is calling me."

With plans to avoid Nick for the remainder of her vacation, she had a quick shower—trying not to picture Nick's naked body all soaped up in there moments ago—dressed in a pair of jeans and black knit sweater and made her way to the kitchen for a bite.

So much for avoiding Nick. There he was sitting at the kitchen table looking good enough to eat. Even though she glanced everywhere but at him, she couldn't help but notice that he still looked uneasy after the events of last night.

She dropped a kiss onto her father's cheek, gave Murphy a scratch on the head, and took a seat beside her mother at the table. Margaret handed her a bowl and Rachel grabbed for the box of cereal. "Did you have a nice time at dinner last night?" Rachel asked, looking for a distraction.

Her father's brown eyes lit with laughter, and he shook his head from side to side. "We sure did. And afterward, we stopped in to visit with the Denbys. That Travis is one heck of a funny guy. I sure miss seeing him and Tori hanging out together. He told me the funniest story—"

As her father continued with his litany on why Travis was the funniest guy he knew, Rachel was only half listening, because when she tucked her feet beneath her, she couldn't help but notice the intense way Nick was staring at them—like he had some sort of freaky foot fetish.

Wait a minute!

Last night, hadn't he been touching her feet before he went all carnal on her? So it appeared that any and all feet turned him on, male or female.

After her father finished his story, Rachel scarfed down her cereal and prepared to excuse herself, but Margaret put her hand over Rachel's to stop her. Her mother's blue eyes were soft and a little sad. All thoughts of Nick and his weird foot fetish vanished when an abnormal quiet fell over the room.

"What?" Rachel asked.

"It's about Grandma Reddy's special ruby. We need to fill Mason in on what's happening."

Rachel took a moment to think about the story behind Grandma's prized possession. On Christmas day, many years ago, before Grandpa first headed off to war, he'd given Grandma the stone as a promise ruby as opposed to a promise ring assuring her he'd return home safely. And he always had, time and time again. In Grandma's heart and mind, it was a magical stone and naturally love stemmed from it. After the war, during those few times they were apart, she knew if she kept it close and wished upon it, they would be reunited. Even on his deathbed she held the ruby tight, knowing he'd always be with her in spirit until they were reunited again in heaven.

Her mother turned toward Mason. "She left me a note before

she passed away and wants me to announce the fate of her stone on Christmas morning."

"Do you mean one of us will inherit it?" he asked.

Rachel shot Mason a glance and thought about how each child would love to have that ruby—for their own special reasons. But who would be the lucky recipient?

As the middle girl Rachel always felt a little lost in the shuffle. Holly was the oldest and most responsible. Tori, the youngest, was the most fun-loving and family-focused, and then there was Mason, the youngest and only boy. Even though Grandma always made every one of them feel treasured, Rachel felt Grandma had a special place in her heart for Mason, partly because he was the only boy, and partly because he looked so much like Grandpa Reddy. At times she heard her call him "Grandma's special grandson." Rachel paused to consider that a moment longer. She'd originally assumed the stone would go to Holly, the golden child, but after thinking things through she now had a sneaking suspicion the stone would actually go to Mason. After all, there was no denying that Mason always got whatever he wanted. And now he's got the man Rachel wants, too!

Margaret squeezed Rachel's hand and it plucked her from her musings. "We'll all find out soon enough," her mother assured them all. "Until then I placed the ruby on the fireplace mantel for us all to enjoy."

Needing a reprieve from all the emotions churning inside her, and the sudden burst of animosity she felt toward her brother, she glanced outside. "If you'll all excuse me, I'm going to hit the cross-country trails."

"Oh, sounds like fun," Mason piped in.

Nick turned to Mason and gestured toward the door. "Want to go?" Obviously, Nick hadn't realized Mason was mocking her.

Mason pulled a face. "I just don't have a taste for skiing. I think I'll have a nap instead, since I didn't get to sleep until the wee hours of the morning." Just then Nick stifled a yawn, like he'd barely gotten a wink himself.

Rachel shivered, not wanting to think about what had kept the pair up all hours of the night.

Mason arched a brow. "So, what do you say Rachel? Can Nick tag along with you?"

Tag along? Hell no! The last thing she wanted was for Nick to accompany her on her cross-country excursion. In fact, she just wished he'd make his way back to New York.

"No," she bit out, not bothering to mask her strong opposition. God, she just knew if she spent any more time with him, it'd be harder and harder to keep her hands to herself and her emotions in check.

"Whoa, did somebody wake up on the wrong side of the bed or what?" Mason shot back.

Rachel didn't like the inquisitive way her mother was staring at her. "What?" she asked, darting her mother a glance, then winced at her temperamental behavior. Rachel prided herself on always being very even-keeled, but the news of her grandmother's ruby combined with Nick's surprise visit and Mason's shocking announcement, had her acting like a deranged smack addict.

He mother shrugged. "Nothing, dear," she said, and went to work on making another pot of coffee.

She glared at Mason and hedged. "I like to go fast. For exercise.

Most people can't keep up." Okay, she really needed to calm down and stop rambling.

Mason's eyes raced over Nick in sheer appreciation. "You don't think *he* can keep up?" He tilted his head and asked, "Can you keep up, Nick?"

Nick sat there exuding confidence. "I can keep up."

Bloody hell.

"But if she really doesn't want—"

Thomas cut Nick off. "Of course she wants you to go, Nick. She'd have no reason not to, isn't that right, Rachel?"

Rachel turned to her father and balled her hands under the table. "Yeah, that's right. I have no reason not to," she said through clenched teeth, and fought not to glance at her mother and study her reactions.

She took a quick swig of coffee, jumped from the table, and made her way to the porch. "Coming?" She cast her words over her shoulder.

Twenty minutes later, both she and Nick were speed skiing through the trails with Nick hot on her heels, easily able to keep up, or even fly by her should he desire. His closeness made her more breathless than the exercise.

In the distance a puff of smoke rose over Grandma's cottage. *Grandma Reddy* . . . Oh, how Rachel wished she were here to talk to. She'd know just what to do about this crazy situation, just how to get Rachel through the holidays unscathed. As Grandma filled her thoughts, she hadn't even realized her strides had slowed.

Nick moved in beside her. "You okay?" His voice startled her and she faltered. Nick slipped his hand around her waist to steady her. When he packaged her body to his, everything inside her ached for him. God, why did he have to touch her like that? Like he meant it.

Rachel's chest rose and fell with her deep intakes of breath. She stepped back, breaking free from the circle of his arms. "Yeah, just thinking about Grandma."

Nick, who was not one bit winded, planted his pole beside him and leaned on it. His dark hair fell forward and his blue eyes glistened in the early morning sunlight. "Were you two close?"

Rachel smiled and shaded her eyes against the glaring white snow. "Very. We spent a lot of time together. Every day after school she'd bake fresh cookies for us kids." She chuckled and tapped her hips. "Even when some of us didn't need them."

Nick laughed. "She sounds like she was wonderful."

Beneath the laughter she heard longing in his voice and it sparked something in her memories, something he'd said to her last night. "Why would you be spending the holidays alone, Nick?"

He paused for a long moment. "I'm the only Grant left. My parents are gone."

She placed her hand on his and watched his throat work when he swallowed. "I'm sorry."

"Don't be." He gave an easy shrug and glanced heavenward. "Believe me, they're in a better place."

Her attention glided over his face, assessing him. "Were you close?"

His body tensed. "We mixed like oil and water, and the truth is, I did my best to keep my distance." He cast his gaze downward, veiling his expression, but she didn't miss the turbulence in his eyes and vulnerability in his voice. Her heart squeezed and she sensed that he was lowering his guard and sharing something very private and extremely personal with her. Emotions swept though her and everything inside her reached out to him, wanting to comfort him, to soothe him, to take him in her arms and make all those old painful memories go away. "It was especially bad around the holidays," he added, his honesty knocking her off balance. "The fighting, screaming . . ." His voice fell off as a shiver wracked his body.

She watched the play of emotions across his face, and her heart lodged somewhere in her throat as she processed the information. She'd been so selfish, so busy considering her own wants and desires that she never stopped to consider Nick's.

His eyes lifted to hers and empathy stole over her as she softened like whipped meringue. "I've only ever wished for one thing at Christmas, and Mason has made that come true." His words came out a little raspy and the need in his eyes touched her soul. "You have such a great family, Rachel."

Her chest tightened and she felt guilty for snapping at them all earlier. "Yeah, I do."

"They're all so kind and welcoming, letting a stranger into their house for the holidays."

"You're not a stranger, Nick. You're with Mason so that makes you family, too," she assured him, and in that instant she vowed to make this an extra-special holiday for him.

His face softened, and she felt the tension ease from his body. "Thanks, Rachel." When he squeezed her hand, it created a new closeness between them, a friendship, an inherent trust that affected her heart as much as it affected her libido. His smile came slow. "So, I told you my Christmas wish, now it's your turn to tell me yours."

To find someone loving.

Someone caring.

Someone who would put her needs first.

Someone just like Nick.

God, if she only had Grandma's special, magical ruby. She'd hold it close and wish things were different between her and Nick. Heck, what does Mason need with the stone anyway? He already has the perfect man.

"Well," he probed. "What is the one thing you want for Christmas? The one thing you'd wish for, or ask Santa for."

"I don't have a Christmas wish."

He shot her a dubious glance. "Sure you do, everyone does."

"Not me." Rachel turned her gaze to a spot behind him in time to see a bunny hop across the path. "Look," she whispered, thankful for the distraction.

Nick spun around and his eyes widened. He made a clicking sound with his tongue. "Damn, where the hell is my gun when I need it."

Her mouth dropped. "Nick!"

He gave her a teasing grin. "I'm kidding, I'm kidding." With blue eyes that were alive and adventurous, he looked like an exuberant kid on Christmas morning, and Rachel couldn't help but share in his excitement. "Come on, let's follow it," he whispered.

They both went to work on removing their skis and slipped off the beaten path. Nick led the way, following the tracks, which gave her a nice view of his magnificent backside. Keeping up a rigorous pace, they weaved in and out of trees, dodging the frost-tipped branches along the way.

Nick glanced back at her, a playful grin curled up the corners of his mouth. "Need me to slow down?"

His soft chuckle warmed her insides and she had to admit, she loved this playful side of him. She also had to admit how much she enjoyed being around him.

Never one to back down, she worked not to sound breathless and shot back, "It's the Christmas season, Nick. I was being charitable when I was leading." With that, Nick laughed out loud and she couldn't help but join in.

A few minutes later, Nick stopped abruptly and she nearly crashed right into him. He pitched his voice low and gestured with a nod. "Check it out."

Rachel looked around him to see the quaint cottage at the edge of the frozen lake. "That's the Myerses' old cottage. I think it's abandoned now."

"Want to investigate?"

"We probably shouldn't."

"Why not?"

"What if someone is inside?"

"Are you afraid of getting caught?" When she didn't answer, he arched a brow and pressed on. "Or perhaps you just don't have a taste for snooping around?" When she caught his coy grin, and the mischief in his eyes, she suddenly suspected he knew she'd been poking around in his things.

Heat flared her cheeks as she moved past him. "Try to keep up." Again Nick laughed out loud and Rachel smiled as pleasure resonated through her.

Rachel circled the house, and spotted fresh footprints in the snow. She glanced around. There was no vehicle, but she did spot a snowmobile beneath the small carport. Then she remembered Melissa Myers, the family's only daughter, who was around the same age as Holly. She'd heard she went overseas for work and wondered if she'd come home for the holidays.

Nick stepped up beside her as she lifted her hand to knock, but a low sexy moan coming from inside the cabin stopped her. She inched forward and peered into the window to see two naked bodies sprawled out on a bearskin rug.

"Ohmigod," she whispered.

"What is it?" Nick shaded the sun from his eyes and peered in. His nostrils flared and his breathing quickened.

Rachel perused the man and let out a slow breath when she recognized those broad shoulders, that tall muscular build, those piercing hazel eyes and the cast on his leg. Holy hell. It was none other than wild man Jacob Wiley, getting it on with Melissa Myers.

Jacob pulled Melissa to her feet, secured her wrists with cuffs and fastened them to a bolt hanging from the ceiling. Once he had her immobilized, he put a bar between her legs, spreading them wide. Melissa's eyes dimmed with desire as Jacob walked around her, trailing a flogger over her body, stopping every so often to tap her ass with it. Desire thrummed through Rachel's veins, taking her by surprise.

Adventurous and uninhibited, Melissa tossed her head from side to side, her pleasure apparent.

Rachel's body buzzed to life and she began to quake, aroused beyond anything she'd ever known. There was something undeniably exciting and primal about what she was watching. Her breath grew shallow and she felt a little shaky, a little unstable. Nick must have sensed it. He snaked his arm around her waist and held her back to his chest intimately. Jesus, she couldn't believe how incredible it felt to be held by him.

She turned her thoughts back to the sexy show and wondered if this turned Nick on as much as it did her.

"Holy fuck," he murmured. The lust in his tone answered her question and pulled her into a cocoon of need and desire.

Completely engrossed in the action, Rachel aimed a longing glance their way. Her pulse leaped and her body fairly vibrated. As a storm brewed inside her, her words came out breathy. "We should go." But she was so turned on by the activities inside the cabin, she pressed her nose against the window, her actions contradicting her words. It was wrong, she knew, but she couldn't seem to help herself. She'd never experienced the pleasure of submission before, and by the look on Melissa's face, there was a lot of pleasure to be had.

Teetering on the edge of ecstasy, her body began burning from the inside out. She made a low noise in her throat, and she could almost hear the snow sizzling beneath her boots.

Okay, she needed to get out of there before she turned around, ripped Nick's clothes from his body, and had her wicked way with him. She summoned all her control and made a move to inch back, but Nick stopped her, caging her between his body and the glass window. He put his mouth close to her ear and spoke in a whisper. "Not yet." His voice bombarded her body with rich, evocative sensations and she nearly liquefied under his touch.

Heat stained Rachel's cheeks as she watched Jacob lavish his woman with lots of delicious attention. He ran his tongue over her breasts, her cherry red nipples, her flat stomach, and her sopping-wet sex. He thrust a finger inside her and spent a long moment bringing her to the edge. Before he let her tumble over, he brushed the tip of the flogger over her clit, then whacked her ass. Rachel felt her own cheeks sting in response. But God help her, it was a sting from pleasure, not pain.

She and Nick remained still for a long time, just watching and enjoying. Jacob stood in front of Melissa and positioned his cock at her entrance. As Rachel's senses exploded and her body hummed in anticipation, Jacob angled his head. His hazel eyes locked on hers as she spied his private activities. When Rachel's mouth dropped open in surprise, he shot her a wolfish grin.

Startled at getting caught, Rachel pushed backward off the door, knocking both her and Nick to the snow-covered ground. "Oh shit." She scrambled to her feet. Both giddy and panicked, she held her hand out to Nick. "We need to get out of here."

Stifling a laugh, Nick climbed to his feet and they both ducked back into the woods. Once they were under the cover of the trees, Rachel sank to her knees, let out a breath she hadn't realized she was holding and plopped against a tree.

Nick's blue eyes glistened with mischief and laughter. "Well, that was fun."

Oh yeah, it was fun all right. Fun, exhilarating, titillating, and right up there with one of the best times she'd ever had. "That was naughty, Nick. Really naughty."

"Yeah, naughty but nice, right?"

There was nothing she could do to keep the pleasure from her voice. "Do you think he knew we were watching the whole time?"

"Yeah, he's obviously an exhibitionist, as well as a guy who likes a little bondage."

She spent a moment thinking about the way Nick had pinned her to the bed last night and how exciting she'd found it. Her sex muscles moistened and she rippled in remembrance as she replayed that erotic moment in her head. Heat moved through her blood and warmed her cheeks at the way his big strong hands had restrained her, just like Jacob had immobilized his woman. She gulped air.

Did Nick have bondage tendencies? Did she?

Of course, none of the guys she'd been with had ever fully explored her desire or spent the time to understand her needs and pleasures.

Nick tossed a snowball at her, pulling her back to reality. "Hey, what's going on in that pretty head of yours?" When she glanced at him, his simmering blue eyes flitted over her face like he was studying the blush on her cheek, like he knew her every budding fetish.

She shook off the lust, slipped back into her skis and said, "Come on. Let's get back. I'm getting hungry." Except it wasn't food she was hungry for.

Ten minutes later, they neared the mouth of the path and she could see her homestead off in the distance. She stopped to take a breath and from behind Nick put his mouth close to her ear. "Thanks for letting me tag along, Rachel." The soft warmth of his voice made her weak.

Rachel sucked in air and closed her eyes for the briefest of seconds while she took a moment to formulate a response. "My pleasure," she whispered, unable to believe how close she felt to Nick, how comfortable he was to be with, and how much fun they'd had together. A tightness gathered around her heart, and she knew she'd gotten in way over her head. Everything from the way he touched her, shared private memories with her, to watching that sexy act with her had played havoc on her emotions.

How could she have let herself fall so hard? Then again, how could she not? He was everything she'd ever wanted in a man, and the truth was, she was already half in love with him before he'd ever stepped foot in her parents' home. No wonder she couldn't carry forth with her plan to seduce Luke.

She did a quick tally. Okay, so it appeared she couldn't have Nick, yet she couldn't bring herself to engage in a frivolous affair to help her forget him either.

So what the hell was she supposed to do now?

Chapter Five

Arms folded, legs crossed, Nick leaned against the living room archway and perused the room. Tonight was Travis Denby's annual Christmas party and an excited energy trickled through the Reddy house as the clan prepared food and gifts to take to their neighbors. The fresh scent of gingerbread and baked ham casserole wafted through the house, and Nick's stomach grumbled in response. Bing Crosby crooned in the background and soft firelight danced along the poinsettia leaves lining the metal grate. Nick pushed off the wall, stepped over Murphy as he slept in front of the lively flames, and walked through the old house, examining the photos adorning the walls. From baby pictures right up to graduation, he could follow the progress of each offspring. His glance settled on Rachel's beautiful smiling face and his heart clenched.

Rachel . . .

Over the last few days, Rachel had gone out of her way to fill his every waking hour with activities that she somehow knew he'd enjoy—activities that Mason wanted no part of because he didn't quite have a taste for them. From sliding on the duck pond, snowball fights at the park, trekking up to her late Grandma's cottage with Murphy in tow, to horse-drawn sleigh rides through the wintry trails, Rachel had given him everything he'd missed out on as a child. If she were trying to make this the best Christmas he'd ever had, she was doing a damned fine job.

As he moved through the archway and into the kitchen, something brushed against his hair and he glanced up. Mistletoe hung from every threshold and he couldn't help but laugh. The good people of Haven really did have an affinity for the plant.

A tap came on the porch door just as Thomas came sauntering down the creaking staircase. Earlier in the evening when he'd come in smelling like wood and chain-saw oil, Margaret had ushered him up to the bathroom to shower and change before they made their way to Travis's. Unlike his own father, who'd always reeked of scotch and anger, Thomas was a wonderful man, an affectionate father, and a devoted and loving husband. In turn, it was easy to tell how much Margaret adored him by the way her face lit up whenever he entered the room. Even after all these years, they still acted like schoolkids around each other.

Damned if he didn't want the exact same thing.

Standing just inside the kitchen archway, his heart lodged somewhere in his throat as he looked around, watching Margaret open the porch door for Buzzy, who came in carrying homemade pies and gifts, followed by Rachel's big sister, Holly, and her new man, Cole.

This was the kind of family he'd always dreamed of having, the kind he'd missed out on while growing up. From warm cookies and sibling rivalry to Christmas parties and . . . *mistletoe*. Okay, okay, so he loved all the mistletoe. Goddamn it! So what?

As Thomas made his way into the kitchen to help the women pack their goodies, Nick searched for Rachel. Through the kitchen archway, he spotted her near the mantel, examining Grandma Reddy's stone. From the turmoil in her eyes, it was easy to tell how much she treasured Grandma as well as her prized possession. Rachel had told him all about the ruby and its so-called power, but truthfully, while the story was a heartwarming one, he didn't put much faith in its magical abilities.

His glance raced over Rachel and his entire body shuddered. She was dressed in a hot little black number that hugged her curves to perfection—and she was undoubtedly the most gorgeous woman he'd ever set his eyes on. His gaze panned the length of her, taking pleasure in her lush backside, long sexy legs and . . . *bare feet*. God, if she didn't start wearing socks soon she was going to be the death of him.

She darted a quick glance over her shoulder, then carefully gathered the stone into her hand. For a brief second her eyes slipped shut and her mouth was moving, like she was making some sort of secret Christmas wish with it. Which made him wonder exactly what she was wishing for, because despite his probing, she'd yet to tell him.

He made a move to go to her, but Buzzy touched his arm and stopped him. He turned to her. Her eyes narrowed and her lips pursed as she perused him. "Nick, are you having a nice Christmas?" she asked. "I see Rachel's been keeping you busy outdoors."

He shifted under her scrutinizing stare. Now how did she know that? Had she been keeping tabs on them? "Yeah, I've indulged in every outdoor winter experience that Haven has to offer."

"Mason doesn't seem to mind." She gestured with a nod to Mason and Jack, who were both laughing over rum and eggnog at the kitchen table.

Nick shrugged. "Why would he?"

She pinched her lips, and little white lines formed around the edges of her crimson-colored mouth. "Those two look good together, don't you think?" She offered Nick an apologetic smile and put a comforting hand on his arm. "Don't take it too hard, I never thought you two were right for each other anyway."

Understanding hit like a wrecking ball. Nick held his hands up. "No, no, you've got it all wrong. Mason is my friend, not my *partner.*" Jesus, just because he'd come home with Mason for the holidays didn't mean he was gay. He guessed Buzzy had never picked up on the "vibe" thing Mason had talked about.

Buzzy's eyes widened in delight. "So you two were never partners?"

"Work partners, not lover partners," he explained, and glanced over his shoulder to see Rachel pulling stockings out of a wicker basket. "If you'll excuse me, I need to give Rachel a hand," he said, and made his way past her.

Nick moved in beside Rachel and glanced at the stockings as she hung them one by one, and it was then he spotted one with his name stitched on it.

His entire world shifted and in a soft, barely audible tone, he asked, "Who did this?"

She gifted him with a dazzling smile as she secured his Rudolph stocking to the mantel next to Mason's. "I did."

He exhaled slowly, and the sudden urgent need to gather her into his arms and just hold her tight had his head spinning. Emotions clawed at his insides. "Why?" It was shocking how much that gesture affected him and warmed his darkest mental corners. As though moving on their own accord, their hands connected, her fingers curled through his, and he noted just how comforted he felt by her touch.

They stared at each other for a long time; then Rachel broke the silence. Her voice hitched when she explained, "Because I told you, Nick. You're here with Mason so that makes you one of the family."

Breaking the intimate moment, Margaret moved in beside them, a tray of refreshments in her hand, and a strange new twinkle in her eyes. "Hey, you two." They both turned to her and she pointed to the ceiling. Mistletoe hung in clumps above them and when Nick glanced back at Rachel he caught her moistening her lips, her dark eyes flaring hot.

In that instant, the air around them charged. Unable to help himself, Nick grinned and mimicked the kid from the skating pond. His gaze shifted to her lips, and his voice dropped an octave. "You gotta kiss her."

Sweat collected on his forehead when he pressed his mouth to hers. At that first sweet touch, his heart twisted and his knees nearly gave out. Discretion aside, he pulled her in tighter. Her body molded against his as he stroked his tongue against hers, exploring, tasting . . . *needing.* As her warm familiar aroma enveloped him, his senses exploded and his cock thickened in his unforgiving dress pants. *Oh Jesus . . .* She tasted like cinnamon, sugar, honey, and candy.

She tasted like forever.

Some small coherent part of his brain heard Mason from the kitchen, then a click of the door as he made his way out to the driveway to warm up the vehicles. At the sound of his voice, Rachel abruptly broke the kiss. The temperature around them dropped a few degrees as she blinked up at him. Her eyes were dark, solemn, and he spotted a quick flash of angst before she hastily excused herself.

As he watched her dart across the room, his conversation with Buzzy suddenly rushed through his brain, and all the pieces of the puzzle known as Rachel fell into place. Oh Jesus, just like Buzzy, Rachel thought he was Mason's "partner," as in Mason's boyfriend, which completely explained her hot/cold behavior toward him. They clearly wanted each other, that feverish kiss had proven that, and both of their reasons for pushing the other one away centered around Mason.

His heart missed a beat. God, he loved her caring, nurturing nature, sacrificing her wants and desires for her brother, like any good sibling would. Honestly, he'd never met a woman quite like her, and expected he never would again.

He loved the way she responded to his caresses, his kisses. He loved the way she touched his heart and understood his every need. He loved the warmth and friendship and intimacy between them, but he especially loved how she went out of her way to give him the Christmas he'd missed out on as a child.

Hell, he loved a lot of things about her, or rather, he loved *everything* about her.

He loved her. . . .

Oh God, he loved her.

He glanced around, thinking about all the Haven festivities, the smiles, the lively conversation, the kisses under the mistletoe, the laughter, and the love. He wanted all this, but there was only one woman he wanted it with.

Rachel.

She was special and warm and loving and caring. She was fun and generous and kind. . . .

She was home.

The home he'd always longed for, and never thought he'd ever have. Maybe never thought he *deserved* to have until Rachel had shown him otherwise. Nick felt a strange fullness in his chest and taking a breath seemed almost impossible. What was between them wasn't about wild flings or sexual affairs. This was about so much more. He sensed she felt it every bit as much as he did and, like him, was trying desperately to fight it. Oh God, he needed to talk to Mason. To confess his feelings. To tell him he was utterly in love with his sister. Nick had tried to keep his hands to himself, not wanting to jeopardize his business relationship with Mason, but once Mason understood that Nick wasn't looking for a quick roll in the hay with his sister, that he wanted to play for keeps, surely that would change things.

AFTER BREAKING THE KISS WITH Nick, Rachel threw on her parka and boots and rushed outdoors. Forgoing a drive, she hustled to Travis's on foot. She was so glad her baby sister, Tori, was coming home tonight because after that powerful, intimate moment, she really needed someone to talk to. Of course, she could always talk to Holly but she was so happy and so caught up in her new man that Rachel didn't want to bring her down.

Travis greeted Rachel at the door with a big kiss, ushered her cold body into the warmth of his home, and took her coat. Inside the already crowded room, she made her way to the refreshment table, and was sipping on a glass of rum and eggnog when her family arrived. She watched Nick put his arm on Mason's shoulders, pull him away from Jack and guide him to a secluded spot in the corner. From her distance she couldn't hear the conversation, but by the look on Mason's face and the intense way his glance kept going from Nick to Jack to her, and back to Nick again, she'd hazard a guess that it was a pretty serious one.

A few days previous, Rachel had vowed to give Nick the full Reddy Christmas experience, at the expense of her own emotions, that is. For some inexplicable reason fulfilling his lost childhood had become more important than her own well-being. But after that mind-numbing, soul-touching kiss, she knew she was done for.

She was completely and utterly in love with Nick, and any more time spent in his arms would be emotional suicide at best. But how, oh how, could a man who was gay kiss her with such fevered passion?

Feeling achy, hot, and needy, she'd spotted Sheriff Jack coming her way. She drew a rejuvenating breath and tried for casual, despite the turmoil brewing inside her. "Hey, Jack. How's it going?"

"Not too bad. You?" He went to work on pouring himself a drink, and glanced over the trays of squares, tarts, cakes, and cookies.

"Couldn't be better," she lied. Unable to help herself, her attention strayed to Nick, and her eyes moved over his face. A second later, their gazes met and locked and bombarded her with want. As his visual caress slid over her skin, a shiver worked its way to the tips of her toes. Her focus shifted to the door in time to see Cole's younger brother, wild man Jacob Wiley—the same Jacob Wiley she'd watched having sex—and Melissa Myers enter. Her jaw slackened. Nick turned to see what had garnered her attention.

Visions of the way Jacob had taken control of Melissa's satisfaction rushed through her mind and aroused her. Every nerve ending in her body came alive, and her sex clenched with need. Conscious of the way Nick was watching her, she felt color rise high on her cheeks as she pictured his deft fingers tying her up and working her body in such a delicious manner. Her breath grew shallow and her tongue darted out to wet her suddenly dry lips. Oh God, she couldn't believe how much she wanted that, craved that. With Nick.

The sound of Jack's voice brought her attention around to him. "Have you heard about Misty?"

"What about Misty?" Margaret asked as she stepped up beside them and reached for a glass.

Rachel's father joined in, his eyes moving over the assortment of sweets with longing. "Yeah, what about Misty?"

"She went into early labor." Jack paused to take a drink. "She was helping the police department hand out teddy bears, and I had to rush her to the hospital in the backseat of my car. It came on pretty quickly."

Rachel's eyes widened. "Is she okay?"

"Oh yeah, she's fine. Josh arrived at the hospital shortly after we did. He's with her now." He paused to tap the scanner at his side. "I'm just waiting to hear more."

Her mother filled her drink glass with punch, then questioned, "What about tomorrow's parade, and the display at the department store? Who's going to step in for the two of them and play Santa and Mrs. Claus?"

Thomas turned to Rachel and flung his big burly arm around her. "I'm sure Rachel would love to do it."

Her mother piped in. "Oh, Thomas, that's a great idea. Maybe Nick could help out, too."

"Hello?" Rachel waved her hand. Didn't they realize she was standing right there? "I'm right here, maybe you should be asking me."

Her mother's blue eyes glistened like she knew something Rachel didn't. "It's a great idea, don't you think, Rachel? Nick could play Santa and you could play Mrs. Claus."

Rachel pursed her lips and gave an adamant shake of her head. "Actually, I—"

Nick stepped up behind her and pressed his chest against her back. He deliberately put his mouth next to her ear and the heat of his breath made her quiver and lose her train of thought. Distracted by his close proximity, she fumbled with her words. "I . . . we . . ."

"We'd be happy to," Nick said.

Chapter Six

The strangest emotions stole through Rachel as she watched
Nick take on the role of Santa Claus wholeheartedly. Just listening to him chuckle jovially and seeing his juvenile antics—
honestly, he really was simply a big kid at heart—had her laughing
as she watched him, in spite of herself. Seated beside Nick in the
department store Christmas display, dressed in her Mrs. Claus
outfit, Rachel worked to keep herself composed as she kept his
basket stocked with coloring books and candy canes.

One after another the kids came, whispering all their Christmas wishes and dreams to Santa. As the hours ticked by, the crowd
began to dwindle and the department store soon cleared of shoppers. Rachel stretched out her arms and yawned when security
started making their rounds and Sheriff Jack stopped by to offer
his thanks for all their help.

Nick climbed from his big sleighlike chair and turned to her.

"Why don't you go get changed, Rachel? There are a few things I'd like to discuss with Jack. Then I'll come find you."

Rachel saw the spark in Nick's eyes and wondered what the hell was going on. Was Nick angry that Jack had been spending so much time with Mason? Or was it something else entirely? Either way, it was none of her business and she was itching to get out of the uncomfortable costume. All that fur around her neck—not to mention the wig—was giving her a rash, and the waistband was so tight it made it hard to breathe. Obviously, Misty was a lot tinier than Rachel, or at least she used to be before her belly shook like a bowl full of jelly.

Rachel walked to the back of the store, bypassing the "holiday theme room" where they had a romantic bedroom display set up, complete with a Christmas tree, electric fireplace, king-size bed, lights, artificial green swag, and a plush carpet on the floor—all items for sale, of course.

Once she found her way into the changing room, she immediately went to work on removing the constricting floor-length red velvet outfit; the only problem was the damned zipper seemed to be stuck. Rachel worked at the metal teeth, twisting and turning the fabric, pulling and . . . *ripping*. Oops.

After all that work, she'd only managed to get the zipper down a few inches. Perhaps if she turned the dress so she could see what she was doing, she'd be able to line up the teeth and free herself. Rachel shimmied inside the dress, and managed to get one arm out through the neck hole. Okay, now that seemed to have made matters worse. She tried, unsuccessfully, to get her arm back in. Goddamn it! She was stuck. Completely and utterly stuck. Now what the hell was she supposed to do? She shifted and pulled and tugged and flopped around the room like a mental patient captured in a straitjacket.

Exhausted and frustrated, she finally plunked herself down on the bench and let out a long-suffering sigh.

A knock on the door startled her and she straightened, well, as straight as she could get under the circumstance.

"Rachel, are you okay?" Nick asked. "You've been in there a long time."

"I'm fine," she croaked out. "You go on ahead without me. Get a ride with Jack. I'm going to hang out here awhile. I have some things to do."

Silence and then, "Okay."

She was far too embarrassed to go out there and ask Nick for help. Instead, she decided to stay put, and after Nick left, she'd go find a pair of scissors and cut herself free.

She sat there for a good fifteen minutes. Ample time for Nick to change and get a lift home with Jack. Too bad her arm had gone numb in the process.

Rachel pressed her ear to the door and met with silence. Satisfied that Nick had left, she inched the door open and peered into the dimly lit room. What she saw turned her knees to pudding and had her blood going from simmer to inferno in record time. She sucked in a huge breath.

"Nick?" she questioned.

"That's Saint Nick to you."

Still dressed in his Santa suit, with a pack of toys over his back and a pair of handcuffs dangling from his fingertips he stared at her. His eyes were dark, smoldering, undressing her with each sweeping caress.

Oh. Good. God.

As he gave her a look that conveyed his hunger, one thought filled her mind—just how hot she was for Santa.

"Need a hand?"

Oh, she needed a lot of things. . . .

He crooked his finger and motioned her close and in that instant lust overshadowed rational thought. Like a puppet on a string she blindly obeyed, completely lost to her needs and desires.

Looking wild and untamed, he gripped her dress on either side of the zipper and in one fluid movement pulled. She gasped. The sound of ripping reached her ears, but that wasn't the reason for her sharp intake of breath. It was the dark, carnal way Nick was looking at her and the primal way he tore her clothes from her body that had erotic noises rising up from her throat. Her dress fell to the floor in a heap, leaving her standing there in nothing but her lacy bra and underwear. As sexual awareness leaped between them, her sex clenched and the low groan crawling out of her throat conveyed just how much she liked his take-charge attitude.

Her glance rushed to his handcuffs and his bag full of toys. Her breasts swelled, and she wondered if he could see the hardening of her nipples. "What . . . what do you have in there?" When he merely offered her a wicked grin, she rushed on, "And what do you plan on doing with those?"

"You see, Rachel, you haven't told good old Saint Nick your Christmas wish yet, so I'm here to hold you captive and—*pump and probe*—that information out of you."

Pump and probe . . .

Her body quivered, her pulse kicked up a notch and the look on his face told her everything—not only did he understand her budding fetishes, he planned on fulfilling them. Her body shifted into overdrive, anxious for him to do just that. Jesus, no man had ever taken the time to discover her desires before, let alone fulfill them.

Fire licked over her thighs and she questioned in a shaky voice, "Do you plan on interrogating me?"

His soft chuckle curled around her and the heat from his mouth triggered a craving deep inside her. "Well, that's one way to put it." With his eyes full of want, he shot her a look of passion and intimacy and in that instant she knew it better than she knew her own name, Nick Grant really and truly wanted her, as much as she wanted him.

Holy hell, and halle-friggin'-lujah, she had to have been mistaken about his sexuality all along! Right? Because only a heterosexual man could look at a woman like that.

He captured her hand in his and tugged until her body pressed against his. Through his thick velvet costume she could feel his cock press insistently against her stomach. His very thick, very impressive cock, to be precise.

"Come with me," he murmured into her mouth.

She peered past him and darted a glance around. "What about security?"

"Taken care of."

"How?"

"Jack."

When she opened her mouth, he pressed a finger to her lips to silence her. "I'll ask the questions from here on out."

Breath rushed from her lungs in a whoosh, and she slammed her mouth shut as his voice, and the sexual promise lingering beneath, played down her spine.

One hand slipped around her waist, and splayed out on the small of her back. His touch was intimate, determined, and the feel of his fingers sliding over her skin brought on a shiver.

"Cold?" Nick asked, his eyes moving over her half-dressed body.

The tender concern in his gaze warmed her heart. She shook her head. "Hot," she admitted honestly.

That seemed to please him. A wide grin split his lips and prompted him into action. He nudged her forward and guided her through the department store until they came to the display room. As she took great pleasure in the festive ambience she couldn't help but notice how gorgeous and romantic it was. But what did he plan on doing with her there? In the middle of the department store? She gulped air.

"Nick?"

Equal measures of excitement and uncertainty rushed though her when she felt a cold metal handcuff close over one wrist. Nick inched her backward until her knees hit the bed. Without his eyes ever leaving hers, he gave a little shove and she fell onto the cushiony bedspread.

She tilted her head to see him, and the warm firelight from behind fell over his body like a halo, but the look in his eyes told her he was anything but angelic.

Her body reacted with urgent demands as he stroked his hand over her arm, lifted it above her head, and secured it to the bedpost. He reached into his bag and pulled out another metal cuff, securing her other arm to the opposite post.

Gaze riveted, he stood over her; his dark eyes were smoldering with passion and need. The intensity in his gaze was almost frightening. She writhed on the mattress as her body beckoned his touch. Nick caressed her inner thigh, and slid his hand downward, widening her legs as he went. Lust washed over his face when he came to her feet. Understanding his fetishes and suddenly feeling very naughty and playful, she wiggled her toes, enticing and teasing him.

His nostrils flared and his grin turned lethal. "So that's how you want to play it, is it?" He dropped his sack and reached inside to pull out a flogger with soft suede tresses.

Oh. My. God.

As he leaned over her, his rich scent singed her senses and the sound of the flogger hitting his palm nearly took her over the edge. Without preamble, he got right to the point. "So tell me, what is it you want for Christmas, Rachel?"

As desire flashed inside her, she opened her mouth but no words came. Her brain stalled when he began ripping the big velvet coat from his body. His pants quickly followed and a moment later he stood before her in nothing but his boxer shorts, his huge cock straining for release.

"Tell me, Rachel." He inclined his head, as though mulling something over. "Come to think of it, I can't remember where you were on my naughty-or-nice list." Her gaze shifted to watch him slap his flogger against his leg, and she bit down on her lip to suppress a moan as blistering heat exploded inside her. "If you were on my naughty list, then there will be no presents for you, only punishment."

Her breath hitched and her heart thumped in her chest. "I've been nice, Santa," she countered, her blood flowing thick and heavy. "Very, very nice." Dear God, was that her voice?

Nick cocked his head, doubtful. "Is that so?"

She nodded, unable to mask her enthusiasm for the sexy game Nick was playing with her. "I definitely think I deserve a little something special from Santa."

Nick ran the suede tresses over her skin and his delectable foreplay brought on a shudder. He spoke in whispered words and she heard the raw edge of longing in his tone as his eyes grew dark. "I'm not convinced you've been nice."

She angled her head until her mouth was lined up with his cock. Feeling wild and out of control, she decided to make him as crazed as he was making her. She inched closer to the edge of the mattress and murmured, "Why don't you get rid of those shorts and I'll show you just how nice I can be?"

His breath grew shallow and his cock jumped inside his shorts at her sultry invitation. "Holy fuck, Rachel." God, she loved the way he reacted to her, the way his body was so needy for her. He tore off his underwear and positioned his cock near her mouth. In a thoughtful gesture, his hand slid around her head to cradle it, making the position more comfortable for her.

Rachel flicked her tongue out to taste him, drawing lazy circles around his head before she plunged forward and took him to the back of her throat, eager, but unable to devour every magnificent inch of him. Her body vibrated and her sex began rippling, aching to feel his girth inside her. When he groaned, she felt him swell and sensed the urgency rising in him. He began moving his hips, easing his cock in and out, and her hands ached to touch him, to stroke him, to feel his silky softness. She licked and sucked and moaned in delight as he fed his cock into her mouth. Tiny drops of pre-cum dripped from his slit, and she eagerly lapped up every delicious speck.

"Mmmm, so nice," he murmured. Then a violent shudder overtook him and he pulled back far too quickly for her liking.

"No," she murmured, but her protest was lost on a moan when he slapped her sex with the flogger. Goddamn, that had to be the most erotic thing she'd ever felt.

"So it seems you have been nice, after all." His voice came out deep, sexy. "Then you'd better tell Santa what you want from him." Rachel knew he was giving her the opportunity to tell him exactly what she wanted, exactly what she needed. When he wet his lips, she sensed his restraint. "Tell me your secret Christmas wish, Rachel."

A bevy of fantasies rushed through her head, and the furtive brush of the flogger against her flesh had her spilling all her sinful little secrets. Lost in a haze of lust, she said, "I want Santa to kiss me."

"Where?"

The fire in his eyes licked her from head to toe. She opened her mouth in invitation, and ran her tongue along her bottom lip. "I think Santa should start here."

Nick leaned over her and pressed his mouth to hers; his touch was soft, yet commanding. A savage growl rumbled up from his throat as his tongue moved inside and thrashed against her cheeks. Held captive beneath his erotic assault, Rachel stirred, and the sound of the metal handcuffs clanking against the bedpost raised her passion. A moan escaped her lips and her body lubricated.

Nick inched back and met her glance. "Mmm, nice, very nice. Maybe you deserve a little something more from Santa."

She nodded and her sex began throbbing. "More kisses," she said, barely able to reply.

"Where?"

She arched her back and said breathlessly. "Here."

He gave her a playful look. "You'll have to tell me exactly where."

She practically sobbed with need. "My breasts, my nipples."

Nick pulled the cups of her bra down until he exposed her quivering breasts. He stared at her in sheer appreciation before he inched forward and made a slow pass with his tongue, giving her pleasure beyond her wildest dreams. Her hips came off the bed and she pulled on her handcuffs. A moment later he greedily drew her nipple into his mouth, ravishing and relishing her with dark hunger. Delirious with pleasure, her muscles spasmed as he sucked deeper, biting and nibbling on her nipple until she cried out in ecstasy.

He inched back and his eyes ran over her quivering body with pleasure, before lingering on the metal restraints. "I must say I do love having you at my mercy."

It occurred to her that he liked to take on the role of dominant as much as she liked to take on the role of submissive. Nick's nostrils flared and his voice took on a husky edge when he asked, "Is there anywhere else you'd like Santa to kiss?"

She bucked forward. "Here."

"Where?"

Oh God, he wanted her to say it, he wanted her to be wild, uninhibited . . . *naughty.*

He raced his fingers over her body. "I don't understand, Rachel." He circled her belly button with his lips. "Is this where you want my mouth?"

She shook her head wildly.

"Then where?" His hand slid to her hips, tracing the pattern of her curves and the devilish gleam in his eyes didn't go unnoticed. "Here?"

He continued to touch her all over, everywhere but between her legs. As her senses exploded, she blurted out, "My pussy. I want you to kiss my pussy."

"Your what?" he asked, pushing her even further, encouraging her to open herself up to him completely, to free herself of any inhibitions as she handed her pleasures over to him.

"My pussy, my cunt," she said, unable to believe how wild, reckless, and *naughty* that frank language made her feel. God, Nick was such a master at reading her wants and needs.

He grinned. "Such naughty, naughty words from a nice girl, don't you think?"

She nodded in agreement and decided to push a little herself. "Maybe I need to be punished after all."

His sexy grin turned her inside out. "Oh, you most certainly do. And I think I'll start here." He cupped her drenched cunt. "Because I believe a tongue lashing is in order."

With single-minded determination, Nick inserted himself between her legs, gripped her panties, and eased them down her legs. He leaned forward and pulled her aroused scent into his lungs. That first sweet touch of his tongue to her clit had her hips coming off the bed, and Nick splayed his hand over her stomach and pushed her back, immobilizing her, and she nearly erupted then and there. God, she loved how he understood her every desire.

He stroked her with his tongue, and pulled her engorged clit into his mouth for a long thorough suck. She drew a breath but could barely inflate her lungs. "Nick," she murmured, tossing her head from side to side, going wild beneath his invading mouth. *"Please . . ."*

"Please what?" he asked from between her legs.

"I want you to fuck me."

"Oh, I plan on it, sweetheart, but first I need to taste you." With that, he inserted a finger, his mouth moving back to her clit, slowly building her orgasm. He brushed his tongue over her swollen bud while his thick finger found the sensitive bundle of nerves inside her. She fisted her hands and writhed as the scent of her arousal saturated the room.

Pressure culminating, he offered her another finger for a deliciously snug fit, and began to pick up the pace. He ravaged her with fevered hunger, knowing just what she needed to take her over the edge.

As though sensing her climax, he murmured, "That's it. Come for me, baby."

Taking her all the way to the moon and keeping her hovering on the precipice, he burrowed deep and his fingers stroked her with need. When he applied more pressure to her clit, she moaned without censure and responded with a hot flow of release. As her control obliterated, soft quakes began at her core and continued onward and outward dancing along every nerve ending. Nick plunged deeper and her body burned as she gave herself over to her orgasm.

"Nick . . . So good." She called out his name and concentrated on every erotic pulse of pleasure between her legs. Nick remained between her thighs for a long time, drinking in her creamy essence and gifting her with slow, soothing laps of his tongue until her muscles stopped spasming and she found her way back to earth.

When her tremors subsided, he slid up her body until their eyes met. Moisture glistened on his mouth, and the warmth, trust, and easiness between them touched her deeply. Oh God, she'd never experienced such an intense level of intimacy with anyone before.

His fingers tangled through her hair and she grew needy for him again. "Is there anything else you want from Santa?"

Oh God, she wanted everything from Santa. She wanted him in her arms, her bed, and in her life. Forever. But did he want that, too? Or was this just a wild Christmas fling for him?

Once again, his lips found hers and his kiss was so full of emotion and tenderness a lump lodged in her throat.

"Tell me," he murmured into her mouth. "Tell me what you want?"

"I want you inside me."

Chapter Seven

Just seeing her lying there, sprawled out before him, his to do with as he pleased, brought out the animal in him. Sweat collected on his brow and he was ready to explode just from the erotic sight of her.

With his body aching to join with hers, he trailed the back of his hand over her breasts, her stomach, and her beautiful pussy, unable to rein in his lust. She looked sexy as hell with her dark hair spilling across her pillow and her chocolate eyes dimming with desire—for him.

Oh fuck, he needed to be inside her.

Now.

He hungered for her with an intensity that made him shake.

"Nick?"

"Yeah?"

She swallowed. "Are you okay?"

"No," he whispered with effort. He sucked in air, barely able to control himself. The need to ravish her pulled at every fiber of his being and it was all he could do not to dive between her legs, spear her with his cock, and ride her furiously. Jesus H. Christ, he had *never* been so mad with need before.

Her body shuddered as his eyes moved over her and her rich sexual scent singed his senses, spurring him on. Crazed with lust, he licked his lips, her honeyed taste still lingering on his tongue.

Hands shaking, he tapped her thighs, and she read his intent. Fueled by need, she opened her legs wide, offering herself up to him so nicely. Flames flickered in the electric fireplace, the rays dancing over her naked body, and glistening on her pretty pink lips.

A low tortured growl cut through the silence around them and he worked to leash his control. Moving hastily, he reached into his sack and pulled out a condom. He quickly sheathed himself; then he buried his face in her neck, tasting and inhaling her scent as his cock probed her opening.

"Nick, please, fuck me." The sheer need and desperation in her voice stirred every emotion inside him.

In one quick thrust, Nick pushed his cock all the way up inside her hot tight center, and knew in that instant he'd found heaven. He closed his eyes and savored the sensations.

She writhed beneath him, begging for more. As need sang though his veins, he began fucking her, long, hard, and deep. She moved with him, both giving and taking and finding an erotic rhythm that nearly rendered them senseless.

He angled her body for deeper thrusts and in no time at all, Rachel let out a low moan of ecstasy. Her muscles tightened around him and he felt her hot juice drip over his shaft. Breath labored, she whispered, "I need to touch you."

Her words wreaked havoc on his senses. "Fuck . . ." he bit out, barely able to move as her hot pussy hugged him tight.

Nick grabbed the key to the handcuffs, reached up, and unlocked her. She raced her fingers over his body and through his hair, bringing them face-to-face.

"Nick, baby, are you okay?"

Unable to speak, he shook his head.

She brought his mouth to hers. "Come here." The love he saw shining in her eyes filled him with warmth as they crossed some imaginary line and gave themselves to each other. "It's time for me to take care of you, the same way you've been taking care of me."

Take care of him? Fuck, she'd been taking care of him since he'd arrived in Haven, giving him something he'd never had before, and now she was giving herself to him. "Rachel, I . . ." Oh God, he loved her. He loved her so fucking much.

She pressed her finger to his lips. "Let's just feel, not think."

He nodded, no longer able to speak as a barrage of emotions and physical sensations rushed through him. Nick collapsed onto the pillow beside her and she climbed over him, positioning her legs on either side of his body.

Eyes full of want, she pulled open her pretty pink lips and impaled herself onto cock, and he was almost certain he'd lost his mind.

She began riding him, her beautiful breasts swaying with the movement. As pleasure engulfed him, he cupped her breasts and ran his thumbs over her hard nipples. God, she was so perfect, everything he'd ever wanted and she made him feel the way no other woman had ever made him feel. "You're so beautiful, Rachel."

Desire clouded her eyes and once again she erupted all over him. Her hot cream singed his cock and he bit back a growl, forcing himself to hang on because he needed in some primal, elemental way to mark and claim every inch of her body as his, once and for all.

Giving her no reprieve, he gripped her hips and flipped her onto her back. Her eyes widened with curiosity and a flurry of emotions passed over her face. "Nick?"

"Turn around, Rachel."

She nodded. The way she trusted him, and so readily handed herself over to him touched him deeply. His heart pounded so hard in his chest he could barely see straight. Nick grabbed a pillow and positioned it under her stomach. He grabbed the flogger and slapped her ass with it, leaving a bright red mark. Her gasp of pleasure told him just how much she liked that. Using the palm of his hand, he stroked her lush cheek, soothing the sting left behind. She wiggled her ass, conveying without words what she wanted.

He spent a long time treating her ass to a seductive lashing, then reached into his sack and pulled out a bottle of lubricant. She watched him carefully. He put a generous amount on his shaky fingers and then widened her back passage. Her muscles tightened and her breathing deepened.

Leaning over her, he whispered into her ear. "I need to fuck you everywhere, Rachel." Jesus, his voice was rustier than a bucket full of nails. "Do you understand that?"

"Yes, I need you everywhere, too." He heard the eagerness and need in her tone.

He eased one finger inside her, teasing her open, stretching her, preparing her for his girth. As he tested her tightness, he sensed she was venturing into unknown territory. "Have you ever done this before?"

She shook her head. "I'd never trust my body to anyone else the way I trust it to you, Nick."

Emotions ripped through him and he needed to connect with her in a way he'd never connected with another. "Rachel," he whispered, his voice wavering, conveying the depth of his feelings with that one simple word.

Once he had her prepared, he positioned his cock at her opening and slowly offered her an inch at a time until she got used to the fullness.

Her fingers curled into the sheets, and a low whimper escaped her lips as she opened her body to him.

"Are you okay?" he asked.

"Better than okay." She arched upward, taking him all the way inside her. Soon they joined as one, and Nick had no idea where his body stopped and hers began. They began moving in tandem, as fierce possessive need raced through his body.

With his blood pulsing hot, he reached underneath her and stroked her clit, needing to make this good for her. She moaned in bliss and his cock tightened in response. Oh God, he could barely hang on. Soon Rachel's erotic whimper filled the room and when her juice poured over his hand, he felt his orgasm take hold. He stilled his movements, leaned over her, and held her tight as he released inside her.

"Oh, sweet Jesus," he murmured as he rode out every erotic pulse. He stayed inside her for a long time, not ever wanting to leave the comfort of her body.

After a long moment, he felt her shift beneath him. Nick eased out of her and moved in beside her on the bed. He gathered her into his arms and held her tight, loving the easy intimacy between them. God, she looked so sexy and rumpled it filled his heart with love. When she smiled up at him, he felt giddy, and suddenly understood what it was like to be a child on Christmas morning.

"You're a wild, naughty woman, Rachel. I'm not sure Santa should bring you anything after all."

She snuggled in tighter. "Oh, I think Santa has already given me everything I've ever wanted."

"Everything?" He glanced at his sack of toys.

She followed the movement and grinned. "Then again, if Santa has any other tricks up his sleeve, or toys in his bag . . ."

As her beautiful brown eyes glistened with renewed interest, his entire world shifted, and before she could finish her sentence, he silenced her with a kiss, needing to be inside her again. He pulled her tight and over the course of the night took her again and again.

Chapter Eight

Rachel had lost count of the times she and Nick had made love throughout the night. Nor did she have any idea what time it was, but she suspected morning would soon be upon them.

When Nick pulled her impossibly tighter, a surge of love rushed to her heart and she tilted her chin to see him. Everything in the way he touched her, kissed her, and made sweet passionate love to her all night long had told her that he was interested in more than a simple Christmas fling, which was the best Christmas present Santa had ever given her. Her heart thudded with longing as she soaked in his warmth.

"Nick."

"Yeah."

"I have a confession to make," she said, not wanting to keep any more secrets from him.

He angled his body and propped his head onto his palm. "What's that?" He trailed a finger over her skin and she shivered under his touch.

"I want to let you know why I'd been acting so strange."

His sexy smile made her toes curl. "You? Acting strange? Never . . . " he teased.

She crinkled her nose and whacked him. "You see," she rushed on. "I thought you were gay. I thought you were Mason's *partner.* I even made a wish on Grandma's stone that things were different between us. But after last night, I know you were never gay."

Nick let out a long-suffering sigh, and pulled away from her. Unease moved through her as he inched back, taking his heat with him. "What?" she questioned.

"I have a confession to make, too."

When she caught the strange look in his eyes, worry gnawed at her and she had a moment of doubt—about his sexuality and about this being more than a holiday fling. She braced herself. "You do. What?"

"You see, Rachel, I wanted to see what it was like to be with a woman, but I have to confess, I don't really have a *taste for it.*"

Rachel's eyes opened wide and she sat up straight in the bed. Her sheets pooled around her waist and, suddenly feeling very exposed, she quickly grabbed them to cover herself up. "You've got to be kidding me?"

Nick laughed out loud, ripped the sheets from her body, and pulled her back to him. "Hell yeah, I'm kidding you."

She whacked him again and let out a relieved breath. "Don't ever do that to me again."

"That's what you get for pretending you never knew me." He furrowed his brow. "Although I must say, I still can't figure out why you did that."

"I guess I have another confession to make. I was crooning to my mother about this guy named Nick that I met at work, so when Mason showed up with you, I didn't want her to know you and the man I was already half in love with were one in the same."

His eyes darkened; his nostrils flared. "You were already half in love with me?" His fingers bit into her skin and the intensity in his gaze nearly robbed her of her next breath. "So now are you going to tell everyone that?"

She shook her head. "No."

He gave her a perplexed look. "No?"

"No, I'm going to tell them that I'm completely and utterly in love with you."

Warmth and passion moved over his eyes and a flurry of emotions pressed against her heart. "Just like I'm completely and utterly in love with you, Rachel. And I plan on telling anyone who will listen." He pulled her in close for a soul-searching kiss, and Rachel could hardly believe she'd found a man who was sweet, compassionate, and loving. A man who put her needs before his own. A man who loved her as much as she loved him.

As her body began sizzling with need, she broke the kiss and whispered softly into his mouth, "I'm pretty sure my mother already knows, and I'm sure that's why she suggested we play Santa and Mrs. Claus, so we could figure a few things out for ourselves."

Nick laughed. "Actually, I'm pretty sure we were the last to know."

Rachel shook her head and chuckled. "Somehow this has to be all Mason's fault."

His passion-imbued eyes moved over her body and a savage sound rose up from his throat. Heat flooded her pussy. Nick swallowed, dropped a soft kiss onto her mouth and said, "Seriously, Rachel. I do have a confession to make."

With that, Nick climbed from the bed. Her lascivious gaze went from his tight backside to the video camera set up in the corner. Her pulse kicked up a notch, and her jaw dropped open.

"You didn't?"

He gave her a wickedly delicious grin. "Oh yeah, I did."

"How? Why?"

He turned the video on and the television screen filled with images of the two of them making love.

"Because you have other fetishes that we need to explore."

"Ohmigod," she whispered. "How did you know?"

Nick cocked his head. "Santa sees all, Rachel. In fact, he keeps a list. And Santa knows just how naughty you really are, and just how much you like watching."

Her heart leaped with excitement. She purposely wiggled her toes at him as she patted the mattress beside her. "Is that right? Maybe you should tell me what else Santa knows?"

He climbed into the bed beside her, pulled her close and said, "I think Santa should show you instead."

Mistletoe Bliss

BY
JODI LYNN COPELAND

Chapter One

His lips were like candy. His tongue just so dandy. And his rock-hard pecs beneath her palms—anything but made of jelly.

Had the half-mile trek from her snowbank-lodged rental car frozen Victoria Reddy's brain cells, or what the hell was she doing letting her ex-lover kiss her?

Only kissing didn't fully describe what Travis Denby was doing to her. She hadn't made it more than two feet inside his home when he'd pulled her into his arms and waged a sensual assault on every deprived female hormone in her body. Then there were the sexual neurons. Those babies were firing on all cylinders and then some.

Soft yet deliciously firm, Travis's lips pressed against hers. The silky, wet warmth of his tongue moved with the same quiet command, rubbing, caressing. Reminding her with potent familiarity that he knew exactly how she liked her loving and that he was equipped with all the right moves to deliver.

Strong, knowing hands lifted from her waist to grip her forearms. Through the layers of her coat and sweater, delectable heat sizzled from his fingertips to her skin. That warmth zinged up her arms and back down again, arrowing straight to all the best parts. Her nipples beaded to hungry, aching life. Liquid longing pooled in her sex.

Tori sighed into his mouth. *So, so good.*

Hard to believe she'd been fighting to catch a breath against the blustery wind and frigid, snowflake-laden night air mere seconds ago. That had to have been a nightmare. She must still be on the flight from Miami to New Hampshire, lost now in a naughty dream.

Once she arrived in her hometown of Haven, there wouldn't be time for physical gratification. She had a week to spend with her parents and siblings before she was due back in Miami to meet with a client who held the power to take her real-estate career from quickly blossoming to stunningly full bloom. She intended to spend those seven days proving what a responsible adult she'd become: a businesswoman on par with the rest of the career-successful Reddys.

If she was going to enjoy a little naughty fun—real or imagined—the time to do it was now.

Giving in to pleasure, Tori let the dream unfold. A cocoon of thigh-tingling bliss surrounded her as she speared her fingers through Travis's coal black hair and sank into the heady decadence of the kiss. He tasted of hot, virile male and rum-spiked eggnog. Two things she'd never been able to resist. Two things she savored with an eager moan and the responsive stroke of her tongue. His grip on her arms increased, drawing their bodies flush. The press of his solid, muscular thighs was pure carnal invitation. Murmuring gleefully, she pressed back, drew his big body even tighter against hers, and acknowledged the bulge pressing just below her navel. The already near-solid and yet-still-growing bulge.

Mmm mmm mmm . . . She'd forgotten how nicely his stocking was hung.

She hadn't forgotten how wickedly delightful his hard cock felt thrusting inside her, holding her a most-willing captive as he sailed her to the edge of climax. Her pussy throbbed with the forbidden yearning to feel him inside her now—given their past, he ranked incredibly high on the "last man she should want to do" list. But then, this was just a dream.

Praying that she didn't cry out for real when she gave into imagined orgasm, Tori pulled her hands from the thickness of his hair and slipped them down his broad back, lower to cup his fine behind through his jeans.

Was it possible his ass felt even better now than it had a year ago?

Whatever the case, she planned to grope to her heart's content. She definitely planned to keep kissing him, inhaling the intoxicatingly spicy scent of his cologne. Grinding against his increasing erection until it was full blown and then . . .

And then it would be really nice if whoever or whatever was making the distracting whistling sound would knock it the fuck off already. Didn't the responsible party get that this was her one chance at naughty?

Apparently not, because the sound grew louder. High-pitched. Taunting.

Taunting?

Tori's mind broke from the numbness—first frigid and then sizzling—which had overtaken it. Her mouth and hands kept moving for the heartbeat more it took for the identity of the sound to register. Not just any whistle, but a wolf whistle. One aimed at her and Travis, because she couldn't be any further from dreaming.

Holy crap!

Eyes snapping open, she jerked her hands from his ass and her mouth from his own. She took an awkward step back and was rewarded with the doorknob ramming into her butt. Dull ache shot through the right cheek. The vibrant sting of embarrassment followed as she recognized Travis's living room full of guests. Tonight was his annual Christmas party and a good share of Haven was in attendance, including her family. Her brother, Mason, stood less than ten feet away. His eyes sparkled with amusement, and she could guess he'd been the owner of that whistle.

In search of escape, Tori pulled her gaze from her brother's and found it locking on Travis's.

Her heart skipped a beat. Her pulse gave a slow, trumpeting roll. Oh man, her memory hadn't played tricks on her mind. His eyes really were that mesmerizingly green. He also still had that way of looking at her that said she couldn't put anything past him, he knew her every thought. Her every *salacious* thought.

Over a square, stubble-dusted jawline, Travis's mouth curved with good humor. His eyes shone with the same. Then, in a blink, concern overtook his expression. Reaching a hand out, he stroked his knuckles along her cheek. "Are you okay?"

Tori worked past the bubble of desire lodged in her throat.

"Fine." At least, from a no-longer-freezing standpoint. From a wet-between-the-thighs standpoint, not so grand.

Damn, she should have risked frostbite by continuing her trek down the road a mile to her parents' place.

Aware he wasn't talking about her appearance, she offered, "I hit a patch of black ice and stuck my rental car in a snowbank. It's not exactly pleasant out."

"You should have called. I would have come for you."

"My cell died during the plane ride. I only packed an outlet charger." Even if the phone had worked, his would have been the last number Tori dialed. She'd had every intention of avoiding this party. She'd hoped to ignore Travis this week, as well. Instead, she'd groped him.

"Guess we can safely assume Alan's parking the car." Mason's amused voice came from beside her.

Tori groaned. A smart-aleck remark from her brother was the last thing she needed. "I told Mom he couldn't make it," she bit out. "I figured she'd pass the message along."

"Tori?" As if mention of her name conjured her up, Margaret Reddy appeared next to Mason. Her blue eyes flooded with tender warmth as she pulled Tori into a hug. "Oh, baby, I'm so glad you made it to Travis's party."

"I was about to say the same thing," Travis said when her mother released her. His potent gaze swept over Tori, from the tips of her snow-packed boots to the red-and-black parka zipped to her chin. "You look great."

She felt naked. Naked, needy, and eager to nibble on his lips some more. Hating the way he still got to her, she let out a dry laugh. "Amazing what gale-force winds will do for a person's appearance."

"Gale-force winds?" Mason questioned.

"My car got stuck in a snowbank a way down the road."

"It's negative five with the windchill." Her mother's voice rang with disapproval. "You should have called. Your father would have come for you." Thomas Reddy's hot toddy–enhanced laughter burst from across the partygoer-filled living room, and Margaret amended, "Mason would have come."

God, this was *so* not going well. First, the whole groping thing and now her mother thought she was as irresponsible as ever.

Tori shook off her parka to prove she was plenty warm, never mind it was all compliments of Travis. He held out a hand, and she let him take the coat. "It's not a big deal, Mom. I needed a chance to stretch my legs after the plane ride and car tri—" Her oldest sister, Holly's, long blond hair caught her attention from across the room and she stopped short to gasp. Holly acting even mildly flirtatious in public was unheard of. "Does Holly seriously have her arm wrapped around that guy's waist?"

"That would be Cole Wiley." Mason made exaggerated moony eyes. "They're in love."

"Mason!" Margaret admonished. "Be nice to your sister. It's wonderful that she found Cole."

He hung his head. "Yes, Mom." She gave his shoulder a whack, and he laughed. "You know I'm thrilled for them. Holly's long overdue for a good man in her life."

"Sounds like someone else I know," Tori observed.

Mason looked across the room to a tall, sandy-brown-haired guy in a Stetson and his eyes warmed with appreciation. She nodded her approval of her brother's current interest, aware the two wouldn't be knocking boots for long. Maybe one day Mason would settle down, but for now he blew through boyfriends like tissue. "Ah, Sheriff Jack's the lucky man of the season."

"Only because Travis is taken."

"What?" Tori's stricken response burst out. She looked to her left, relieved to find Travis gone.

"Yep," Mason confirmed solemnly. The humor came back into his eyes. "He's head over heels for his business. Worried you, didn't I?"

Travis was gone, but their mother was still there. She eyed Tori in wait of a response. Feeling like she was about to be seen clear through, Tori improvised, "I thought you meant he'd developed a thing for guys. I was surprised, not worried."

Mason smirked. "You still can't lie worth a damn, little sis."

Number one, she was older than him by a year. Number two, did he not know when to quit? Keeping her growl inside, she asked, "Don't you have a sheriff to taunt into handcuffing you to his bed?"

"Don't mind if I do." He started toward Sheriff Jack only to turn back and wink. "When I'm done with the cuffs, I'll be sure to toss them Travis's way."

"Guess this explains why you weren't downstairs."

Travis looked up from checking e-mail. Tori stood in his office doorway, sexy as sin in a red V-neck sweater and snug black jeans. She'd added blond highlights to her wavy, shoulder-length brown hair and had bangs cut in since he'd seen her at Grandma Reddy's funeral in the spring. Otherwise, she looked the same as she had for the past decade. Long limbed and gently curved. Dark lashes fringed her big blue-green eyes, and her soft, pink lips appeared ripe for kissing all night long.

His thoughts threatened to return to her curves and the hedonistic way they'd felt rocking against him. Since he'd only just gotten his cock relaxed, he cut those thoughts off short.

Closing out an email, he stood. "I didn't realize you were keeping tabs on me."

She looked stricken. "I wasn't."

"I promised to loan your dad a book on woodworking with all natural materials. Figured I'd better grab it now, before we both get sidetracked with the toddies." Travis grabbed the book in question from his desk and moved to the office door.

Tori stepped back. Wariness crossed her face before she looked down the hallway to where a cacophony of Christmas music, lively voices, and mouthwatering smells carried up from the first floor. "I didn't see your parents downstairs."

Typically, he could read her most every thought. Now, he couldn't figure out what was going on with her nerves any more than he could guess why she'd responded to his kiss. He'd simply been making use of the threshold mistletoe to get an early Christmas present. He'd planned on getting an earful for it, starting with a reminder that he'd had his chance, and ending with one about her uptight-as-hell fiancé.

Loathing crawled through Travis, though he wasn't sure if it was aimed at her fiancé or himself for granting Tori the freedom to run into another man's arms. At least Alan hadn't made the trip north for the holidays. "They left a while ago. Dad's back's been acting up again."

She looked back at him. "What about your sister and Burke?"

"You remember Josh and Misty?" She nodded that she recalled the high school sweethearts, and he continued. "Misty went into preterm labor earlier tonight. Anna and Burke are due to have baby number four any second, and I guess hearing about Misty made them anxious, because they went home shortly after they got here so they'd be closer to the hospital."

Tori's eyes widened. "Wow, Mom's emails are slacking on the gossip. I had no idea either of them were expecting. You must be thrilled about being an uncle again."

"You know how much I love kids."

Frowning, she glanced back down the hallway. He could almost see the wheels spinning in her head, taking her to the times they'd talked about having children someday. With his own real-estate career as priority one, Alan wasn't liable to fulfill her life-long dream of a big family anytime soon. Travis, on the other hand, found the idea as appealing as ever. Almost as appealing as the way she was chewing at her lush lower lip.

She'd always been a nibbler. As much as she loved it when he played the dominant, she got off on teasing him with her teeth. Nipping at his lips, along his neck, scraping them over his nipples, down to the tip of his cock . . .

Hell, so much for losing his erection. Just the thought of her gifted mouth on his shaft, and his heart was pumping faster, his dick swelling to rock-solid.

Tori's eyes returned to his. Obviously, his revealed his condition. The wariness made a second showing and she took another step back. "About the kiss . . ."

"I greeted every female who walked through my door tonight the same way. There's mistletoe hanging in the entryway."

"Stuck your tongue in my mother's mouth, too, huh?"

He grinned. "What can I say? Margaret's a good-looking older woman. Besides, I wasn't the only one with my tongue in someone else's mouth."

Travis expected a guilty smile. He got narrowed eyes and the sight of her visibly tensing. "I was freezing. You can hardly blame me for seeking out heat." Her expression softened but not her stance. "I came up here to use the bathroom. Someone's in the downstairs one and, after my winter wonderland trek, I'd love to get freshened up. That's if you don't mind."

"Like I said before, you look great. Since you're not going to believe me, the bathroom's this way." He started down the hallway in the opposite direction from which they'd come up.

"I know where the bathroom's at, Travis."

"I've done some remodeling since the last time you slept over." He heard her intake of breath over his word choice and laughed to himself as he moved inside the master bedroom.

She appeared in the doorway after a few seconds. "You did away with the outside entrance?"

It was almost comical the difference in how she looked standing in his room now and in the past. Then, she'd worn a smile oozing sex and sin and, when he was at his luckiest, nothing else. Now, she was fully clothed and looking ready to bolt. It wasn't comical, though, because he wanted the old Tori back so damned bad that being here with this new version twisted at his heart. "The extra door was eating up space."

Refusing to look at the bed and consider all the erotic encounters they'd shared in it, Travis continued to the bathroom and flicked on the light. She joined him, but not without first roping her arms around her chest in standoff fashion.

Her stance loosened a bit and appreciation warmed her eyes as she took in his recent remodel job. Natural hardwood floors, a floor-to-ceiling revolving closet with engraved doors, taupe walls speckled with sky blue accents, and a matching porcelain Jacuzzi tub brought the room into the twenty-first century.

"Nice work," she complimented. "All yours?"

"Most of it." He inclined his head to the atrocious oil painting on the wall beside her. "That's yours."

Tori followed his nod. A sound caught between sigh and gasp escaped her lips, and a tangle of emotions passed through her eyes. Then a lone silent question emerged. *Why?*

Travis responded just as silently. *Because it was the only part of you left behind.*

Chapter Two

Tori closed the bathroom door and stared at the oil painting on the wall in disbelief.

Why would Travis bother to keep it, let alone frame it and hang it in this beautifully remodeled room? She'd gifted him with her butt-ugly, senior high art project years ago as a joke for all the times he'd teased her over it. Had he hung it there to see his day began with a laugh at her expense?

That didn't sound like the guy she knew.

Of course, she hadn't expected that guy to let her quietly walk out of his life for a job either. Regardless of their romantic past, Travis and his family had been friends with the Reddys for years. He was like his father had been before ailing health took over— ever ready to give the shirt off his back or lend a helping hand.

Then there was the fact that it hadn't been humor in his eyes when he'd pointed out the painting. Rather a blatant mix of tender affection and carnal hunger that had her wanting to give him the shirt off her own back, right along with the rest of her clothes.

Warmth flushed through Tori as she reflected on the urgent way he'd pulled her into his arms and kissed her. She flushed it right back out again to consider her reflection in the beveled mirror over the sink. What Travis meant when he'd said she looked great came clear. Her cheeks were stung red from the winter wind, her hair whipped about her head from the same, and her eyes huge and on the hazy side. She looked fresh from the fuck.

Quickly, she finger-combed her hair into a halfway-decent style and then applied the cotton candy lip liner ever present in her pocket. The flavor was far removed from the professional image she'd established over the last year. Fortunately, none of her clients or coworkers were going to be kissing her. Alan included.

Only the lack of kisses coming from Alan's way wasn't such a fortunate thing. It took her already iffy mood and made it down-right sour.

Regarded as the baby of the family, despite Mason being younger, Tori had always felt like she could never be as strong or smart or sensible in her parents' eyes as her siblings. Her relationship with Alan had changed that. He'd gotten her in with a prestigious, southern real-estate firm where she was respected and quickly making her way up the corporate ladder. Then he'd made her the first of the Reddy offspring to get engaged. For the first time ever, she'd accomplished something none of her siblings had.

She'd been thrilled. And then, two short months later, she'd been dumped.

Tori sighed. She might as well accept she was never going to best her siblings at anything so she should give up trying already.

Her mood continuing on a downward spiral, she turned off the bathroom light and moved into Travis's bedroom. He wasn't waiting for her, thankfully. Maybe she'd get lucky and he would be too busy entertaining guests for their paths to cross again tonight.

On the way into his room, she hadn't allowed herself to look around. On the way out, she sized up the place. Outside of a new comforter on his queen-size bed and a flat-screen TV on the wall across from it, the room hadn't changed. Neither had his cologne.

The familiar, spicy scent had taunted her senses downstairs. It taunted her across the room to the small green, rectangular bottle on his dresser now. Tori lifted it to her nose and inhaled. Yep, same stuff. Evident by the way it got her wet and wanting with a mere sniff. She was daring to discover what a second scent would accomplish when footfalls sounded on the wood floor behind her.

Guilty heat singed her cheeks as she spun around. Travis stood within touching distance, his smile pure arrogance. Probably it should be a turnoff. Only it wasn't. He was so far from being cocky that she'd always found those times he played the part of conceit a huge turn-on.

A protective wall of defense rose as she set the bottle down. "I thought you'd returned to the party."

"I was waiting to walk you back."

"Good thinking," she returned derisively. "I'm liable to get lost on my own."

He frowned. "First you're rude to the brother you haven't seen in months, when all he was doing was teasing you, and now you can't hold a conversation without getting defensive. Don't tell me you let Alan suck all the fun out of you."

"Mason was being obnoxious, and Alan didn't suck anything out of me."

The smile returned to Travis's lips. Naughtiness darkened his eyes as his voice dropped to a rough caress. "Not even rum and eggnog?"

A sensual shiver raced along Tori's spine with the reminder of the New Year's they'd mixed cocktails and pleasure, literally. She fought both the white-hot memories and the urge to look away.

He laughed. "Sorry. You know how old habits die hard. I guess the new Tori doesn't have that problem though."

Clearly, she *did* have that problem as his deep laughter rumbled through her like a physical stroke. Apparently, no wall she could build would be strong enough to block either the memories or the scorching chemistry still present. "I'm the same Tori I always was. Now, I just recognize there's a time and place for messing around."

She'd meant messing around in the joking sense. He took it otherwise, going by the way his black eyebrows rose and his attention shot to the bed. The last thing she should do was follow his gaze. Like an idiot, she did anyway. Stared right at the bed and considered how many times she'd lain on it, writhing and moaning in pleasure. How many orgasms he'd delivered while she was up on her knees, down on her back, wrists shackled to the bedpost. They were all her favorite positions when Travis was involved. All ways Alan had never even considered taking her. All ways her pussy shuddered to experience again, right now.

Tori's face heated. Her blood warmed. God, if he gave voice to any one of their past liaisons, there was no telling what she might do.

"Alan's treating you right then?"

Surprised by the question, she looked over to find his expression sedate. Good. That was exactly how she wanted it. Mostly. "He's a good man."

"That isn't what I asked." Eyes narrowed, Travis studied her face in that way that left her feeling completely exposed and vulnerable. "I knew something was wrong the second you stopped kissing me long enough to give me a clear view of your face."

"*You* were kissing *me*."

"Fine, it was mutual mouth-sturbation. The groping was all you." He lifted his hand and gave her cheek a knuckle stroke in the same distracting fashion he had downstairs. "I don't like it when you're unhappy, Tori."

Yeah, well, she didn't like wanting to purr at his touch. He had those damnable woodworker's hands, rough and delicious no matter where they settled on her body.

"I'm happy," she retorted, unable to stop the protectively defensive note from reentering her voice.

"Really?"

Not as happy as she would be with another round of mouth-sturbation or better yet, masturbation, but . . . But there was no point in lying to him. Like Mason said, she couldn't do it worth a damn, which promised to make keeping her broken engagement from her family a huge chore. "In general, yes."

"We're talking about with Mr. Nose to the Grindstone."

"I don't know who your source for information on Alan is, but he *is* a good guy. Yes, he views his work as a top priority but, from what I hear, so do you these days." According to her mother's emails, Travis's custom woodworking business had turned from a small-time, local operation to one that catered to the bulk of New

England. He'd taken a number of others under his employ, but had personally kept the tasks of quality checking every product and meeting directly with buyers to capture their vision and ensure their satisfaction.

"I still take off every Sunday and make time for family and friends the rest of the week. If you were my fiancée, I'd be damned sure to set aside plenty of hours for you."

If?

What the heck was that supposed to mean? Had he lived to regret letting her go, or was he using smooth words in the hopes she would let him into her pants for a no-strings-attached Christmas fling?

Afraid she would ask the question aloud, Tori stepped back and crossed her arms. Purposefully, she added bite to her words. "I'm not going to spend my first night home arguing with you. If that means you want me to leave, it's not a problem. I have plenty of unpacking to do once I get to my parents'."

For a long moment he didn't respond, simply stared at her until the room temperature seemed to notch up a good twenty degrees. Then, a slow, sexy grin formed on his lips. He ate up the space she'd put between them with a single stride. "Guess you do still have some of the same habits. You're still adorable when you're in a snit." His hand rose again, this time to her lips. His eyes followed his fingers as he traced the curve of the lower one. "You still make my cock hard as iron with little more than a kiss."

The breath snagged in Tori's throat. The lump of desire she managed to swallow downstairs returned thicker than ever. Lust fought a battle with good intentions.

Maybe that no-strings fling wasn't such a bad idea.

She hadn't planned on allowing time for sex this week, but it would be far easier to give in to temptation than to spend the week resisting it. Far easier to admit that, until tonight, it had been months since her last kiss. Longer since she'd been touched in the sensual sense by anything more substantial than a vibrator.

Then there was the caressing, stroking, fondling. "I haven't been spanked in a long time either."

TRAVIS'S THUMB STILLED ON THE upward slope of Tori's lower lip. His cock rose to instant attention. Not trusting himself to stop at touching her face when she'd broken out the spanking talk, he let his hand fall at his side. "Care to expand on the 'either' part of that announcement?"

Hesitation passed through her eyes. She looked past him to the open bedroom door, then back again. Now would she bolt?

Her throat worked visibly with her next swallow. In a near whisper, she confessed, "Alan broke off our engagement a few months ago. Your kiss downstairs was the first I've had in ages."

Travis's heart skipped a beat. God in heaven, if sweeter words had ever been spoken he couldn't recall. His source for information on Alan was the one person he could trust not to feed him lies: Tori's father. Thomas hadn't mentioned a breakup, so he must not be in the know. Thomas would be giddy to think his youngest daughter wasn't going to marry a guy all wrong for her. Travis was so giddy he wanted to punch a fist in the air and shout out his gratitude for all of Haven to hear.

Since he didn't know how Tori felt about the separation, he

kept his fist at his side and his expression relatively sedate. "*Our* kiss. Mutual mouth-sturbation, remember?"

The heat in her eyes said she couldn't forget. With her words, she kept to the topic of her broken engagement. "My family doesn't know. I'd like to keep it that way until after the holidays."

"Why are you telling me this, Tori?"

"I needed to tell someone, if only to get it off my chest. You're one of the few people I trust not to go blabbering the news to all of Haven."

Travis staved off an ironic smile, since he'd been considering doing just that. He concentrated instead on the way Tori's gaze had dropped to his mouth. The heat in her eyes warmed, moving into the sweet curve of her lips. There was clearly more to be said. "And?"

"And"——her voice returned to a whisper, this one throaty and laced with sensual promise——"I thought it would help in convincing you to spend the next week sleeping with me, no strings attached."

Well, hell, if the words didn't keep getting sweeter. His body was also getting harder. Too bad going with the want blistering through his blood by yanking off her clothes and tossing her on his bed for a welcome-home fuck was bound to give the wrong impression.

Her eyes betrayed her nerves as they returned to his. "The thing is, I'm up for a vice president position with the real-estate firm. If I can seal a hotel deal with the client I'm meeting with the day after Christmas, I'm pretty much guaranteed the promotion. I don't want to spend the entire time I'm here stressing over it though, and we both know how good sex works to de-stress me." Her cheeks flushed with pretty color. "I mean how well sex works, not that only good sex works to de-stress me. Not that sex with you isn't good. It's great. I just . . . wish you would stop my rambling."

Travis found himself fighting another smile. She really was too cute for words when she got herself worked up like this. What wasn't cute was if Alan had done a number on her heart. "I'm waiting to hear how you can think Alan's such a good guy when he proposed to you one day and turned around and broke your heart a few days later."

"It was two months later," Tori corrected. "And my heart will survive."

The cute factor drained away in a blink then, as she became the woman he last remembered standing in his bedroom: the one who oozed sex and sin. A seductive smile spread across those entirely too kissable lips. It was *her* hand that rose to *his* mouth now. *Her* thumb settling on *his* lower lip, rubbing back and forth, tempting him to open up and suck it inside.

"What do you say, Travis? Are you up for some holiday loving, or should I shop elsewhere? I saw Jacob Wiley downstairs. As memory serves, he's usually good for a quality romp, and I seriously doubt the leg cast will slow him down."

Jacob had been a year behind them in high school, having moved to Haven his sophomore year. With the nearly three to one ratio of single women to men in their little town and Jacob's roguish looks and behavior, the girls had all flocked to him. All but Tori. Though it was foolish to think her words anything more than a taunt, annoyance and a shade of jealousy tugged at Travis.

Lamely, he pointed out, "His brother's dating your sister, which could well make him your brother someday in a roundabout sort of way."

Amusement shone in her eyes. She quit with the lip rubbing to slip her hand down his chest. "You tongue-kissed my mother tonight. I'd say that's a whole lot worse than doing some guy who may never be family."

Her fingers curled into his shirt, their warmth seeping through to his skin, and the invitation there was too damned good to resist. He leaned into her, enjoying the slight widening of her eyes and the subtle flare of her nostrils. "I didn't tongue-kiss your mother. Thomas would've beat my ass. Besides, she never could have lived up to the expectations set by her daughter."

Yanking off her clothes and tossing her onto his bed *would* give the wrong impression. Yanking off just a few of her clothes and tossing her up against the wall for a taste of what they'd both been missing would give her something to think about tonight when she wasn't having sex. No matter his reaction to her Jacob taunt, Travis knew she wouldn't run to some other guy when he called an early end to things. Fun-loving and frisky as she'd been, not even the old version of Tori slept around. She could extend a no-strings offer to him solely because of their history.

It was because of their history, too, that he knew she'd squeal in delight when he grabbed her wrists in his hands and pinned her up against the wall beside the bathroom doorway.

Breath quickening, Tori gave the predicted squeal. Rapturous relief flooded her face and she gave a testing tug at the binding of his hands. "Is that a yes?"

Taking both wrists into one hand, he sliced a hard thigh between her legs and rocked against her sex through her jeans. "It's not a no."

The challenge to turn her down simmered into her eyes. She writhed against his thigh, grinding her cunt in an attempt to soothe the ache he knew blossomed deep in her core, the same one snugging his balls. Meeting that challenge with a taunt, Travis bucked his knee against her crotch and pressed hard into her sweet spot. She blinked several times rapidly, and he could just imagine her plump little clit peeking from its hiding place, eager for a pet.

A euphoric "ooh" fell from Tori's lips seconds before he slammed his mouth against hers. When he'd been kissing her without permission he hadn't dared take too much. He was kissing her with permission now and he dared take all he wanted.

Wildness undulating through him, he sank his tongue between her lips and deep into the soft, moist recesses of her mouth, tasting, teasing. Tormenting with each sensual stroke. Her own tongue moved against his with reckless abandon, desperate need. The same damned breathtaking torment he delivered to her.

Clearly, she still kept cotton candy lip liner in her pocket. The sweet, sticky taste merged with the hot, carnal taste of Tori. Together, they licked over his senses and had his mouth demanding more, more, more. The rest of him craved for more, as well. Just enough of her smoking body to whet her appetite and leave his cock feeling abused.

Tightening his grip on her wrists with his left hand, Travis slipped his right hand beneath her sweater. He slid it upward, along the smooth, warm flesh of her torso to the clasp of her bra. A lovely thing about being smaller-chested, she'd once told him, was that she could wear front-clasp bras without fear of anything spilling out when it shouldn't and he could get to her breasts in an instant. Taking advantage of that instant access, he popped the clasp and palmed the supple, rounded flesh beneath.

She arched up beneath his touch, puffing a hot sigh of need into his mouth. The rub of her pussy against his thigh increased. She gave another tug at her wrists to no avail. Laughing in dark delight, he freed her breast to flick his thumbnail across its nipple. Moaning, she thrust her chest forward. Unlike her breasts, her nipples were large. Big and incredibly sensitive to the point she'd climaxed for him more than a few times from nipple stimulation alone.

His mind consumed with bringing her the kind of pleasure that would have her yearning for more, Travis gave the nipple another flick. The nub became a long, hardened point that he caught between thumb and forefinger and squeezed. Excitement danced over Tori's flushed face. She tore her mouth from his to cry out loud enough to wake the dead. Fortunately for her, his guests were even louder and unlikely to detect sounds coming from the second floor. Unfortunately for him, that cry ripped through his body and stroked at his cock with such painful pleasure he felt ready to come on the spot.

"Put your mouth on my breasts." Her words sighed out in a hot, harried command.

He'd been right the second time, Travis acknowledged. The new Tori had held on to some of the old Tori's habits. Some of his favorites.

Christ, how he yearned to taunt her in to telling him what she wanted in explicit detail. Now wasn't the time. Promising himself that time would come soon, he gave in to her request. Pushed her sweater and bra up past her breasts, and flicked his tongue across a suntanned mound that made it clear she lived somewhere far warmer than Haven.

But he could change that now that she was no longer engaged. He *would* change that.

He'd let her go once believing she would never stay gone. This time he had to show her beyond a doubt nothing was worth staying away from him or Haven.

Starting with the erotic delights to be had in her hometown, Travis pulled the tight, dusky nipple into his mouth and gave it a hard sucking. Tori jerked at her bindings once more. When that failed, she turned her minor writhings to major wrigglings against the hard, powerful press of his knee. Through their jeans, her pussy felt soft and hot and he could guess was dripping wet with her succulent cream. He'd kill to sink his tongue inside her cunt and feast on her juices. Since that wouldn't be happening tonight, he took satisfaction in turning his mouth on her other nipple.

He loved the aroused nub with the alternating circling of his tongue and scraping of his teeth until her breath panted out hot and fast, inches from his ear. Then he sucked it inside and pushed it hard against the roof of his mouth.

With a shuddering moan, she canted her hips hard into his, shooting electric sensation throughout his aching, raw cock. "Oh God, Travis! It's been way, way too long."

And her nipples were still as big of pleasure points as ever, because she way, way, way too close to coming.

Fuck, how he wanted to continue to suck at them. How he wanted to go down on his knees, strip her free of her jeans, and make love to her pussy. Let her have one mind-bending orgasm as a reminder of all they'd shared in the past and a prelude to all those yet to come. But he wasn't about to do that. Not when the whole "why buy the cow when you can get the milk for free" analogy kept rattling through his head.

Tori was getting the cow, make that bull, no matter how many days of taunting and how many nights of cold showers and masturbation lay in his future. Only his days and nights weren't unlimited. He had six more until she flew back to Miami, and he planned to spend at least half of those buried, balls deep, in the velvet luxury of her beautiful pussy.

Regret sighing through him, Travis withdrew his mouth from her nipple. As if she could predict his next move and was primed to prevent it, Tori tightened her thighs around his leg. He kept going anyway, sliding his knee free, releasing her slim wrists, and taking a step back.

She didn't look cute now, with her lips plump and red from his kisses and her exposed, rigid nipples the same. She looked like *his* woman. Caveman tendencies rose with the thought, urging him to strip her naked and toss her on his bed more than ever.

"Unfortunately, it's going to be even longer," Travis said to himself as much as her. "I have a houseful of guests, at least some of whom are bound to be looking for me."

Bold to the bone in true old Tori fashion, she closed the space between them and gripped his cock through his jeans. "This won't take more than five minutes, I swear."

The blood blazed through his veins as she pumped his stiff flesh. He bit back his groan. "Your dad's liable to show up in three. I told him I was coming up to grab that book for him a long time ago." Unwrapping her hand from his erection, he backed toward the door. Damn, the view was just too incredible. It had his cock jerking against his zipper and his feet shuffling so fast he'd be lucky if he didn't fall and break his damned neck. "See you downstairs. And don't worry, Tori, your secret's safe with me."

Chapter Three

The smell of fresh-baked cookies tantalized Tori's senses as she descended to the first floor of her parents' old farmhouse. When she reached the living room, Murphy, the family's Labrador retriever, stood up from in front of the stone fireplace to greet her hand with a "you know you want to pet me" lick. Tori happily obliged, petting the dog as she took the time she hadn't last night to appreciate the gaily decorated room. A Christmas tree laden with years of handmade ornaments took up the corner near the fireplace. Poinsettia plants lined the metal fireplace grate and a bevy of stockings hung on the mantel, including one for Nick—a business associate of Mason's who'd come home with him to experience the warmth and joy of a Reddy family holiday.

One thing Tori *had* noticed last night was that mistletoe flanked every archway in the house.

Mistletoe had supposedly been responsible for Travis's greeting kiss. Knowing how often he stopped by her parents', would he use that excuse to kiss her here without fear of who might be watching?

Not that she'd feared who might be watching last night, when she all but begged him to take her up against his bedroom wall, with his door wide-freaking-open. Yeah, she'd come to recognize there was a time and place for messing around, all right.

Even with reverting to her formerly "a little too fun-loving" self and nearly paying the price of discovery for it, she'd hoped to get Travis alone again during the course of the party. That hadn't happened. And she wasn't sure a holiday fling would happen either, since all he'd whispered as he'd helped her into her parka was that he would think about it. She'd figured she would lie awake all night thinking about the possibility and the sexually frustrated state he'd left her in. Between her weariness from traveling, her late-night, icy-cold hike, and the lull of her childhood bedroom, she'd fallen asleep in minutes. If she'd dreamed of all the wicked things she wanted Travis to do to her, she couldn't remember.

Pushing him from her mind, at least as much as was possible, Tori went into the kitchen. Dean Martin crooned "Let It Snow" from the stereo in the adjoining dining room. Her mother hummed along, swaying her trim hips side to side, as she rolled dough for Christmas cookies on the granite countertop.

Nostalgia swept over Tori for all the mornings past, when she'd come downstairs to find her mother doing much the same thing. She loved the respected professional image she'd obtained in her coworkers' and clients' eyes since hiring on at the real-estate firm. Sometimes, though, the thought of moving back to New Hampshire, getting to see her parents and lifelong friends whenever the mood struck, was almost too good to pass up. Of course, if she nailed her morning-after-Christmas meeting and secured the VP position for it, moving anytime in the foreseeable future wouldn't be an option.

Vowing to use part of her promotion bonus to send her family plane tickets so they could do Easter at her place, she went to the coffeepot on the counter. Margaret looked over when Tori opened an overhead cupboard door and took out a Santa mug with a stocking hat for a handle.

Tori smiled. "Morning, Mom."

"Morning, baby. Did you sleep well?"

Did she really have to call her baby? She got that it was a pet name, but it seemed like one Tori had outgrown twenty years ago. Not wanting to hurt her mom's feelings, she gave her frown to the coffeepot as she poured herself a cup. "Better than I have in weeks. There's nothing quite like my old bedroom."

"It's not the bedroom. It's the whole family being here. So long as we're all together, anyplace will feel like home."

Sort of an odd observation for her mother to bring up out of the blue. It did bode well for Tori's hopes of having Easter at her place—with someone else in front of the oven.

She lifted her mug in salute. "Hear! Hear!"

Margaret picked up a matching mug and clinked it against Tori's. They took a sip in unison. After setting her cup down, Margaret grabbed a spatula from the end of the counter that butted up against the oven. She held it out to Tori. "I need seven dozen cookies cut, baked, and frosted in time for the Santa and Mrs. Claus display at the department store this evening. No excuses about being kitchen-challenged either." She shook her head, sending her long silver hair dancing about her shoulders. "How all of my off-spring inherited their father's inability to cook, I'll never know."

Tori stuck her tongue out at the spatula, but accepted it. A glimpse at the oaken, rectangular table that centered the kitchen showed her mother hadn't set up for the cooling and frosting part yet. She went to the drawer that held the waxed paper only to find it now held paper and pencils. "Where's the waxed paper?"

Margaret nodded at a floor-to-ceiling pantry across the room. "In the pantry."

"That's new." Tori looked around the kitchen and discovered the pantry wasn't the only update. A good deal of modernizing had been done since she'd been home this spring. New appliances, new countertops, ivory-toned cupboards, and warm cranberry walls.

Had the rest of the house been updated?

Tori was about to ask when she reached the pantry. Between the painstakingly detailed engravings on the door and the lovely overall craftsmanship, she knew it was Travis's work. Her parents really adored him. If they were to have a holiday fling, she was going to have to be extra careful to see that none of her family found out. Knowing how his family felt about her, the same ap-plied as well.

"Where's Daddy?" she asked as she covered one end of the table with waxed paper. She didn't bother to ask about the rest of the family. She'd gotten the lowdown last night.

Holly would either be writing like the wind in the hopes of making a pressing book deadline, or rewarding herself for making progress on the story by getting frisky with Cole. Nick and her other sister, Rachel, who were standing in for Josh and Misty by playing Santa and Mrs. Claus, had agreed to spend the morning setting up the display. And knowing Mason, he'd worked his charms to earn himself breakfast in Sheriff Jack's bed.

"He snowmobiled over to Travis's. Travis loaned him a book last night and your father managed to set it down and then forget all about it. Considering how many toddies he had, God only knows where it ended up."

Tori laughed. Her father *had* been feeling good, which made it a somewhat favorable thing that her car was parked in a snowbank. Her mother had terrible night vision so, after collecting her luggage and defunct cell phone from her rental, Tori had driven her parents home. "I heard Anna's expecting."

"She *was*. Buzzy said she went into labor around two this morning. She had a little girl just before eight. Misty delivered a boy a few hours earlier. He's barely five pounds and had some trouble breathing on his own at first, but Buzzy says he's doing great as of her last check."

Laughter bubbled up a second time with mention of her parents' incredibly nosy neighbor. Her need to know could get annoying at times, but Buzzy's overall good heart made up for it. "Where would we be without Buzzy?" Tori returned to the counter. She leaned against it, sipping her coffee as she waited for the oven timer to go off. "I'm surprised Travis isn't at the hospital."

"He'd just gotten home from there when your dad called to see if he could come look for that book." Her mother glanced over, smiling. "Dad said Travis sounded like he was the father, the way he was going on about the new addition to the Denby clan."

Tori felt a frown tug at her lips. The talks she and Travis used to have about children were just one of reasons she never saw his ending their relationship coming. She'd thought they were going to last for the long haul. Then the second she'd gotten a job offer in another state and showed a little interest in accepting it, he'd urged her not to worry about them, but to snap up the position. He had his parents to look after, his sister and her family, and Tori had her dreams to follow.

"He's always been so good with kids," Margaret said as she finished filling another sheet of cookies for the oven. "Hopefully, he will find the right woman soon to have them with."

Tori's belly roiled. The coffee suddenly felt like acid eating its way down her throat. Her mother looked over like she was expecting a response. What was she supposed to say? That the thought of Travis having kids with some other woman made her want to find said woman and stab out her ovaries?

The oven timer sounded and Tori expelled a relieved breath. *Saved by the bell.*

She took the first of two trays of cookies from the oven and transferred them to the waxed paper. She returned the still-hot cookie sheet to the stovetop and was about to grab the second cookie sheet when her mother said, "I was hoping we'd get some time to visit today."

An eerie sense of foreboding washed over Tori. Hesitantly, she asked, "What's going on?"

"Nothing too much. Your sisters and brother already know so I wanted to fill you in as soon as possible." Margaret wiped her flour-dusted hands on a dish towel and then leaned against the counter, mimicking Tori's pose. "When Grandma Reddy passed away she left behind a note about her special ruby."

Tori's foreboding fell to the wayside as a mixture of sorrow and guilt rose. She'd always been close with her grandma, but the last year—Grandma's last year alive—she hadn't been home nearly enough. Work had taken precedence in a way she couldn't help. Not if she wanted to be successful. "What did the note say?"

"I can't share that yet, but the fate of the stone will be revealed on Christmas morning."

The fate?

"Did she leave it to one of us kids?" The ruby had meant everything to her grandma. Grandpa Reddy told her it would keep their love strong and them safe while they were apart. It had done just that time and again, and her grandparents had sworn it was magical in that way, that love naturally stemmed from it.

Tori wasn't sure she believed the stone held the power to either bring or keep a man in her own life, but she would like to get her hands on it to find out. More than that, she would love the stone to be left to her so she could show the entire family she was responsible enough to see to its long-term welfare. Given that whole "not around the last year of Grandma Reddy's life" thing, the odds of that happening were pretty much zilch.

"You'll find out soon enough," Margaret assured her. "Now grab that other batch of cookies out of the oven before they burn. And remember when you're getting them off the cookie sheet— each one you break is another you have to remake."

TORI PULLED INTO THE DRIVEWAY of Grandma Reddy's old cottage and parked next to Holly's rental car. Thankfully, Sheriff Jack's dad had been able to use his trusty plow-mounted tow truck to free her own rental from the snowbank. After last night's bitterly cold trek, she wasn't feeling up to hiking the path from her parents' place to the cottage out back.

Stepping from the car, she took a moment to look around. Evergreens and elms surrounded the cottage, with paths for various recreational activities cut in throughout the wooded area. The duck pond between the cottage and main house was visible down one of the paths. Tori winced as she recalled the time she'd told Rachel she could perform a better figure eight than her any day. Not only had Tori *not* completed a figure eight, she hadn't made it back to the house without first having to go to the emergency room to have her ankle set and put in a cast.

Just one more time I failed to shine.

Shaking off the depressing thought, Tori made her way up the recently shoveled walkway to the wreath-bedecked door. She considered letting herself inside, then opted against it. Holly might not be alone. She could have blown off writing to blow Cole, period.

The thought triggered a spurt of envy followed by a fresh smile. The prim and ever professional Holly she'd known six months ago would have turned three shades of red over the idea her family was thinking of her and sex. The new Holly still might not be super keen on the idea, but she also wouldn't demand a change in topic.

Tori righted the wreath's slightly off-tilt red bow, then, knocking, called out, "Is it safe to come in?"

A handful of seconds passed, and Holly opened the door in navy sweats, with her long blond hair in a ponytail. "I'm not in a 'killing off my characters and anyone who dares to interrupt my time with them' mood, if that's what you're asking."

"Actually, I thought you might be ravaging Cole's naked, shackled body."

Holly laughed. "Don't I wish! Sadly that won't be happening until I meet my minimum daily page count." She stepped back to let Tori in. "Cole took Jacob to have his leg checked for healing progress."

Tori stomped the snow off her boots on the welcome mat. She considered taking off her coat, then decided against it. There was no telling how this visit with Holly would go; she may well want to make a hasty exit. "I don't know Cole as well as his brothers, but from what I do know of him he seems like a great guy."

Devotion entered Holly's eyes. "That he is." She went to her notebook computer on the wooden counter in the kitchenette and saved the open file. With a glance over her shoulder, she asked, "How's Alan doing?"

"Swamped with work as ever, but good." Tori bit her tongue around the response. It wasn't a lie—they worked together and she knew for a fact he was doing good. Still, the idea of leading her family into believing everything was hunky-dory between them didn't set well.

Holly moved to the open sitting area and took a seat in front of a crackling fire. "Mom was disappointed that he couldn't make it for Christmas. I think she was hoping to see that he was as much for family as he is for business."

Tori stood transfixed by the fire. In a heartbeat she was two years in the past. Grandma Reddy had gone away for a special weekend with the girls, and suggested Tori and Travis have a special weekend as well, by taking advantage of her empty cottage. They'd used it, all right. The sofa. The rug. The kitchenette countertop.

God, she must have come thirty times that weekend.

Almost as good as their lovemaking was the way he'd first indulged her appetite with his amazing cooking skills and then her funny bone by watching her favorite slapstick comedy for the fiftieth time. A sad smile twisted at Tori's lips. She hadn't watched that movie once in the year they'd been apart.

Holly's words caught up with her. Absently, she shrugged. "I'm sure Alan will have kids someday. Right now it just doesn't fit with his career plans."

"*Alan* will have them? Don't you mean both of you will?"

Tori gave her head a hard shake as she realized her mistake. This was exactly why she shouldn't be thinking about Travis around her family. "Of course." Her smile felt too bright, so she rushed out the reason she'd come here. "Mom told me about Grandma's ruby."

Holly's expression became the cool, composed courtroom mask she'd perfected years ago. "I don't want it."

"How could you not?" Tori asked, shocked. "It was Grandma's most prized possession. What she swore kept her and Grandpa together and safe all those years. Besides, you're the natural choice to receive it."

"Because I'm so freaking responsible, right? The golden child."

"Better to be viewed as ruled by responsibility than lacking it altogether."

"Whatever. I don't want it." Holly regained a soft smile. "With luck, it will go to Mason."

Tori stiffened with how quickly her sister tossed out Mason's name. It was the response she'd feared. "You don't think I stand a chance."

"Everyone stands a chance. I suggested Mason because he's Grandpa's likeness. Dad's, too, for the most part."

"But my chances are slimmer than most, don't you think?"

"I have no idea."

She should change the subject before they started fighting. But, damn it, she wanted an honest answer. "You have an opinion," Tori pressed. "If it was your ruby and you were going to leave it to one of us four kids, where would I fall on your list of potential recipients?"

Disbelief shone on Holly's face. "Oh my God, why are you making such a big deal out of this?"

"Why are you refusing to answer? You're a lawyer for cripes' sake. Direct responses should be a given."

"A retired attorney," Holly shot back, eyes narrowed, "and I would never mix business with family."

Really, really she should drop this. But she still just couldn't. "You don't think I'm dependable enough to see to its long-term welfare."

Hesitation flashed in Holly's eyes. She glanced at the fire, then back at Tori. "Okay. Fine. You want an answer, then no. I don't know that I do. Your specialties are family and fun. Two incredibly wonderful things. Sometimes, though, that fun has a way of getting in the way of better judgment. Like the time you got so engrossed in getting the old geezer decorations together for Dad's fiftieth birthday party that you forgot all about getting the cake out of the oven."

Was she serious? "I was fifteen," Tori said defensively.

"Yeah, and that cake was my present! It took every ounce of effort I had to get the recipe right. Then there was last Thanksgiving, when you mixed vegetable oil with the salad dressing instead of olive oil. We were scraping our tongues off for days."

"Mom just said to use oil. How the heck was I to know what kind of oil she meant? That wasn't a result of having fun either."

Holly raised a hand and starting ticking off fingers. "The time you snuck beer and smokes into Old Man Denby's woodshed and nearly burned it to the ground."

"Only *almost* and that was Travis's influence. Not to mention nearly as long ago as the cake incident." Not to mention a really good memory even if they did both end up sick and grounded.

Tori focused on the heat of frustration burning her cheeks and not that of arousal for how far they'd gone in the woodshed that day. It was her first experience with sex and the first time she saw Travis as more than a friend. "I might have made a few blunders in the past, maybe even a few hundred that were directly a result of getting carried away with making things more fun, but I'm not like that anymore. I think before I act. Ask questions if things aren't concrete."

"Well . . . in that case, I'd have to reconsider where you'd fall on the list."

"I'd still be in last place, wouldn't I?"

"Tori!" Holly bit out. Her face regained its courtroom mask. "I seriously need to get back to work, or my editor's going to take a wet noodle to my ass. How about we catch up tonight, after the Christmas parade? We can crash Rachel and Nick's Santa and Mrs. Claus display, then head to The Tavern for happy hour."

And then what—Holly could recount a hundred more stupid things she'd done? Reminding herself she'd asked for this, Tori feigned a smile. "Sure. See you then." She went to the door, turning back when she reached it to offer an authentic smile. "For the record, you're buying."

THEY WERE AT THE TAVERN to have a good time, Tori reminded herself as she followed Holly through the L-shaped seating area to a wooden booth near the back of the bar. She was *not* going to think about the ruby, or the fact that her sister thought she was as irresponsible as ever.

A middle-aged blonde she'd never seen before came to take their drink order. "Irish coffee," Holly said, sliding the coat from around her shoulders.

Outside of that time Tori had gotten sick on beer and smokes in Old Man Denby's woodshed, she wasn't much of a drinker. The last year, as she'd concentrated on rising to the top at the real-estate firm, she hadn't touched so much as a glass of wine. She remedied that now. "I'll have a Chablis."

The server departed, and Tori took off her parka and hung it on the hook attached to the booth's side. Awkward silence descended as the seconds passed and neither sister spoke. Tori frowned. They used to be quite close. Was the silence now because of her idiotic behavior at the cottage, or simply because of how much time had gone by since they'd last chitchatted?

Determined to end the silence, Tori asked, "How's Jacob's leg?"

Holly was back to wearing her courtroom mask as she grabbed a handful of peanuts from a wooden bowl in the center of the table. "Not completely healed, but the doctor said no surgery."

"That's a relief. I realize Jacob's hardly a saint, but it's a crock when he has to suffer for coming to a woman's defense." She still couldn't believe Jacob had taken on an abusive husband. Haven had always seemed such a place of security, where nothing bad ever happened. Thankfully, the jerk hadn't returned to The Tavern since Cole took a page out of Jacob's book and hung the guy up by his belt loop.

"It is," Holly agreed. "But he's digging all the extra female attention he's getting for it."

Tori laughed. "Oh yeah. Like he needs help in the getting-a-woman's-attention department."

Holly joined in on her laughter, and just like that the awkward tension melted away. By the time their drinks arrived they were talking and laughing like old times. And, God, that felt so good. Simple talk, simple laughter. No stress. No thought to impressing anyone.

"Mind if we join you?"

Tori's head snapped up at the sound of Travis's voice. He stood at the head of the table looking near edible in a black leather bomber and blue jeans. His black hair was sexily wind tousled and his alluring smile was out in full force. She glanced away and found herself staring at his groin. Instant tension, this time of the sensual variety, tightened her shoulders and attacked her sex with dampness. Another look away, this time to the side, found Sheriff Jack and Mason standing behind Travis. This was supposed to be a reunion date with Holly, a girls-only event, but they could hardly turn down her brother and his man. Travis she should turn down, if only to avoid sitting thigh to thigh with him, feeling the heat rising off his hard body when she knew she didn't dare touch.

She smiled. "Of course not." Holly agreed, and Tori scooted over in the booth.

Travis slid in beside her. His powerful thigh came to immediate rest against hers, their knees tapping together, and her pussy throbbed with the thought of the last time that knee had connected with her body. In his usual reading-her-mind fashion, Travis looked over and knowing, primitive hunger flashed in his eyes. Swiping nervously at her lips with her tongue, Tori focused on watching Mason slide into the booth next to Holly.

Sheriff Jack grabbed a chair from a nearby table and planted it at the open end of the booth. "How's the writing progress going?" he asked Holly.

"I got my daily page count in." Accomplishment sounded in her voice.

Mason grinned. "Which means she gets to end the night by letting Cole in."

Holly flipped her middle finger at him. Everyone laughed at the behavior that would have been so un-Holly prior to Cole, and Tori felt the tension drain away again.

Sheriff Jack turned his smile on her. "How are things for you, Tori?"

Even as she cherished the camaraderie, she acknowledged that this was her chance to show everyone present how far she'd come professionally. "Excellent. In fact, I'm on the cusp of a huge promotion."

"Nice. And your man?"

The tightness returned to her shoulders even before she felt Travis's stare. She sipped at her Chablis before offering, "He's fine. Keeping busy with work."

"You know what they say about all work and no play," Mason said.

She could sense a remark about "a totally not right for her Alan" coming, so she pushed at Travis's thigh with her own. "This place needs music."

Travis slid from the booth. "I'd better assist. No telling what kind of noise you southern girls listen to."

Mason came to his feet. "We'll make it a threesome." He gave Sheriff Jack's shoulder a squeeze, and then followed Tori and Travis toward the jukebox.

Tori groaned. So much for escaping her tension when the two men causing it were hot on her trail. Saying hello as she passed friends and neighbors, she continued to the back wall of the bar. The mistletoe hanging over the jukebox came into view seconds before she would have planted herself beneath it.

The sprig of green leaves and red berries would be the perfect excuse to kiss Travis. Much as she craved that very thing, it was the last thing she should do. Kissing another man once when she was supposedly engaged was bad. Kissing another man twice when she was supposedly engaged would be about as irresponsible as it got. Having a little fun at another's expense wouldn't raise her maturity level in anyone's eyes either but, for all the ribbing Mason had been doing, she couldn't resist.

Hiding her smile, she started to slide a quarter into the jukebox only to stop with it midway in. "Damn. It must be broken. It won't take my quarter."

Travis moved up beside her. "That's strange. I swear it was playing when we came in."

Mason held out his hand. "Let me see." She gave him the quarter and stepped back. He easily slipped it into the jukebox. "It's not broken."

"Nope. But you two *are* under the mistletoe. Pucker up, boys."

Mason looked first shocked and then appreciative. Travis shot her a look that said she would pay. Thinking about all the naughty ways he could take it out of her sweaty, nude body, she inclined her head. "Get to it. None of this cheek stuff either."

Accepting the challenge, Travis pulled Mason into his arms and laid a firm but close-mouthed kiss on his lips. Her brother's shocked look returned, like he didn't think Travis would go through with it. Tori was a little surprised herself, but mostly turned on. She rubbed her tingling inner thighs together.

What the hell? Since when did watching two guys kiss arouse her?

It had to be how long she'd gone without sex nipping at her. Whatever the cause she was more aware of Travis than ever when they slid back into the booth minutes later. Every slide of his thigh against hers warmed her further. Every pull of his full lips around his beer bottle had her belly tight with longing. Every time he looked her way, his eyes full of that damned understanding, her pussy grew more liquid.

By the time they left the bar more than an hour later, she felt like one big, wet, quivering hormone. Mason led the way to the exit. He stopped short when he reached the door. "Tori, can you grab the door?"

"What, is your arm broken?"

He held up his hand to examine the palm. "No, but I think I got a sliver off the booth seat when I slid out. My hand's throbbing like a beast."

"Big baby," she taunted playfully, then opened the door for him to move through.

Mason looked to Travis. "After you."

Travis started for the door. When he reached the threshold and stood directly beside Tori, Mason nodded up at the ceiling. A smart-ass grin formed. "What do you know? Mistletoe. Pucker up, kids."

Tori groaned. Damn, she should have seen that one coming. Since she hadn't, she leaned into Travis intending to get away with a cheek kiss. Her brother planted a hand against her shoulder and shoved her up against Travis before she could make her move.

Her mouth darted past Travis's cheek to slam against his mouth. Instant heat flooded her with that familiar and delicious press. Strong arms surrounded her. The scent of his spicy cologne came next. She sighed as his broad chest rubbed against her breasts, pinging her nipples to hard, needy life. His tongue slipped between her lips. Erotic sensation shot to her core, further liquefying her pussy. She drank it in, drank him in as she roped her arms around his neck, ground their hips together, and just let go.

"Get a room."

Mason's amused remark cut through the sensual haze. Time and place—and the fact that neither were good ones—registered. Face blazing, Tori unwrapped herself from Travis's shoulders.

She glared at her brother. "I will," she ground out. "Next time I see my *fiancé*."

With a last scowl, she pushed through the door and hurried out to Holly's rental car. Her sister smartly kept quiet as they climbed inside and waited for the heater to defrost the layer of fresh ice on the windshields. The passenger-side window started to clear away, and Tori noticed Travis climbing into his truck a few spots away. She'd assumed he'd ridden with her brother and Sheriff Jack. Since he hadn't and she also couldn't stop quivering like a human vibrator from that damned kiss, she opened her door.

"What are you doing?" Holly asked.

"I need to ask Travis a quick question . . . about the sleigh ride."

Aware how bad the lie sounded, Tori jogged over to Travis's truck and rapped on the window. He rolled it down to ask drily, "Looking for your fiancé?"

"I'm looking for an orgasm. Have you thought about my offer?"

"Yep. But I'm going to need a little more time to deliberate."

"Why?" she asked, unable to keep either the wanting or the impatience from her voice. "It's sex, not rocket science."

A horn sounded behind her. Travis nodded his head out the window. "You're keeping Holly from getting her jollies."

Yeah, and he was keeping Tori from getting her own. Making a mental note to add masturbation to her bedtime routine, she hurried back to Holly's car and climbed inside.

Chapter Four

Gathered in the Reddys' dining room, sharing breakfast with the entire family minus Holly and Tori, who'd yet to wake, Travis finished off the last of his food. A few seats away, Margaret lifted a still heaping plate of cinnamon and apple pancakes in offering. "Ready for more?"

Travis sat back in his seat to pat his stomach. "They were incredible as always, Margaret, but if I eat another it's going to require undoing my jeans."

"Speaking of undoing your jeans—morning, Tori," Mason said from beside him.

"Mason, be nice to your sister!" Margaret admonished, but it was clear she fought a smile.

Travis turned in his seat to find Tori standing in the dining room's open entrance. Her cheek was red with crisscross imprints as if her pillowcase had been rumpled beneath it while she slept.

Her hair looked like it had gone a round with a windstorm, and her too big gray sweatshirt hung off one shoulder to expose her smooth, suntanned skin. She looked completely endearing, and he was hard in an instant.

"Yeah. I mean, jeez, she hasn't even had her coffee yet," Rachel added, amusement sounding in her voice.

Travis pushed back his chair and stood. "Still take it black?"

"Yes, but I can get it myself," Tori answered without looking at him, and then disappeared into the attached kitchen.

Travis grabbed his empty coffee mug from the table. "I can use another cup myself. Anyone else need a refill?"

Mason handed over his mug with a wink. Travis considered the way Mason had been teasing Tori the last few days as he moved into the kitchen. With the two being the youngest of the Reddy siblings and closest in age, they'd always taunted each other. This time, though, it seemed Mason had one goal in mind and that was to push her Travis's way every chance he got. Did he know about her breakup with Alan? Better yet, did he know that Tori wanted Travis and for more reasons than no-strings sex?

He set the questions aside for the time being as Tori's backside came into view. Unlike her oversize sweatshirt, her black leggings were skintight. The sweatshirt rode up in the back, sending his cock into a throbbing fit with the way it put her shapely ass on display.

Damn, but if he didn't already have enough temptation eating at him.

She glanced over when he joined her at the counter. He set down Mason's half-empty mug and topped it off. After doing the same with his own, he asked, "Sleep well?"

"Not at first." A slow, taunting smile played at her lips. "But a little masturbation and I was out like a light."

Travis groaned. Now that just wasn't fair, painting those open-thigh, pussy-creaming, fingering-fucking fantasies in his head. "Sounds like we were getting off together separately."

Tori leaned closer to whisper, "We could be getting off together together."

The warmth of her breath coasted along his ear and chased a shiver through his body. He fought fire with fire, sending her a wickedly naughty grin. "And I could jerk down your leggings, stick you up on the counter, and slam my cock into your pussy right here, right now." Letting the words hang, he picked up the two coffee mugs in one hand and moved past her. He reached back at the last second to swat her butt with his free hand. "See you tonight, sweet cheeks."

"How can every single one of you have other plans? This is an *annual* event." Hands on her hips in her parents' living room, Tori gave her family a censorious look. Her favorite part of the Christmas season was the annual sleigh ride. She'd been looking forward to it for months, and now it appeared she was going to be enjoying it alone. Or at least, alone with Travis.

Slipping into her boots, Holly shrugged. "Sorry, but I haven't made my daily page count. Now that dinner's over I need to get back to work, pronto."

Her mother gave Tori an apologetic look as her father helped her mother into her coat. "Your father and I have plans with Travis's parents. You know how seldom they get out."

"Sheriff Jack has the evening off," Mason said from his relaxed position on the recliner. "The last till after I head back to New York and I'm not about to *not* take advantage."

Tori pushed out a breath of frustration. They were all valid excuses, so why did they sound so planned? Had her family overheard her kitchen exchange with Travis this morning? God, she never should have dared such naughty words with them less than twenty feet away. "Where are Rachel and Nick?"

"They left to snowshoe the path out by the Myerses' old cabin a few hours ago," Holly said. "I guess they got sidetracked along the way."

Considering Rachel and Nick hadn't come home until early this morning and, soon after, confessed to being involved, it was safe to assume they were doing more than snowshoeing. Either way, they wouldn't be back on time when Travis was due to arrive with the horse-drawn sleigh any moment.

She should be thrilled about the idea of alone time with Travis, Tori mused as she zipped up her parka. Time to tempt the hell out of him until he really did lift her up on the counter and slam his hard cock into her pussy. And she was sort of thrilled. It was just that this sleigh ride was supposed to include her entire family, everyone laughing and having a good time, arguing over which neighbor had the best Christmas display, sipping rum and eggnog as they traversed the countryside and the brightly decked-out town.

Outside, Travis pulled up in the horse-drawn sleigh. With a last disappointed look at her family, Tori tugged on her gloves and went to the door. "I guess I'll see you all later."

Her father came over to pull her into a big, burly-armed hug. "Have a good time, honey."

She only had a second to consider why he'd hugged her like she was going back to Miami instead of out for a couple hours when Mason tossed out, "Give Travis a kiss for me."

Groaning, because the freaking man would not let her catch a break, she opened the door. An icy wind slammed into her face. She yanked up her hood and tied it tight around her throat. Evening was setting in, the Christmas lights in the trees out front having just come on, and fat snowflakes fell all around her. It was a beautiful night, if not also a freezing one.

Her teeth on the verge of chattering, she crossed to Travis's sleigh. His *one-horse* sleigh. "Why don't you have the big sleigh?"

"What would we do with all the extra room?" The sensual heat that darkened his already potent green eyes beneath his black stocking cap said he had plenty of suggestions in mind.

Did they involve more mouth-sturbation? What about more spankings? Despite the cold, Tori's ass tingled with lascivious warmth. She eyed Travis accusingly. "You knew it would just be you and me."

"Your family apologized at breakfast for not being able to make the trip this year." Releasing one of the horse's reins, he pulled back the thick plaid blanket that covered his lap and the whole of the bench seat. "C'mon up. I promise not to bite."

The wolfish tilt to his mouth said otherwise. Uncertain it was a wise move, given this alone time felt more and more orchestrated, she climbed into the sleigh. The bench seat felt minuscule with his big, hard, deliciously masculine body next to hers. As it had done last night in the bar, his thigh pressed hotly against hers. The blanket covering their laps and legs somehow made that simple press feel incredibly intimate, spiking warmth through her body and toasting her numbing cheeks. The urge to use its camouflage to slip her hands into his lap and fondle his cock was almost too powerful to pass up.

Mmm . . . Coming up here might not have been the wisest choice, but it was definitely the most pleasing one.

Tori licked her lips. Was her family looking out the window or could she get away with a little "thanks for picking me up" nibble?

Before she could risk a move, Travis signaled the dappled gray into action. The sleigh pulled out of the snow-packed driveway and onto the road . . . in the wrong direction. "Where are we going?"

"I need to drop by Anna's house."

"She's home from the hospital already?"

"As of this afternoon."

Tori expected the next ten minutes to be laden with sexual tension and not nearly enough nibbles. Instead, they were light with talk and laughter. Things got a little more serious when they discussed their jobs, but still it was easy friendship, the kind she'd never known with any other man not related to her. She'd gotten along well with Alan from the time they'd met, but she'd never shared her thoughts, hopes, and dreams with him the way she always had with Travis. She'd never wanted Alan with the fierce, consuming hunger she felt for Travis.

The thought brought the beginnings of tension. Before it could mount, Travis pulled the sleigh into the driveway of his sister's two-story, log home. He climbed out on his side, and came around to help Tori down. Together, they moved up the shoveled path to the front door. Burke opened the door without their having to knock, a little boy with his father's warm brown eyes and his thumb in his mouth perched on his hip.

With a welcoming smile, Burke pulled Tori into a one-armed hug. "It's great to see you again."

"Aunt Tori!" A girl's excited squeal came from the living room at Burke's back. Within seconds, Anna and Burke's six-year-old daughter, Allison, had her arms wrapped around Tori's legs. Between the deep green shade of her eyes, her coal black ponytail, and her strong facial structure, she could have easily passed for Travis's daughter.

The thought set heavy on Tori, as did the girl calling her "aunt," the way she'd done when Tori and Travis were together. She chased the sensation away with a mock gasp. "Allison, you've gotten huge!"

"I'm six." Stepping back, Allison smiled in a way that revealed a gap where one of her front teeth used to be. "I lost my first tooth this morning."

"Wow. You're having a busy week in this house."

Brendan, the couple's four-year-old, came flying down the staircase on the other side of the room. "Hi, Aunt Tori. Wanna see the baby?"

"That's not a question you need to ask Tori." Anna came down the stairs at a much slower rate. She held a pink-blanket-wrapped bundle snuggled in the crook of one arm. "She's a baby-aholic."

Tori peered at the sweet little face peeking out from its taco-style wrappings. A pang of longing speared through her. "Oh my goodness. She's so tiny and beautiful."

"She won't be tiny long with the way she eats." A mother's unconditional love shone in Anna's eyes. "Ready to hold her?"

"I can't," Tori bit out. She searched for an excuse that wouldn't involve admitting the truth: She couldn't hold the baby without tearing up with the want for her own. "I had a cold a few days ago and I feel like it could still be lingering in my throat."

Travis came up beside Tori and held out his arms to his sister. "No colds from this end, so you'd best hand her over."

A torrent of emotions pricked at Tori's eyes as he took the baby into his arms and held her like a pro. Damn, she hadn't been prepared for this. She thought she'd been speaking the truth when she told Alan that kids could wait, that she wanted to focus on her career every bit as much as he did. Now, she had to question those words. Now, she had to wonder if his ending their engagement wasn't in fact the best thing to ever happen to her.

"Want to play Barbie, Aunt Tori?" Allison asked.

Though they would be leaving soon, Tori grabbed hold of the offer with the eagerness a kid took hold of her stocking on Christmas morning. "Of course I do, sweetie."

Twenty minutes later, they said their good-byes. Travis closed the door behind them, and they started down the path to the horse-drawn sleigh. "Despite what you might hear, holding a baby doesn't lead to pregnancy," he commented.

Tori feigned a confused look. "What are you talking about?"

"You were afraid to hold Mckenna."

"I wasn't afraid." Not wanting to leave the words as a lie, she added, "Not of holding her and catching some pregnancy bug."

Travis studied her face for a long moment, leaving her feeling stripped raw. "Why did Alan break things off?"

"I've always hated the way you can guess what I'm thinking."

"Not always." Salacious heat entered his eyes as he climbed onto the sleigh. "Sometimes you love it."

Hell, he was right again. Sometimes, like now for example, she loved it so much she didn't know if any man could ever rise to the expectations he'd set.

Tori stiffened, her booted feet planted in the snow on her side of the sleigh. Did she really feel that another man would be hard-pressed to fill Travis's shoes, and, if so, why hadn't she realized it before this?

Not ready to return to the cocoon of blissful intimacy and heat the blanket provided, she pretended to tie her bootlace. "Alan said I'd never be content without kids. There was a chance he might have wanted them down the road, but he claimed that I want them now."

"He might just be a good man, after all."

The respect in Travis's voice brought her to her feet. "You honestly think I'm ready for kids? That I'm responsible enough to make a good mother?"

"I don't have to think it, Tori. I *know* you'd make an amazing mother, as much because you are responsible as because you know how to have fun."

Warmth rushed through Tori, another round of that delightful heat that touched on her emotions as much as her panties. He sounded so sincere, and looked the same. His faith in her abilities was more than she could handle right now.

Affecting a careless smile, she scooped a handful of snow into her glove and climbed onto the sleigh. "I told you I was still fun." Travis glanced over, mouth open to speak. Before he could say a word, she bathed his face with snow. "Fun enough to do that."

Shock flashed on his face. Then his eyes twinkled with devilish merriment as he spit out snow. "You do realize this is war?"

"What I realize is that you throw about as good as I paint."

Leaving the taunting words hanging in the air, Tori jumped out of the sleigh. Laughing all the way, she hustled through the nearly knee-deep snow for a nearby evergreen. A snowball plastered her butt just before she would have reached the tree. Her feet threatened to come out from beneath her with the force of the impact. She fought to regain her balance and was almost there when a second snowball slammed into her backside. This one took her down. Hard.

Her belly hit first, face and hands slamming into the snow next. The breath whooshed out of her. Parting her lips on instinct had her eating a mouthful of powder.

Strong hands gripped her around the middle, lifting her slightly and turning her onto her back. "Holy shit, are you okay? I thought you were expecting that."

She attempted speech but only managed a garbled "fine." She blinked the snow out of her eyes. Then she blinked again, and her heart pummeled against her ribs. Travis knelt in the snow beside her, his big, bare hand descending toward her face. His lips opened a fraction—inches from her own. The heat of his breath bathed her frosty chin and cheeks and sizzled her blood as he wiped the snow from her mouth with the rough pad of his thumb.

His lips came closer. His nostrils flared. "You're adorable, Tori," he spoke in a rough semiwhisper. "Absolutely adorable."

Tori gulped down air. Oh, Jesus. He wasn't looking at her like a guy who wanted to sleep with her for a night or two, and then say good-bye. He was looking at her like he wanted to keep her by his side, now and forever.

Survival instincts had adrenaline cruising through her system, giving her the energy to lift her snow-laden arms. She pushed against his chest and shoved him aside. Shoved aside hope and longing, and the kiss she'd spent hours, days—hell, maybe the last year—craving. "We should get on with the ride."

EMOTIONS CHURNING THROUGH HIM, TRAVIS veered the sleigh down the road leading to his house. He wasn't convinced Tori was ready to buy the bull, but this week was flying past and he would be damned if he let either it or her slip away.

Bundled up on the seat beside him, her blue-green gaze held the same conflicted feelings it had an hour earlier, when he'd nearly kissed her on Anna's front lawn. When he'd ached to do so much more. Thankfully, Tori had shoved him aside, or they might still be there now, melting the snow with the heat of their thrusting bodies.

Buzzy would have had a field day with that one. Somehow, the old but endearing biddy would have found out. She always did.

Was that what had happened tonight? Had Buzzy found out about Tori's broken engagement and shared the news with the Reddys? Something had to have triggered them into turning down this sleigh ride that was a standing tradition.

"Where to now?" Tori asked curiously.

Travis turned a smile on her. All thoughts of Buzzy fell away as needful desire coursed through him, quickening his pulse and rousing his cock. A few other women had passed through his life the past year, but none that fit him the way Tori did. If she'd changed during her time away, became a "new" Tori, it was only minimally. She was still the perfect balance of playful fun and loving sincerity. Perfect for him.

Fuck, he wanted to take hold of her chin and kiss those sweet, sexy, and yet incredibly naughty lips.

Soon. Damned soon. First, there was the horse to attend to.

"The barn," he supplied, pulling up his tree-lined drive. "It's getting too dark to safely take the sleigh all the way to your parents' place." He directed the horse into the two-story, brown barn out back of the house.

Inside the warmer confines of the barn, Travis climbed from the sleigh. Tori lifted the blanket from her lap and started to follow. Not a chance was he letting that happen.

"Stay put and keep the blanket on while I get things taken care of," he advised.

She shot him another curious look, but then sat down. He made fast work of sliding the barn door shut and attending to the horses, both the one that had pulled the sleigh and the three other geldings he'd acquired from his folks when their health no longer allowed for properly taking care of them. Even working quickly, the nightly chore seemed to take forever. His expectation heightened and his dick stiffened further with each passing second. He was all but hobbling with his hardness by the time he returned to the sleigh.

Tori had pulled off her gloves and taken down her hood. Her blond-streaked brown hair fell in lush waves around her shoulders. Painfully aware of the heavenly sensations of the silky strands wrapped around his hand—better yet, his cock—he climbed onto the sleigh.

She laughed when he pulled back the blanket. "I'm pretty sure I can handle getting out by myself."

"I'm sure you can." Ever-mounting hunger reflected in his voice, tugged at his balls. He sank onto the bench seat and re-covered their lower halves with the blanket. "But I was hoping you'd want to stay up here awhile longer."

Surprise flickered over her face. Understanding dawned next with the widening of her eyes. She swallowed hard visibly. "To do what?"

Travis slipped his hand beneath the blanket and then between her thighs. "Make good on your offer."

Chapter Five

An unbidden sigh left Tori's lips as Travis's thumb found her sex. Beneath the camouflage of the blanket, he stroked her labia through her clothes. Erotic heat pulsed through her, the heady sensation sharpened intensely by her inability to see his sensual play and know what would come next. The lust consuming his dark, burning gaze suggested everything. That same lust smoldered through her, her heart thumping as it screamed a single silent word.

Yes!

His thumb ceased its rubbing to press between her folds. Her pussy lubricated, hips thrusting forward on primitive instinct. She yearned to grab hold of his hair, grind her aching cunt against his hand, and shout her elation. The hesitation she'd known on Anna's lawn reared its head, stopping her from doing that. The ugly oil painting on his bathroom wall, his remark about how he'd treat her if she was his fiancée, the way he'd looked when he said she'd be an amazing mother and then again when he'd nearly kissed her a short while ago . . . All those things and so much more seemed to imply he wanted more from her than uncomplicated sex.

The press of Travis's thumb let up. Doubt flashed in his eyes. "Has the offer been rescinded?"

She clenched her sex, feeling the loss of his touch deep down inside. "Should it be?"

"Go with whatever your head's saying."

Her head was saying he was a big boy and he knew her terms. Her head was saying he was a big, big boy, and he knew how she liked her loving. Her head was saying he was a big, big, big boy, and if he didn't get his hands on her this instant, she was liable to implode from unfulfilled desire.

He knew her terms.

The thought repeated in Tori's head, a silent chant of encouragement to take everything she craved and give back the same. To indulge in rare naughty fun.

If she secured the VP position, her free time would go from light to none at all for at least the next several months. Even when her work schedule lightened, she wasn't liable to have time for dating and she'd never sleep with some random stranger. A stranger wouldn't know her body, know her mind. Know if he took her nipples into his mouth and sucked long and hard enough, she wouldn't be able to stop from coming.

Her nipples hardened. The soft cotton of her bra taunted the stiff points, making them burn for the feel of a warm, damp mouth. Of *Travis's* warm, damp mouth.

He knew her terms.

Once more the thought rallied through her mind. This time she grabbed hold of the words and let go of her hesitation. Her sex fluttered in wild anticipation. Her pulse galloped. It felt like forever and a day she'd waited to get her hands on his fine-ass body. She couldn't wait a second longer.

The briskness of the air and the roughness of their surroundings ceased to exist as she hitched her bent leg up on the seat and took hold of his coat zipper. Fingers trembling with the urgency of her want, Tori jerked the tab down and pushed her hands beneath the parted sides. Rich heat lifted through his thick sweatshirt. The spicy scent of his cologne tangoed with the fresh scents of winter and the muskier scent of the barn, the result altogether too satisfying.

Liquid warmth flooding her belly, her pussy, her toes, she shoved the shirt up his chest and palmed his deliciously hard abdomen. Flicking her gaze to his, she spoke in a hot, throaty bedroom whisper, "My head's saying you're wearing way too many clothes."

Travis's muscles contracted beneath her touch. His lips parted to release a sigh of pure pleasure and promise. Dark, feral hunger slipped into his eyes, over the strong lines of his face. Beneath the blanket, the hand between her thighs moved. Not knowing where it would touch down next had her breath quickening and body strung taut. Then her breathing screamed to a euphoric halt as his fingers landed on her zipper, tugged it down, and dove inside her panties.

A lone big finger slipped between her slick folds. The pad found her clit, circling with slow, teasing strokes. A second joined in, picked up the pace. One of those deft fingers pressed against the swollen bundle of nerves and electric excitement shot through her with the force of a lightning bolt.

Desperately, Tori fisted her hands against his abs. Arching up on the sleigh seat, she cried out with the exquisite pressure. Her ass fell back against the seat, and she tore her hands from his chest to capture one of his beneath the blanket.

"My offer. My lead," she murmured raggedly.

She'd spent these last days longing for the feel of his cock thrusting between her lips, the taste of his hot seed spilling onto her tongue. She *had* to have them both, now, before she lost her mind to passion completely.

Reluctance to give up control flickered through Travis's eyes. But then he sat back on the seat and gave himself to her. A decadent feeling of power rippled through her. It drove her crazy when he took control, turned his wicked wiles on her. It drove her nearly as mindless when he rescinded it. When he trusted her so completely with his body.

Letting the blanket fall to the sleigh floor, Tori climbed onto his lap and took his stubble-dusted chin in hand. The hard line of his cock rubbed delectably along her pussy as she settled against his powerful thighs.

Murmuring her delight, she dropped her mouth to his and nibbled at his full, tasty lips. "Tell me what you want, Travis."

"Everything." The word chased out a rough caress.

Leaning back a fraction, she rocked into the powerful cradle of his thighs. "Not good enough."

His dick jerked. A low groan rumbled from his throat. "I want to feel your lips nibbling everywhere."

And oh how she wanted to nibble.

Bliss rocketing through her, Tori bent her mouth to the crook of his neck. She flicked her damp tongue against his bare, salty skin. Her hips rocked again on instinct and her clit tingled with the sweet friction.

Ah God. So good, so tasty. So Travis.

"Here?" she asked patiently as if her heart wasn't beating a mile a minute.

"That's a good start."

Tugging his shirt back up, she turned her mouth on a nipple, tonguing, biting, sucking at the small disc until it peaked beneath her ministrations. "And here?"

"Keep going."

Shivering with the anticipation of finally gaining access to his luscious cock, she slid down his legs to the softness of the blanket on the sleigh floor. On her knees, she jerked down his zipper. He lifted his hips, and she tugged at his jeans and boxers in tandem. One inch of pure virile masculinity revealed itself. Two. Springy black hair skated into view. She tugged another inch and his dick sprang free. Thick. Long. Pre-cum pearled at the purple head.

Her tongue went wild in her mouth. Palming his thighs, she bent her head to his groin and swirled her tongue around his weeping tip. Her pussy pulsed with the dark, sensual taste of his seed. The need for more raged through her. "How about here?"

Travis's hips arced toward her face. His hands, which had been subserviently dormant until now, threaded through her hair. "Oh fuck, Tori," he groaned, fisting his fingers. "Definitely there."

His savage approval made her wetter, hotter, hungrier. The taste of his fluid no longer enough, she parted her lips and drew his steely length deep inside. His full-bodied shout echoed off the barn walls. His pelvis thrust hard, ass leaving the seat and the jeans falling to his calves. He came back down in a slouch position that spread his thighs and put his tight balls on display. Laving her tongue up and down his cock, she took his testicles in hand. Squeezing, shaping. Building forceful pressure that had him slouching even farther.

Tori reached for his ass, the highly sensitive opening of his anus her target. Before she could make contact, his hands pulled from her hair and shot to her breasts. Through three layers of clothing, he found and pinched her tight nipples. A sensation, which should have been slight, registered as wickedly fierce for the overly sensitive buds. She opened her mouth to cry out, and he pulled his cock free of her lips to hoist her off the floor and sunny-side up across his lap.

Grabbing hold of the waist of her open jeans, he tugged both them and her soaked panties down to expose her ass to the kiss of the forgotten cool barn air. And then to the lick of his hot breath as he taunted, "You know what happens to naughty elfs?" A rough, warm palm smoothed across her butt cheeks. "They get spanked."

His palm made another pass over her ass. A wicked thrill whipping through her, she tightened her cheeks. His hand lifted. Sensational heat engulfed her pussy. The seconds ticked past. One. Two. Three. Pleading tickled at her lips. She wriggled against his thighs. Four seconds. Five. Tori whimpered, then moaned.

Why the hell was he putting it off when he knew how badly she ached for this? Was it words he wanted? The dirty kind that never ceased to get them both hot and horny?

"Spank me, Travis," she panted. "Make my ass sting so bad that stars dance before my eyes."

As if that had been his cue, his hand fell hard against her backside. A delicious stinging ache flitted through her cheeks and deep into her pussy. Greedily, she ground her cunt against his lap, her clit pulsing for more, more, more.

"That's for making me kiss Mason," he rasped, his voice a mask of tight control.

Another swat fell across her tender rear, only this time it wasn't his hand. The unmistakable crack of the horse reins bit into the air and then into her soft flesh. The height of pleasure-pain burst through her ass, her sex, her spinning mind. Mini tremors wracked her pussy.

"That's for taunting me with talk of masturbation."

His palm returned to pet her quivering butt, and then he came at her again. No hand or reins this time, but the warm, wet, carnal smack of his lips.

Climax poured through Tori with the startling shift. The heat of release singed in her blood and gasped from her lips. She clutched his bunched jeans and panted for air.

Jesus, so good.

Nothing she'd experienced with Alan could compare. Only Travis could make her feel this consumed, this replete. And yet, still so desperate for more.

"And that's because your ass looks so damned pretty in pink."

Her ass wasn't the only thing pretty in pink. With the rush of her orgasm, Tori parted her thighs and provided a rearview peek-a-boo glimpse of her creaming pussy too tempting for Travis to let pass. Their positioning didn't allow for the indulgences of his tongue. Pulling the jeans and panties over her boots and free of her legs, he sank a finger between her sex-slicked folds.

Still-spasming muscles contracted around his invasion. She writhed on his lap, her fingers digging madly into the bunched-up legs of his jeans. "Yes! Finger-fuck me."

As it always did, her dirty talk went straight to his dick. Between the sinful stroke of her lips around his shaft moments ago, and the hot sweet scent of her excitement in the air, and the feel of her arousal soaking his thighs now, his cock was primed to explode.

Gritting his teeth with the pressure that her wriggling put on his balls, he filled her passage with another finger and moved them together in a pump-and-play motion. Tori's breath jerked out in gasping puffs. Her wriggling turned to grinding and then help- lessly erratic rubbing. He slipped his thumb between her pretty lips and pressed at her clit.

"Ohmigod, again!" she cried out, sex convulsing around his fingers.

With his next upward thrust, hot, silky honey rained down, drenching his already wet thighs and washing onto the raw, burn- ing tip of his shaft.

Travis's cock bucked fiercely. Blood sizzled through his veins. Unable to wait a second longer, he stuffed a hand into his coat and jerked out the condom he'd stored there pre—sleigh ride. After making quick work of the wrapper, he rolled the rubber down his excruciatingly throbbing length. A glance at Tori had him nearly coming on the spot. Lower lip caught between her nibbling teeth and her eyes huge and hazy, she watched his every move.

"Tori, baby?" Her gaze lifted to his, the unquenchable need there telling him what her mouth wasn't ready to. Love, lust, and endless desire wrapped around his cock. Thickly, he beckoned, "Time to go for a ride."

Her passion-plumped lips quirked. "I thought you'd never ask."

Relenting her grip on his jeans, she came to her feet and onto his lap in one fluid move. Eyes trained on his, she held her pussy lips apart and sank onto his cock. A groaning gasp of ecstasy broke from his lips as the heat of her sex scorched him to the bone. Taking hold of his shoulders, she moved up his shaft nearly to the tip and then dropped back down again with a great, shuddering moan. Tension slicing through him, Travis met her on the downward thrust, picked up her pace even as he pushed up the bulk of her coat and shirt.

He flicked open the front clasp of her lacy black bra and buried his face against her lovely breasts for a long, worshipping moment. Pulling back just a bit, he traced the contour of first one straining nipple and then the other. Tori arched against his mouth, thrust her breasts snug to his face. Reverently, he kiss-licked a path along the velvet-soft skin that separated the two, and then sucked the first glistening point hard into his mouth.

The pumping of her hips increased. Fingernails bit delectably through his clothes and into his shoulders. He sucked harder at her nipple. Twisted. Scraped his teeth along the sensitive sides. Her hips stilled and she released an impassioned gasp. Entire body trembling in his arms, she rode the crest of release, showering his cock and flooding his thighs a third time.

He watched her face as she rode out the climax, pupils huge, lips parted, tiny gasping moans falling out second by second. The sheer look of ecstasy hit him low in the gut, popping sweat onto his brow and tightening his balls to a sadistic level.

He'd wanted to make this night the best she'd ever had. Wanted to make memories that would last forever. The only problem was that he couldn't last forever. His dick was playing a ready-to-release-or-not game, and the only option was ready.

Slipping a hand between their joined bodies, he found the bead of her clit and stroked it back to the edge of climax. Hers came swiftly, with little effort at all. Even knowing how badly he needed to come, his took him by surprise. Crashing down hard, overwhelming his every ability as it rolled through his body like a damned tidal wave of sensation and emotion.

The last of her release ravaged through her, and Tori slumped against his chest, catching her breath as he fought to do the same. The cold registered first. His skin was exposed from just below his waist to just above his ankles and every one of those inches, outside of the ones still buried inside her, were suddenly ripe with gooseflesh. Aware she had to be just as cold, he lifted the forgotten blanket from the sleigh floor. He draped it around their bodies. The side covering her back dipped to her ass, but she didn't make a move to re-cover it.

"You're going to freeze."

"Already numb." She tipped back her head. Satisfaction gleamed in her hazy eyes. "Not one. Not two or three. But four incredible orgasms. How do you do it?"

Laughing, he kissed the succulent corners of her mouth, wishing he'd had the presence of mind to kiss her more when they'd been making love. "It's a labor of love."

The satiation fled from her eyes. She went stiff in his arms. Holding her share of the blanket to her chest, she moved off his lap and onto the seat beside him. A wary glance to the barn door told him her next words before she spoke. "I should get home."

Disappointment barreled through Travis. But then he'd hardly expected her to declare her undying love tonight. He also wasn't convinced she was ready to end the night. It was simply a matter of laying out the right motivation to make her stay.

Heedless of the cold when he knew he'd be forgetting all about it again in seconds, he shook off the blanket and went down on his knees on the sleigh floor. "I could take you home," he offered sincerely. Then he took her thighs in hand, spread her legs, and turned a sincerely hot and wanting grin on her pussy. "Or we could go for number five."

The wariness stayed in her eyes a little longer, right up until he licked the length of her slit. Then it was only passion as she buried her fingers in his hair and offered herself up to his seeking tongue and orgasm number five.

Tori inched her parents' front door closed, mindful if she made any unexpected sounds this time of night Murphy would assume her an intruder and launch into a barking fit. Without turning on the lights, she felt her way through the living room to the stairs.

"Sneaking in?"

A scream barreled up her throat at the unexpected voice. She recognized it as Mason's then, and turned to glare at him despite the blackness. "I'm almost twenty-seven. Last thing I knew that was well past the age of curfew." He flicked the end-table lamp on to low. She blinked as her eyes adjusted to the light and discovered he sat kicked back in their father's recliner. An open book lay across his lap, but the bleariness of his eyes suggested he'd traded reading for sleeping some time ago. "Why are you downstairs?"

"I was waiting for you to get home. Alan called a few times tonight. I figured it must be important for him to be so persistent, and wanted to let you know right away."

He what?

The blissful remnants of the last several hours she'd spent with Travis faded to panic. Automatic defense rose, stiffening her limbs. What could be so important for Alan to track her down here? That he *would* have to track her down registered, and Tori breathed a sigh of relief. "Nice try, but that's impossible. Alan doesn't have Mom and Dad's number."

Mason gave her a skeptical look. "You go away for the week of Christmas and don't leave your fiancé a number to reach you at?"

"He has my cell."

"Your cell hasn't left your nightstand since you put it there two days ago. Alan also didn't call." Smirking like the smart-ass he was, he stood from the recliner and used his added height to stare her down. "Have something you'd like to share, little sis?"

"Yes." Her knee with his balls, both because he persisted in acting like she was younger and because she was growing seriously tired of the "push Tori at Travis" trip he was on. For the sake of not waking the entire family when he yowled over his damaged family jewels, Tori took a gentler approach. "My head with my pillow. Good night, *little bro.*"

"Night, Tori." She was midway up the stairs when he spoke again, this time without a trace of humor. "A little fodder for your dreams. Sometimes love isn't enough, and then sometimes it's everything."

Chapter Six

Tori had set no-strings terms for Travis and expected him to adhere to them. In hindsight, she should have made certain she was ready to adhere to those same terms. The last few days they'd spent more time together than apart, both for innocent encounters when one or both of their families were present, and those not-nearly-so-innocent ones when they managed to sneak in alone time.

With each kiss, each caress, each pump of his succulent cock inside her needy body, she was growing closer to him. Remembering all those minor details and facets of his personality she'd managed to expunge from her mind because she loved them so incredibly much.

Just as she was coming to love him again.

The needle Tori was threading through a kernel of popcorn missed its mark. A droplet of blood pooled up on her fingertip.

Sucking the digit between her lips, she vetoed the notion of loving Travis. It was Mason in her head, making her think that way. Mason who knew jack about the topic. The most meaningful relationship her brother ever had was precisely of the jack variety, as in the jack-off one he had with his hand.

The thought triggered memories of the previous night, when she'd shared in a round of mutual masturbation with Travis. Watching the duo of emotions and sensations pass through his eyes as he fondled himself to climax had been the most intimate experience she'd had in ages. Hearing his sighs and groans of encouragement as she'd done the same had formed some invisible bond between them so strong that she swore she'd felt his release deep down inside her. For that moment, it seemed they were joined as one, the way they should have been joined as one in name long ago.

She didn't want his name. But if that was the truth, why did her heart beat a wild tattoo and emotion clog her throat? "Damn it."

Rachel looked over from her cross-legged position on the living room floor, where she, too, was hard at work on stringing popcorn. With their parents in bed early, and Mason and Nick out doing some truly last-minute shopping, Tori and her sisters had taken on the annual Christmas Eve event.

"Another broken kernel?" Rachel asked.

No. The prelude to a broken heart.

Tori lifted her bleeding finger. "Pricked my finger."

"You okay, Tori?" Holly asked from the sofa. "You sound like you're missing the mojo in your life."

"I'm fine. I just can't get over how fast this week went by." She wasn't even sure if she would see Travis again before she had to leave for her evening flight tomorrow. He'd been over for dinner tonight but then left to help Burke assemble toys in preparation of the morning.

"You have to be excited about getting back for your meeting," Rachel pointed out.

Holly glanced out the window and crinkled her nose. "Not to mention to leave the arctic behind."

Tori followed her gaze out the window. The snow had been falling nonstop since early afternoon and the weatherman predicted it would change to sleet, making the road conditions questionable for Christmas Day.

Was it so wrong to hope her flight would be canceled?

God, she wasn't ready to leave. Not her family and not Travis. If neither of them had adhered to that no-strings rule and they both had fallen back in love, did they stand a chance at making a long-distance relationship work any better now than they had in the past?

How did her sister plan to make it work? "I'm looking forward to it. I just wish we lived closer." She looked to Holly. "As much as I miss you guys, I can't imagine how you're going to handle leaving Cole here while you return to Houston."

"We'll figure it out," Holly responded confidently. "Besides, it's not like I can't take a road trip whenever the mood hits."

Therein lay the major difference between their situations. If and when Tori's promotion came through, time for road trips would be a far-off thing. Even when she could find time to travel, then what?

"What happens if you decide to take things to the next level? Do you think he would move to Houston for you and leave his brothers behind?"

"If it came to that, I'm sure he would."

Therein lay another major difference. Travis hadn't been willing, or maybe able—she still wasn't sure which—to follow her to Miami the first time, and she couldn't see him leaving his ailing parents now. What about her? Was she prepared to leave her career behind? She'd worked in real estate before moving south, but the small-time home sales she handled in Haven were nothing compared to the massive deals she made down there. They didn't do a thing to raise her up to the success level enjoyed by her siblings. "Would you move back here for him?"

"If it comes to that, I'm sure I would."

Tori sighed. "I guess that's the mark of true love. A willingness to leave everything behind to be with someone."

"For what it's worth," Rachel put in, "I'm glad that's not something Nick and I will ever have to face. I'm sure we would work something out if we had to, but it's a heck of a lot easier living in the same city to start with." A loving smile settling on her face, she nodded at the gold stand on the fireplace mantel. "Of course, having Grandma's ruby couldn't hurt anything either. It kept her and Grandpa's love strong for years, after all."

Holly's courtroom mask took hold and she bit out, "I don't want it."

"Too bad for you, you don't have a say in the matter," Rachel said. "Either you or Mason is the natural choice."

The lack of her name in that list stung at Tori. She frowned at Rachel. "You don't think I stand a chance?"

"You have as good of a chance as I do. It's just that Holly is Holly, and Mason is the only boy. Not to mention a near carbon copy of Grandpa."

Not to mention since she started focusing on sex with Travis, she'd pretty much forgotten about focusing on how her family viewed her. She'd pretty much forgotten everything but how good the two of them went together.

Holly shot Tori a look of disbelief. "You're going to let her get away with that?"

Part of her wanted to interrogate Rachel the same way she had Holly. A far bigger part was back to thinking about Travis. Thinking that maybe her family viewing her as irresponsible didn't matter so long as he held on to his faith in her abilities. And that still didn't help their situation one damned bit. "I'm sure Grandma chose the right person for the job."

TORI WAITED UNTIL THE HOUSE was dark and silent to creep down the stairs to the living room. The Christmas tree lights had been left on for Santa—a tradition long in the keeping—and they afforded a magical sort of glow to the room. The thought of magic had her gaze going to the fireplace mantel and the ruby that had brought her down here. She still didn't know that she bought into the whole "magical" concept, but she did believe that through the ruby was the best way to reach Grandma Reddy.

Grandma had always spoken and acted from the heart. If there was someone to tell her what path her life should follow next, it was her. Lifting the ruby from the stand, Tori curled it into her fist and closed her eyes. "I probably don't deserve divine guidance, considering how little I was around the last months you were with us, but if you have any pull up there, I could use some help, Grandma. A sign. Something. Anything."

"Mom sure did love that ruby."

Tori jumped with the sound of her father's voice. Feeling like a kid who'd been caught opening her Christmas presents early, she slapped the ruby back on the stand. "It's a beautiful gift Grandpa gave her."

Thomas came up beside her to give the ruby a loving caress. "It is, but it's the sentimentality that matters. Grandma would have loved a paper clip the same."

"Or a really awful oil painting."

"What?"

"Nothing." Only, as much as the words had come out of nowhere, they weren't about nothing. Travis had kept her butt-ugly painting, framed it and hung it in his home, and she couldn't help but feel it was because he considered it a talisman for their love.

Smiling, her father wrapped an arm around her shoulders. "We haven't had any alone time this week. How are you, honey?"

"Good. Enjoying the time off from work."

"I have to admit I never thought you'd be one to chase the corporate ladder."

Defensiveness nipped at Tori. "I have a good head on my shoulders, Daddy. As good as Holly or Rachel or Mason."

"I've never doubted your intelligence." A knowing smile tugged at his lips. "Or your reliability. All you kids are bright—take after the old man in that way. I just know you've always wanted a big family."

Her heart skipped a beat with the sincerity of his words, ones she'd ached for years to hear. Happiness washed over her only to be overtaken by sorrow with the rest of his admission. "People change. I still want kids. Eventually." *Or now.*

Damn, how had things gotten so confusing? She'd set out to de-stress by sleeping with Travis and instead she was so stressed she could barely see straight.

Doubt shone in her father's eyes. "What if Alan decides in ten years he still isn't ready?"

She answered with a noncommittal shrug, refusing to lie to him.

He hesitated a beat, hope replacing his skepticism, before asking, "What if you shopped around a little longer before saying 'I do'?"

She also wouldn't get his hopes up. "I know you love Travis, Daddy, but—"

"Obviously you care about him, too, for his name to be the first thing out of your mouth."

"Of course I care. We've been friends since second grade."

"He still loves you. I think it's half the reason he spends so much time with me, because it makes him feel closer to you."

Of all the words he could have spoken, those ones hit home the hardest. Her pulse raced wildly. Then petered out as memories of the past rose up to eat at her belly. "If he *still* loves me, why did he let me go in the first place?"

"I'd say that's a question only Travis can answer."

Tomorrow Tori would fly home. Tonight Travis was determined to show her that she was already there.

Killing the lights on his truck, he coasted up the Reddys' drive. It was after one in the morning and the last thing he wanted was her entire family for an audience. Icy wind whipped at his clothes and huge chunks of snow plastered him as he slipped out of the truck and into the frigid night. Feeling like he was sixteen again, hoping to get Tori to sneak out so they could fool around, he snuck around to the back of the house and blasted her dark window with a snowball.

The bedroom lights remained off. He tried a second snowball and then a third without success. Daring a fourth was asking to get caught, because Murphy had to be primed for barking.

Fuck. What now? He'd promised to spend Christmas morning with his parents and Anna and her family. By early afternoon, with the weather report grim, Tori might already be gone.

Travis returned to the front of the house. He started for his truck, intending to climb into the warmth and consider his next move. The sight of Tori leaning up against the driver-side door froze him in his tracks.

Acres of snow illuminated her face in the darkness. It showcased her tousled, blowing hair, and lips as soft as they were ripe and inviting. His cock stirred automatically, his mouth feeling suddenly as dry as sandpaper.

She arched an eyebrow. "Looking for someone?"

He joined her at the side of the truck, keeping his hands stuffed in his pockets when all they ached to do was touch. "I didn't know if I'd get back here before you leave tomorrow."

"So you came to tell me to watch out for the door hitting my ass?"

Ah, hell, why bother with the not touching?

Catching her chin in his hand, he stroked his thumb against her luscious lower lip. Always so inviting. Always so damned gorgeous. "That, and a little good-bye mouth-sturbation."

Anticipation flickered in her eyes as he took her mouth with his. He slipped between the lushness of her lips, tasting, teasing, wanting more. Tori shoved her cool bare hands beneath his coat and sweatshirt, took hold of his waist, and gave it to him.

Rubbing their groins together, she feasted on his mouth, licking, sucking, nibbling . . . Good God, the girl could nibble. Her mouth left his to travel down his neck. Her hips picked up their tempo, grinding her pussy against the swelling ridge of his cock while her lips painted a hot, damp path that felt erotic as hell against his otherwise icy flesh.

Her nails nipped into his sides, and ecstasy, raw and intense, shivered through him. "Keep that up and there won't be any snow left in New Hampshire."

Returning her lips to his ear, she whispered, "I want you, Travis. One last time. Please."

"Where?" He almost laughed with the question. Why the hell did it matter where, so long as it meant burying his famished dick inside her gorgeous pussy?

"The woodshed."

This time he did laugh. "Last time we fooled around in a woodshed, it almost burned to the ground."

"Oh, there's going to be fire. The kind that singes so fast and hard you can't help but be burned."

Chapter Seven

No thinking, just fucking.

The only problem with that reasoning, Tori recognized, was that they wouldn't be fucking. They would be making love. Fast, hard, dirty love in her father's woodshed.

Shudders of sensual delight fizzled through her as she took Travis's hand and they hurried through the wild night to the woodshed out behind the house. He closed the door and pulled the string on the bare lightbulb. A dull glow cast over his face, accentuating the dark, needful hunger in his eyes. Logically, she knew it wasn't much warmer inside the small building than it was in the frigid outdoors. But from the second she shook her coat off and yanked her sweatshirt over her head to reveal her bare breasts, the place felt like a sauna.

His gaze hot on her breasts, he divested his coat and shirt, tossed them onto the woodpile next to hers. Her mouth watered as his solid pecs came into view. What she wouldn't do to spend the rest of the night worshipping his awesome body. She didn't have the rest of the night. She had a few stolen minutes and a starving, damp ache between her thighs that demanded he drive his cock inside her, pronto.

Thankful she wore sweatpants, because her trembling fingers weren't up to handling a zipper, Tori kicked off her boots and shoved her pants down her legs. Travis's gaze shot downward. Latching his eyes onto her mound, he attacked his own zipper. His boots and jeans were off in an instant. His thick, jutting cock was sheathed with a condom from his coat pocket just as fast. Then he was grabbing her around the waist and lifting her up his body, rubbing the weeping tip of his erection against her pussy in demand of entry.

Wrapping her legs around his waist, she shifted her hips and welcomed him inside. He drove into her with an urgent impaling. A desperate cry tore from her lips as erotic sensation rocked her to the core. He slammed his mouth against hers and gobbled the sound up whole.

Tilting her hips, she took his shaft deeper, until his balls pummeled her ass with each grinding pump. He groaned with the primal play. Moving his hands to her butt, he lifted her up and down his cock, the rigid length caressing her swollen clit with each furious pass. Tension balled in her belly and worked its way lightning quick to her toes. Mini shudders quaked in her pussy. More as he drove his short nails into her soft cheeks.

One of his hands left her butt. Seconds later, a lone finger found her back entry. The pulse raced at Tori's throat. The breath hitched from her mouth into his. She closed her eyes on a rapturous sigh as his finger slipped between her cheeks to massage her sphincter muscles. Orgasm grabbed hold fast and furious. Pulling her lips from his, she tossed back her head and shouted his name as her hot cream flooded around his cock. He shouted hers right back as he gave into his own release, pounding deep inside her until the last drop of cum left his body.

Clinging to his warmth, she slowly returned to earth. To reality. To the fact that she still had no answers as to where her future might lie. Was his showing up here tonight when she'd been prepared to go to his place the sign she'd asked Grandma for?

Too soon their frosty surroundings set in. She fought off a shiver, not wanting Travis to release her. He read her mind as always and set her on her feet anyway.

He shuddered as he yanked on his sweatshirt. "Damn, it's cold."

Once again thankful for her easy-on-and-off sweats, she hurried into her clothes. She watched as he pulled on the rest of his, committing the salacious sight to memory just in case. Emotion clogged her throat with the thought she might never see him again. At least not for a very long time and then never in this capacity.

She forced a bright smile. "Thank you. I knew I'd have a great time this week—I always do with my family—but spending time with you made it even better."

Travis caught the sorrow she tried to hide behind her phony smile. How could she ever think to get it past him? "Do you really love your job down there, Tori?"

A frown touched at her eyes, but her voice rang with cheer. "Of course. It's great. I get to meet people from all walks of life. Be wined and dined on the corporate budget. Wear a stunning wardrobe I'd never be able to afford elsewhere."

Stand there and lie to him about loving each of those things.

Maybe she didn't realize any better. Unlike the sorrow behind her smile, her happy tone sounded authentic. "The people thing is you, the rest I don't buy."

"I'm a different person than you used to know. You said so yourself—the 'new Tori.'"

"I was wrong. You're not. I also don't think you're happy down there. I think you've just talked yourself into believing you are because you think a successful career will make you a better person in your family's eyes." He hedged a moment, then added, "I think that's the same reason you agreed to marry Alan."

Surprise overtook her expression. That same wall of defense she'd first shown him this week lifted into place with the crossing of her arms. "I suggest you think again. Alan and I had a wonderful relationship. If it wasn't for the whole kids thing, we would still be engaged."

"Did you love him?"

"Absolutely."

Travis's gut twisted with the sincerity of that single word. He'd wanted to believe she'd never felt a thing for the man, that their relationship had been nothing more than a fluke. He could accept he'd been wrong on that front, so long as he wasn't wrong on this next one. "The way you love me?"

The surprise flickered back through Tori's eyes. Quietly, she admitted, "The way I *loved* you was special." She turned her back on him to push open the woodshed door. "I need to get to bed. I doubt I'll get much sleep tomorrow night. Flying always leaves me restless."

She needed to run was the truth of it, evident in the way she'd

turned his word of love into the past tense because she wasn't prepared to admit what he knew each time they touched.

Travis had sworn he wouldn't let her go a second time. Faced
with the reality of her leaving and the off chance her life down there
was what made her the happiest, he knew he had no other choice.

"Good-bye, Tori. If you decide I'm right after all, you know
where to find me."

What the hell am I doing?

The question resonated through Tori's head as she moved
through the gusting wind and fast-falling snow to the front porch.
How could she walk away from Travis when she knew nearly every
word he'd spoken was the truth?

She did love meeting new people through her work down south
and she had loved Alan for a short time, but most everything else
about her life down there rubbed her the wrong way. It left her
stressed, feeling out of sorts, and nothing like she was.

She was the person who recognized and adored Mason's teasing. The girl who respected her parents and the lifelong love they
shared, and wanted the same for herself. The woman who'd fallen
for Travis years ago and would never get him out of her heart. And
that was okay, because standing on the precipice of a good-bye that
felt too damned much like forever, she knew *in her heart* was exactly
where she wanted him to be.

An unstoppable smile curved Tori's lips, warming her in a way
not even the frigid weather could touch. She whipped around on
the porch. Her pulse sped as she caught sight of Travis opening his
truck door fifty feet away. Leaving her. Leaving them.

Oh hell, no. Not on his life was he getting away with that a second time.

Heart in her throat, she shuffled down the porch steps and grabbed a handful of snow. She quickly packed it and took aim for his butt. The snowball missed its mark, slamming into the back of his head.

Rubbing his hand over the point of impact, Travis turned around. His gaze settled on her face as she trudged through the snow toward him. Emotions stormed through his eyes. "You do realize this is war? No excuses about needing your beauty sleep either."

Fine by her, because she didn't want sleep. Now that she'd accepted who she was and where she belonged, and that she didn't need divine intervention or even a magical ruby to show her the way, she wanted to go into his arms and spend the rest of the night making love.

Tori's smile grew. The warmth inside her burned brighter with each step. When she reached him, it took every ounce of restraint not to wrap her arms around his broad chest and never let go. "You know what they say, all's fair in love and war."

"Are you talking about your job again?" he asked soberly.

"No. The big family with the man I can't imagine being without."

His lips twitched. "Where do you plan to have this family?"

For once, she could read him as clearly as he read her. He fought the same battle not to pull her into his arms. "I suppose Miami would work. But Haven is where I belong. With you."

Clear and consuming love moved into Travis's eyes. "Fishing for another fiancé?" he teased.

"That depends. Are you up for the job?" It was Tori's turn to sober then, because there were still those questions of the past eating at her. "Why did you let me go, Travis? If you loved me, how could you possibly tell me not to worry about us, just follow my dreams? I get that you wouldn't move south because of your parents' health. But couldn't you have at least come after me and tried to talk me into coming home?"

"I wanted to," he admitted slowly, quietly. "Almost did twenty damned times. In the end, I knew I couldn't. Not without having to live with the fear that you gave up a dream you believed in to be with me."

The ache in his voice clenched at her heart. She'd thought it had been easy for him to let her go. Never once had she considered he'd done it for her. If that wasn't a mark of true love, nothing was. "I was wrong about that dream. I'm not wrong about the one where we wake up Christmas morning in your bed."

The full, sexy smile Tori adored took over Travis's lips. He pulled her into his arms, against the warmth and solidity of his chest. Bliss sighed through her as he brushed her mouth with an adoring caress. "Is that so you don't have to deal with Mason's 'I told you so' smirk?"

Her brother was going to be such a pain in the ass after this. A wonderful pain in the ass she'd take immense pleasure in taunting right back.

Forgetting all about Mason, she slipped her arms around Travis's waist. The bulge of his groin pressed against her lower belly through the bulk of their coats. Carnal pleasure hummed through her, quickening her breath. With a sultry smile, she ground her hips into his. Her pussy fired to needful life with the responsive nudge of his cock, and just like that she was wet and aching for him like she hadn't had him mere moments ago.

Happy like she hadn't been since Travis let her walk away from him, she gave his lips a playful nibble that promised so much more. "Yeah, because of Mason, and so I can wake up shouting 'Ho, ho—ohmigod!'"

Epilogue

Christmas Morning

The living room staircase gave an old faithful creak as Rachel and Nick descended to the first floor, hand in hand. Mischief glinted in their eyes, making it seem they'd shared a naughty secret . . . or something even better. Nick had been treated like part of the Reddy family since coming home for the holidays with Mason. And, like part of the family, he relaxed onto the living room floor, his back to the overstuffed brown sofa, in anticipation of the gift gifting.

When Rachel would have joined him, Margaret asked from her vantage on the far end of the sofa, "Can you wake Tori, Rachel?"

"Sure, Mom." Rachel pecked Nick on the lips, and then hurried back up the stairs. She reappeared less than a minute later, frowning. "She's not there."

"Maybe she went for a walk," Cole suggested from the love seat.

Beside Cole, Holly looked out the frosted windows. Bitter wind whipped at the shutters, banging them against the house, and a snow-sleet mix danced wildly about the yard, rendering the outdoors fit for neither man nor beast. Or dog. Poor Murphy had come in trembling after seeing to his morning doggy duty.

Settled in his well-worn recliner with Murphy at his feet, Thomas shared a concerned look with his wife. "I can't see her going out on Christmas morning. She's always been eager to see how we like our presents."

Mason glanced up from his designated spot in front of the Christmas tree. He wore a festive Santa hat and a sweater festooned with images of Santa and Mrs. Claus, the same way late Grandpa Reddy had done the decades he'd served in the role as gift distributor. "Maybe her flight was rescheduled for this morning."

Shaking her head, Rachel sank down between Nick's bent legs. Worry lines etched her forehead as she reclined against his chest. "No way. Tori would never leave without saying good-bye."

"You're right," Tori agreed from somewhere behind them. "Maybe I just finally got smart."

Everyone's head turned. A mixture of smiles and questioning looks formed as they spotted Tori and Travis beneath the kitchen archway wearing matching looks of jubilance. Their hair and clothes were dusted with snow, suggesting they'd come in from the unruly outdoors through the kitchen entrance.

Mason nodded at their joined hands, a smart-ass grin in place. "About damned time."

Rachel narrowed her eyes in question. "What about Alan?"

Tori's grin wobbled. She and Travis came into the living room. "We broke up months ago," she confessed. "I didn't want to put a damper on the holiday spirit by sharing the news this week." Her lips fell flat. "And I didn't want to share before that because just once I wanted to accomplish something someone else hadn't already. Just once I wanted you all to look at me and see a responsible, mature adult."

Surprise and then sympathy entered Margaret's eyes. "Oh, baby, how can you think that we don't see you that way? Your father and I love and respect you kids all the same for different reasons."

Holly looked guilty. "When you asked me about the ruby the other day, I never meant to imply you aren't mature, Tori. I . . . I'm going to plead the fifth. The point is this family wouldn't be the same without you."

"Not even close," Rachel agreed. "In fact if I had to handpick a younger sister from the crowd, I'd definitely pick you."

Tori laughed. "Thanks, Rach. And everyone else. I know now that the way I perceived things and the way they really are weren't quite the same. I love you guys all the more for confirming that." She looked at Travis and a glowing smile returned to her face. "And I love Travis."

Beaming from ear to ear, Thomas took his wife's hand. "I might just get grandbabies out of these two yet."

Laughter went up from the group. Mason ended it with a high-pitched whistle. "All right. Enough of the sappy. It's time for the gifts." He grabbed a medium-size, square box from beneath the tree and handed it to Holly. "You first, golden girl."

"That's the 'golden child.' Get it right," Holly corrected, a cool look on her face but humor in her eyes. She peeled the red paper off the box. Mason had wrapped the gift upside down, and the lid fell from the bottom and into Holly's lap. The box's contents—handcuffs and a flogger—quickly followed.

"Mason!" A blush tinted Holly's cheeks. Then she laughed out loud, proving Tori wasn't the only one who'd come to recognize certain truths about herself during these last few days in Haven.

"I figured Cole would appreciate them. Once you meet your deadline, of course."

Wiggling his eyebrows, Cole lifted the cuffs. "Deadline, hell, these babies are getting broken in this afternoon."

A collective laugh went up once more. When it died down, Margaret instructed Mason to pull what looked to be four identical gifts from beneath the tree. They were all shirt-box-size and shared the same metallic, blue-and-white snow-scene wrapping paper.

Hopefulness entered Rachel's eyes. "You discovered Grandma had four rubies?"

Margaret smiled softly but shook her head. "Sorry, dear, but there's just *one* special ruby, which we'll talk about later." She left one of the presents with Mason and passed the others on to each of the girls. "These are for you kids from me."

Seated cross-legged next to Travis on the floor beside Thomas's recliner, Tori got the wrapping paper off hers first. Her face paled as the word *cookbook* came into view. "Oh my God, you expect us to cook."

"That one's actually for Travis," Margaret said. "You're going to be too busy with all those kids."

"*All?*" Tori asked.

"Six or seven."

"Mom!" Travis laughed while Tori looked stricken. "I know I said I wanted a big family, but I meant like three kids. Four tops."

"The more birthdays, the more excuses your father and I have to come home."

"Remember when seeing the four of us used to be reason enough?" Holly teased.

"It's still reason enough, sweetie," Margaret assured. "But I—"

"Wait a minute," Mason interrupted. "You said come home. Where are you going to be?"

Hesitancy shone on Margaret's face. "That's actually the reason for the cookbooks. Your father and I are going to be doing some traveling, and I wanted to be certain you kids had at least a fighting chance of getting home-cooking in our absence. All of Grandma Reddy's favorites are inside, along with a couple of my own." She smiled softly at Holly. "Yes, that includes the chocolate-pecan bread and lemon butter."

"You know I'll look after your place while you're away," Travis said.

Thomas regained his hold on his wife's hand. With a supportive squeeze, he shared the rest of their plans. "We appreciate the offer, Travis, but there won't be a need for that. We've sold the house. To Cole and his brothers."

"*What?*" Tori and Rachel gasped in unison. Tori lamented, "I just decided to move back to Haven last night and now you're not even going to be here."

"You're moving back?" Holly asked enthusiastically. "That's great, because I am, too. I wanted to tell you last night, when you asked how Cole and I would work out living so far apart, but I was afraid I'd let it leak about Mom and Dad selling this place."

Rachel gave her a look that called her a traitor. "You knew?"

Holly's smile slipped away. "I found out the hard way, and was sworn to secrecy right after."

Rachel looked to her parents. "Are you sure about this? This old place has been in our family so long."

"We're sure," Thomas confirmed. "We thought about it long and hard, and it's time to take advantage of our retirement. The house won't really be out of our hands, though. Cole wants us to retain ownership of Grandma's cottage, as well as a room in the bed-and-breakfast. Then Murphy will be here." The dog picked up his head at the mention of his name, and Thomas gave his ears a loving scratch. "You've been here your whole life, haven't you, boy? We can't think to take him away from it at this point."

Mason, who'd so far remained uncharacteristically quiet about the announcement, asked, "You're going to make this place into a B&B?" He looked around and nodded his approval. "I can see that. Yeah, it sounds like an excellent investment."

"Don't get any thoughts about leaving Hilltop Gear to go to work for Cole," Nick warned, only half kidding. "I know your track record, buddy, which is why I made you sign that agreement to work for me for at least the next two years, or pay deadly consequences."

Rachel raised an eyebrow. "Deadly?"

Nick gave a rough laugh. "Maybe it wasn't quite deadly, but your brother's intellect and knowledge of the purchasing industry isn't a commodity I care to lose."

"So long as you have Rachel, you should be safe," Mason informed him. "Someone needs to make sure you're treating her right." Teasing gleamed in his eyes as he nodded back at the Christmas tree. "By the way, I have special boxes for Rachel and Tori under there somewhere, too."

The group enjoyed another round of laughter. All but Tori, Thomas noted. "Tori, you all right? You're not saying much."

"Fine, Daddy. Just adjusting to the idea of this place no longer being our home. I guess it will be, though, in a way." A slow smile crept across her lips as she glanced at Holly. "In a bigger way if Cole decides Holly's worth the long haul."

Holly feigned a cool look. "That would be *Holly* deciding if *Cole* is worth the long haul."

Cole took Holly's hand into his. He kissed the back side, and then addressed her family. "I was waiting for my brothers to get here to bring it up, but I'm shooting for a Valentine's Day proposal with a follow-up ceremony next spring. Don't want to rush her too much. You know how she likes to plan."

Tori, Travis, and Mason all nodded knowingly. "At the B&B?" Rachel asked, while Thomas let loose with another beaming grin and Margaret looked like she was fighting off tears of happiness.

"Where else?" Holly asked, her smile as wide as her dad's.

"I'm thrilled for you guys, seriously. Now about the ruby . . ." Mason nudged.

Margaret sighed. She looked to Thomas and he nodded his go ahead. "We were planning to wait until after the gifts were open, but I can see everyone's going to wonder about it too much to enjoy their presents."

Holly's smile disappeared. "I don't want it," she said flatly.

"Then you'll be glad to know you aren't getting it."

"Really?"

"Not unless your sisters and brother want you to have it,"

Thomas affirmed. "Mom's orders were clear. She wanted to see the ruby go to whomever you kids unanimously believe it should be with."

Surprise passed over the siblings' faces for a few seconds. Then Tori said, "That's easy." She shared a conspiratorial look with her sisters. Together, they smiled at Mason. "Mason's the only one who has yet to find true love—what the ruby is really all about." Going to the fireplace mantel, she lifted the ruby from its gold stand and gifted it to Mason. "May the force be with you, little bro."

Respect warmed Mason's eyes as he looked at each of his sisters, and then their parents. "Thanks. All of you." He came to his feet and reached for the Christmas tree star. "But the force belongs right here." He slipped the ruby into the hollow carved out of the star's center. Like it was made for precisely this reason, the ruby settled into the indentation. The lights at the star's points shone onto the ruby, showering the living room with dazzling rays of red. "Right where it can shine its magic on all of us."

Tears once more glinted in Margaret's eyes. With an adoring smile his wife's way, Thomas handed over his handkerchief seconds before she began to sniff. "That's exactly where Grandma would have wanted it." She wiped at her shimmering eyes. "Oh, and I forgot to tell you her other orders. Wherever the ruby ends up, each of us is required to be there for Christmas. Now and forever."

"There's no place I'd rather be," Holly said.

"Not a chance," Tori agreed.

Affection filling Nick's eyes, he looked to each of the Reddys. "You all played a part in making this my best Christmas ever. I can easily promise that wherever you are, Rachel and I will be."

"God bless us, everyone," Mason put in his two cents.

The words were spoken Tiny Tim—style, the hint of teasing laced through them. But everyone knew the truth. They all *were* blessed, to have found such caring friends and partners, and to have a family whose love would endure no matter where they chose to call home.